LIES SHE TOLD

MARTINA MONROE BOOK 11

H.K. CHRISTIE

Cover design by Odile Stamanne

First edition: February 2024

ISBN: 978-1-953268-18-1

012725h

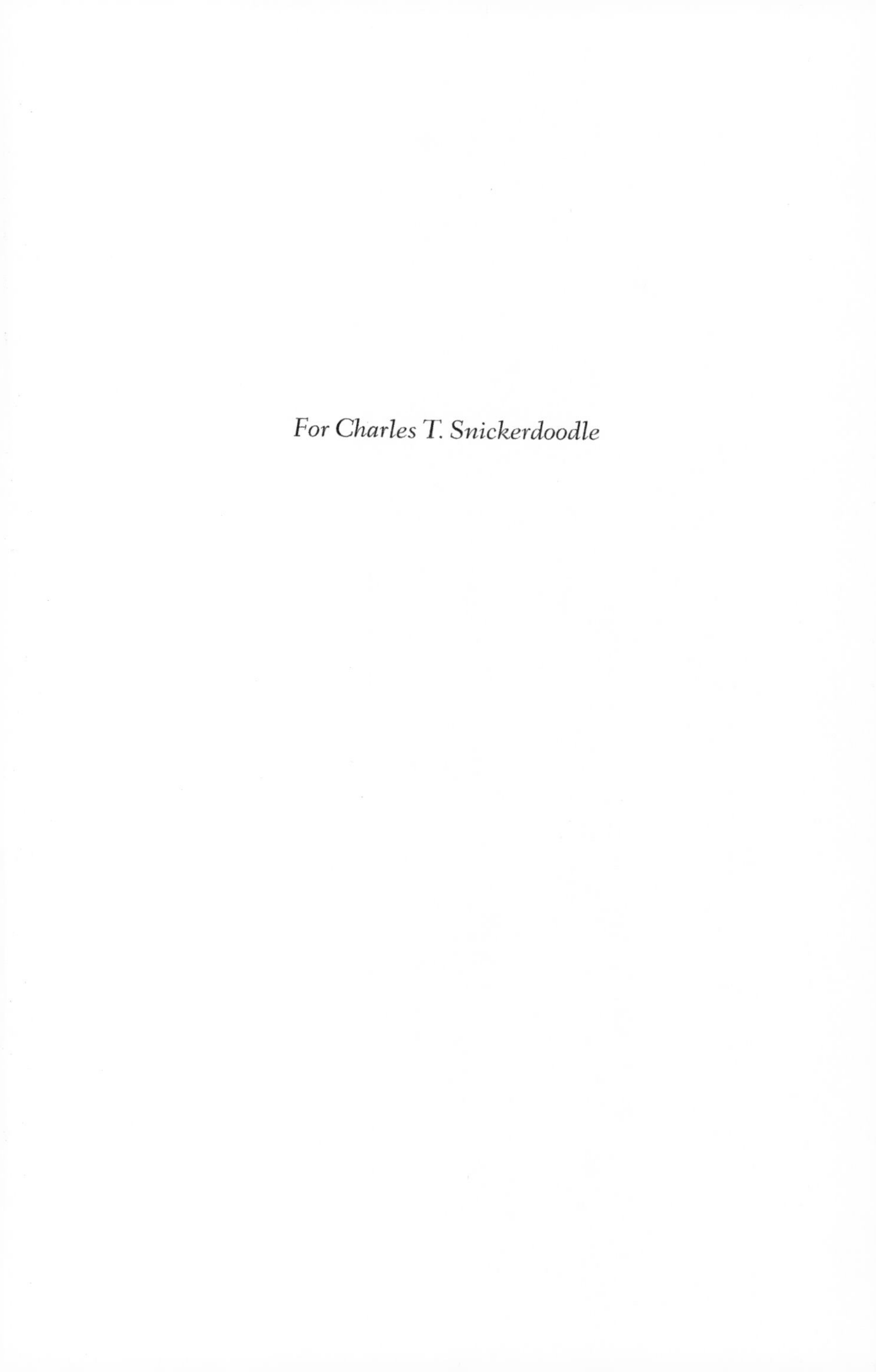

For Charles T. Snickerdoodle

1

CANDACE

SIX MONTHS EARLIER

His blank stare would never be erased from my memory. Nor would I be able to forget those eyes as the weapon was aimed directly at his face. He shook his head and cried, claiming it was all a mistake. Then, boom. Just like a firecracker in the worst night sky.

One shot straight to the head.

Upon impact, he fell and blood splattered. And there were chunks—chunks of what he used to be.

My heart nearly beat out of my chest, unable to fully process what had happened. My ears rang from the gunshot.

It didn't matter if I averted my gaze, because it would always be there.

He was so still.

There were no convulsions. No cries of pain. One shot, and he was out. His life extinguished.

I knew the dead man wasn't exactly a pillar of the community. He was rotten inside. But surely, he wasn't always that way. None of us were born bad. We became our circumstances, our choices, and our mistakes. Maybe he made one too many wrong turns and was trapped in that life.

Barely able to look away, I did for only a moment to see the person who had stolen his life. I covered my mouth with my hand and hoped he hadn't seen or heard me. The next thing I felt was the draft of him running past the bushes I hid behind. The shooter was gone in a flash, just like the man lying dead on the pavement.

With the killer out of sight, I found myself frozen in place. Fight, flight, or freeze. You never know how you'll react. But from that moment forward, I knew I wouldn't—or couldn't—run or fight.

Crouched behind the bush, I surveyed the park. Down the footpath near the playground and a thicket of trees, a large man ran toward the dead man. That running man was a fighter. Not like me. I had stood dumbfounded like a scared little rabbit when I should have fled like my life depended on it. Or at the very least called for help. Why hadn't I called the police?

Should I run? Could I? I stepped out of the shrub and stared down. A chill ran through me as I spotted dark splatter on my jeans. His blood on my denim. They were forever unclean, and I figured I would be too.

Would anybody miss him? I didn't know him very well. All I knew was that he wasn't good, and that he didn't have a wife or a child, at least from what I could tell. He only brought misery, right? Did that make it okay?

The large man arrived, sweating at the temples, spotted me, and said, "Did you see what happened? Did you call the police?"

Not able to answer, I wondered what was wrong with me. It was as if I were having an out-of-body experience. I was trained to assist the sick and injured, so why hadn't I rushed toward the man to try to save him? Was it because it would have been in vain? Or because I thought it was a lucky break? The shooter had accomplished what I couldn't. Or maybe I thought it was God's will. God righting a wrong and smiling down on me. Justice.

"Did you see what happened?" He shook his head. "Oh man, it's too late for this guy. He's dead, really dead."

Yes, he was. He was really dead. Was I glad? Was that what I had wanted? To my horror, I knew it had once been true. But having a moment to consider the implications, I realized he had a mother who would be missing him terribly. She would cry every year on his birthday; her grief over losing a child would never go away. Would she stare at photographs and think about the good times before he transformed into someone she could no longer recognize? Or was she as awful as him?

Everyone was somebody's baby. I didn't want him killed. Those thoughts had been theoretical. Like saying I wished he'd been wiped from the earth. Or hoping he could feel the pain I had.

"Ma'am, did you call the police?" a second, younger guy in a black jogging suit asked.

I shook my head, still unable to speak.

He pulled out a cellphone and dialed, explaining the situation. "There's a man dead. Blood everywhere. Looks like a gunshot wound to the head."

If I were able to break free of my silence, I could explain exactly what had happened because I had witnessed it. And I had seen the shooter. Did he see me? If he did, would he come after me? If I gave a statement to the police, they'd have my name. When it went to trial, he could find me. The prosecution would put me on the stand and my whole life, what I had left of one anyway, would be taken away in that instant.

Crumbling to the ground, whooshing sounded in my ears and footsteps hurried over. Beefy hands caught me just before my head would have smacked down on the cement. My savior yelled out to I don't know to who, to request the paramedics. After that, I stared out at the lifeless man and escaped from the scene into my own darkness.

2

MARTINA

Lowering my firearm, I was filled with a mix of adrenaline and heartbreak. We had found her, but not in time. It wasn't one of those cases where we would smile at the cameras and announce that, after all this time, we had found her alive. Instead, Hirsch would stand at the podium with haunted eyes and describe what we had discovered.

Eliza Mitchell was only sixteen years old when she went missing five years earlier. Despite the faded scent of decomposition, I was sure when I opened the door and shined my flashlight into the makeshift room in the garage that we would find her alive—probably in pretty rough shape, but alive. That's what I was prepared for. Hoping for. But the scene before me stole that hope in an instant.

Standing in the doorway, I yelled out, "Hirsch!"

His boots thudded on the ground as he ran through the door. "Did you find something?"

Tipping my head toward the homemade prison built by our suspect, I explained, "There's a body inside, but it looks like she's been gone for a while. Maybe six months." The hair and approximate size resembled Eliza, and my heart told me it was her. Testing would have to confirm her identity and the medical examiner would tell us for sure, but if I was right, she'd been killed shortly after we had announced the CoCo County Sheriff's Department's Cold Case Squad was taking on her missing person's case.

Hirsch lowered his head and shook it. I knew the look. It was defeat, anger, and sadness rolled into one big ol' ball of despair.

We had found her, but I could only imagine the horror young Eliza had endured during her captivity. Only the medical examiner would be able to tell us exactly what that monster did to her, but I was sure it was inhuman.

Hirsch said, "I'll call the CSI team and Dr. Scribner. We'll gather all the evidence and find out what happened to her."

I didn't think the details would bring the family any solace, but knowing where she was—that would give them something to help them move forward in their lives. To not spend every moment trying to get passersby, or the media, or the police to keep looking for their little girl. Knowing where Eliza was, they could start to heal and hopefully find a way to move forward.

I said a quiet prayer for Eliza and her family, that they would find peace and eventually learn to continue with their lives. Even though Eliza's bright light had been taken, it didn't mean they couldn't continue. From everything I had learned about Eliza, she was warm-hearted, kind, and bright. She wouldn't want her family to suffer.

Hirsch and the Cold Case team's notoriety had given us a bit of a reputation—that if we took on your case, we would find your missing loved one or their murderer would be found and put in jail. Unfortunately, that gave the victims' families perhaps too much hope that we'd find their missing person alive. It was rare to do so and honestly, we had gotten lucky in all the missing persons we had recovered alive.

Vincent stepped toward me, his expression somber. "It's bad, huh?"

I nodded, the weight of the situation settling heavily on my shoulders. "She's been in there a long time. He just left her there—didn't bury her or anything."

"We'll have his face on every news station. We'll find him, Martina."

Our job was only half done. We found Eliza, assuming my ID was on point, but we hadn't found the man who had kidnapped and ultimately killed her.

Based on surveillance and the prior day's search, it seemed our suspect hadn't been at the house for a while. Unfortunately, I thought he must've seen the news that we were re-opening the case, killed Eliza, and fled. Sometimes announcements helped, sometimes it made the perpetrators nervous and forced them to take drastic measures to protect themselves from being caught. It might be exactly what had happened. And it filled me with a heavy sense of failure. If we hadn't done the press conference, maybe she would be alive, and we could have brought her home.

Shaking off the awful realization, I gave myself a mental pep talk and continued on. It was time to put the killer's picture on every network nationwide to alert the public and capture him. He couldn't be allowed to remain free to do this to another human being.

Lock him up and throw away the key.

"Yes, we will. Hirsch is on the phone with the forensics team to come down and recover her and the evidence."

"Is there anything else in there with her?" he asked, peering past me into the dimly lit space.

"Just a dirty old mattress, stained sheet, and empty water bottles..." My voice trailed off, not really wanting to paint the gruesome picture any further.

"Maybe we should close the door then?"

There was a faint odor that we all knew and didn't love. But before I could answer him, my phone buzzed, and I glanced down. "You're right. It doesn't need to be open."

Softly closing the door, I answered the phone, trying to keep my voice steady. "Hi, Mom, what's up?"

"How's it going, Martina?"

Was this a social call? Mom didn't usually call during the day, especially when I was deep in a case. "I'm at a crime scene."

"Oh, I'm so sorry. I'll let you go."

"I have a minute. What is it? Is it Barney? Is it Zoey? Is everything okay?" I asked, my mind instantly shifting to my daughter and dog, fearing something might be wrong.

"No, they're both fine, honey. I was just calling to see how you are and if you wanted to visit Darren with me this weekend."

The short answer was *no*.

It had been six months since I had received the anonymous phone call insisting Darren was innocent. In that moment, I'd caught a glimmer of hope that I would free Darren, and he'd turn his life around, and I would get my brother back after too long. Zoey would be able to meet one of her biological uncles for the first time. There would be hugs and tears and cocoa around the Christmas tree. But that wasn't how it turned out. Life rarely does turn out how we expect. I should have known my brother, who had spent his entire adult life working for the dark side, was still in it.

After his incarceration and guilty plea, Mom and I visited Darren to see him and tell him about the call. He insisted it was someone messing with me. That he was, in fact, guilty as charged. He apologized to my mother and then called for the guard to take him back to his cell. A piece of my heart broke off as I watched my mother crumble. Darren had nearly broken my mom. Despite his confession, Mom visited him almost every week. She insisted she knew her baby and that he was lying. He couldn't have killed a man in cold blood.

Denial.

It was the first stage in grieving, and Mom was stuck there. As her daughter, I tried to be there for her whenever she needed me. Even while standing at a crime scene. It wasn't fair I had to pick up the pieces my brother left, but that was life. It wasn't always fair.

It had been a hectic six months, and part of me wanted to dig into Darren's case to definitively prove to my mother it was all true, but there were higher priorities.

For one, Zoey graduated from high school, and we were preparing for her to go off to college—my baby was leaving for college. Ugh. I didn't want to be reminded. Another big change, and I wasn't sure I was ready. It was just going to be Barney, my little fluffy dog, and me. It was strange to think I had resisted Mom and Zoey's pleas for a pet, considering he was my only remaining snuggle buddy.

"I'll have to check my schedule, Mom. I'll call you later."

I glanced up, realizing Hirsch was probably trying to figure out who I was talking to.

After I hung up the phone and turned to Hirsch, I said, "My Mom. She wants me to go visit Darren."

"Is she still insisting he's innocent?"

"She is."

Hirsch was definitely of the mind that Darren was as guilty as the sun rose each day. Detective Leslie, someone I knew well and had worked with on the original Cold Case Squad, was the one who arrested and investigated Darren. And DA Greggs, someone else I respected, prosecuted him and signed the plea agreement. There was evidence, there was an eyewitness, and he'd pled guilty. The only thing out of place was the phone call claiming Darren hadn't killed the man.

I hadn't admitted it to Hirsch or my mother, but it continued to bother me. My gut was still telling me something was off. Why would someone call me and tell me he was innocent if he wasn't? On an untraceable burner phone. Maybe I should let it go. But that wasn't exactly my style. I needed to put the matter to bed. For my sake and my mother's.

Once we found Eliza's killer, I would look into my brother's case. Because if, by the slightest chance, the phone call wasn't a hoax and my brother was innocent... I *needed* to prove it.

3

MARTINA

Music blared from down the hall, a mixture of some awful tune about summertime and Zoey's voice, carefree and in harmony with the noise. It struck me, hard, that next month the house would fall silent. Zoey would be off to college, leaving only Barney and me to fill the quiet, and Barney wasn't much for making noise. He only made his presence audibly known when someone came to the door, rang the bell, left a package, or if I wasn't paying him enough attention.

Glancing down at the fluffy pup, I said, "Should we go see what Zoey is up to?" He stared up at me with those big, brown puppy eyes, and I took his silent gaze as an enthusiastic affirmation.

Was I losing my mind? Was this what happened when your only child was gearing up to leave the nest, or was it merely a symptom of middle age—or, perhaps, just the eccentricities of being a dog owner? Before Barney, I never quite understood people who dressed their pets in silly outfits or those who walked cats on leashes. But I suspected I had become one of them.

Barney and I hurried down the hall. As we approached, I

knocked on the frame of Zoey's open door. It was a scene I would keep in my memory for all time. Among the glittery posters on the wall and bookshelf stuffed with novels, Zoey wore a shirt adorned with a sparkly rainbow and pink leggings, dancing and singing as she stared down at her bed, which held an open suitcase. Was she packing already?

"How's it going?" I asked with a hint of sentimentality in my voice.

She turned down the volume and said, "I don't know how to figure out what to bring to school. I mean, the dorm room's so small, but I need all my clothes and all my stuff," she lamented, her voice tinged with anxiety. As if on cue, Barney ran up to her, begging for attention, and she lovingly administered scratches behind his ears. "They won't let me take Barney, right?"

"No pets allowed," I affirmed with feigned disappointment, though privately, I knew that once Zoey went to school, it would be just Barney and me. Our downtime would be spent curled up on the couch, him at my feet while I indulged in a true crime documentary or lost myself in a book.

"Maybe just start with packing your favorites."

"That's a great idea, Mom. Plus, Davis isn't that far away, so I could always come home if I need something." She paused, a playful glint in her eye. "You're not going to turn my room into a gym or something, right?"

I assured her with a smile, "I will not turn your room into a gym, I promise."

"I'm gonna hold you to that."

"Consider it held."

Her tone shifted to one of casual curiosity. "So, you're going to visit Uncle Darren today, huh?"

Feeling guilty that my mother had been so upset over Darren's situation, I gave in and agreed to visit him. Even though he was my brother, he was still a convicted murderer. It felt strange to visit San Quentin State Prison to meet with a family member, considering I had visited previously to interview suspects. I, like my mom, had a hard time believing he was capable of murder, but I had to remind myself that throughout our adult years, he had lived in a very different world from mine.

"That's the plan."

"What time is Grandma getting here?"

"In a few hours."

Zoey plopped onto her bed and sat cross-legged beside her suitcase. She looked up at me with a serious expression. "Is he really a bad guy?"

I sighed, contemplating how to explain the complexity of human nature. "Addiction doesn't make you a bad person, nor does a profession of selling drugs. Not alone, anyway. A bad person does bad things to both bad people and good people. It's not that he's a bad person, but he's done some really bad things, and I don't really know him all that well anymore. When we were kids, he was my big brother who used to pick on me. Then the drugs started pretty early on when we were in high school, and... well, we didn't stay in touch."

"But Grandma visits him all the time. She must see something in him, or is it just like a mom thing? Would you visit me in prison if I murdered someone?"

Everybody was capable of murder, but I had a hard time believing Zoey could ever do such a thing, though nothing in life is ever certain. "Of course, I would."

"Everybody has good in them, right? Isn't that what you always say? But we also have a little bit of bad too."

Her questions were leading somewhere. Was Zoey interested in meeting Darren? I had always kept her away from both him and Clark. They ran in dark circles, and considering what had been alleged—that he had killed someone—it was obviously a smart parenting decision. "I do believe that's true. Why do you ask?"

I pondered whether it was truly possible to find good in someone like the man who kidnapped Eliza, kept her hostage for five years, and then murdered her and left her body in a garage. He hadn't been caught yet, despite his face being plastered on every news station. We had volunteers posting his photo everywhere, offering a reward for information leading to his capture in towns across America. It was imperative to catch him before he harmed someone else's child.

"Well, I mean, I don't know... It's like when we were at church last weekend. They were talking about forgiveness and the good in all of us, and I'm just wondering... if maybe... I could meet Darren." Her voice trailed off, leaving the question hanging in the air.

She wanted to meet her uncle. I supposed it wasn't such a strange concept—he was family, after all, and I hadn't talked about either of my brothers much before Darren's murder conviction. I had asked my mother, when she lived with us, not to mention them either. Even so, I still received brief updates from her now and then—like if they were still alive and in the Bay Area. We would get calls every once in a while; usually, one or both of them needing something.

"How about this," I offered tentatively. "I'll talk to Uncle Darren and Grandma and see if he is OK with meeting you."

I felt guilty even suggesting I needed to check with Darren. I had only visited him once since he'd been incarcerated and once before he had signed his guilty plea. Both times, he asked about Zoey, as if he wanted to know her, to know about her. But I didn't like the idea of my daughter going to San Quentin. It was a world I tried to shield her from. But she was becoming an adult and next month would be living two hours away at the

University of California in Davis. My baby, on her own, away from me.

Zoey nodded. "Okay, I'd like to meet him. What's Clark like—your other brother?"

"Well, to be honest, I haven't spoken with him in as long as I hadn't spoken with Darren. But Grandma talks to him. She suspects he's also involved in criminal activity. I'd prefer not to bring him around." Considering fifty percent of my brothers were convicted murderers, I didn't know if Clark was just as dangerous and didn't plan on taking any chances.

"Really? I'd kind of like to meet him too. Do you really think he'd hurt us? He's your brother," she said, with a slight frown.

Family members were capable of horrifying things. Those who hurt us the most were usually the ones who had once loved us—or who were *supposed* to love us. "I'll talk to Grandma and see what she has to say about Clark."

Regardless of what my mother may say about Clark, I would still be a little against him meeting Zoey. More like *a lot* against it.

"Well, maybe he needs our help. Maybe we could meet in a neutral location or something like that," Zoey suggested with a hopeful tone.

I had either raised an overly optimistic daughter, or it was her youth, always being able to see things as potentially good—a glass half full type. I was normally like that too, but when it came to my daughter, I wouldn't let anybody close enough to hurt her if I had any say in the matter.

But I supposed Zoey had a point. After all, I was a volunteer at a rehabilitation center. Would it be any different to try to help my own brother? I'd have to discuss it with my mother and see if Clark was on a path to rehabilitation, like those at the rehab center who wanted help. If Clark didn't want it, I wasn't going to force it. "All excellent points," I conceded.

"Yeah, wouldn't it be just like you working at the rehab center? Which, by the way, how is it going? Do you feel like it's going well, and are you meeting people who are turning their lives around?" Zoey asked with those curious, wide blue eyes.

"It's been really good. A lot of the patients seem to be inspired by how I got sober, and how Grandma got sober, and how we've stayed that way for so long."

"Mom, you're definitely an inspiration," she said, rather dramatically. I was going to miss seeing her face every single day —her bright blue eyes, her sunny disposition, her loud music, her love of glitter and sparkle.

I sat down on the bed next to her and teased, "Don't you think you're packing kind of early?"

"Just getting organized. It's a trial run so I'm not scrambling at the last minute."

That was my Zoey—organized, punctual, planning ahead. What would I do without her? Who would cheer me up in the middle of a terrible case like the one with Eliza, or dealing with my brother's incarceration? Not that it should fall upon my daughter.

Just as my thoughts shifted, Barney jumped into my lap, as if answering my silent question that he would brighten my day —my little puppy with unconditional love, twenty-four hours a day, seven days a week, 365 days a year.

And I could visit Zoey, and we could talk on the phone. I didn't want to be too overbearing. I wanted her to experience college life, but I hated that she was going to be out of my sight, so far away for so long—realistically, for the rest of her life.

I scratched Barney behind the ears and smiled down at him. "Who's a good boy?" I cooed.

My phone buzzed, and I pulled it out. "That's Hirsch. I gotta answer it."

"Cool," Zoey said as she raised the volume of her music and

continued dancing and singing just as she was before I walked into her room.

With a smile, I exited her room and answered the call. "Hey, Hirsch, what's up?"

"They've got him," he said.

"Sergei Antonov?" The man who owned the home where Eliza Mitchell's body was found, and her suspected killer.

"The one and only. Someone spotted him in Humboldt County. Locals brought him in. They're waiting for us. Do you have time to come up with us and bring him back?"

"I sure can. What time are you leaving?" I asked, already mentally preparing for the trip.

"In about thirty minutes. I have to finish up some things at home, but then I'll be ready to hit the road."

"Okay, I'll meet you at your house."

It was a win-win. We caught a horrible killer, and I avoided seeing my brother in prison. A temporary reprieve. With Sergei in custody, I would use my freed up schedule to dive in to Darren's case. Was my brother really a killer, like so many of the criminals I tracked and brought to justice? If he was, what would that do to my mom?

4

MARTINA

SERGEI ANTONOV WASN'T TALKING—NOT to us, not to the locals, not to anyone. The only words he muttered were, "I want a lawyer."

It wasn't unusual. He had tried to cover his tracks, hiding out in a rural community up north, but our media campaign had worked. A local spotted him at a gas station and called it in. The Humboldt County Sheriff didn't hesitate, went in, arrested him right away, and called CoCo County. It was another bittersweet victory. The bad guy would go to prison for the rest of his life, but an innocent life was stolen and destroyed, along with her family. The only solace was that Sergei Antonov couldn't hurt another girl, or another child, ever again. We should be celebrating, cheering, but there was something in my belly stealing that joy. It was what came next.

"What's up, Martina?"

Hirsch knew me too well. "Are we sure he's going away for life?" Would he believe that was the reason for the look of despair I was wearing?

"Kiki and the forensics team aren't finished processing all of the evidence collected at the house, but they've processed enough and are pretty confident we're going to have a solid case against him. He can't hurt anyone else," Hirsch reassured me.

Surely, more evidence would point to him, and he would go to prison—which was where criminals belonged.

The nagging feeling inside me was that my brother was a criminal, and I was going to have to prove or disprove his guilt. He insisted he was guilty, so theoretically all I had to do was line up the evidence and explain it to my mom—and break her heart all over again. What worried me most was what it would do to her. She had already had to increase her attendance at AA meetings due to the stress. But thankfully, she had a strong support system—not just her other AA members and her sponsor, but Zoey, me, and her husband, Ted, too.

"That's great. We don't want anybody else getting hurt," I said, attempting to focus on the positive.

"I know you a little better than that, Martina. What's really going on?"

"Well, I was supposed to visit Darren today. Mom's been pushing me to see him more. I had agreed, but then, when I got the call that Sergei was in custody, I canceled. As you can imagine, Mom was upset, but she said she understood."

"Why does that bother you? Did you really want to see Darren?"

"It's not that. I want to put this to bed, Hirsch. I need to prove to my mom that he's guilty, or not. I have to look at his case."

His eyes widened, and he said, "Are you sure you want to do that? It's possible nothing you can show her will make her feel any different. It's her child; she may never believe that he's really guilty. I can't imagine ever thinking Audrey was capable of something like that. I'm not sure any amount of physical evidence will do it."

"That may be true, but it's kind of nagging at me, too. He

tells me he's guilty, that he did it, but that phone call. I haven't been able to shake it."

It probably wasn't the right time to bring up Darren's case. It had been a long day. As it was, Hirsch had rings under his eyes and his shirt was wrinkled and partially untucked. "Maybe you need to prove it to yourself, too. Maybe that's what this is really about."

Why did he have to be so wise? "I think so."

He sat up straight and ran his fingers through his hair. "Well, at this point, the case files are public record since the case is closed. You know Detective Leslie and I'll help any way we can, Martina, but I don't want to get your hopes up. He signed a guilty plea. Even if you find holes in the case, but don't 100% exonerate him, he will remain in prison until he serves out his twenty-five years."

"What do you mean?" Surely if there were holes, the district attorney would look into it.

"All I'm saying is you have a way of finding holes in everything. Even if you find something that wasn't done exactly how you would've investigated, or how you would've proven it, doesn't mean he's innocent. I just worry about you going down a rabbit hole. Like, what happens if one piece of evidence comes into question? Are you going to fight this, or are you going to try to get him a new trial? He pled guilty. There's really not much you can do. Short of a governor's pardon, I don't think you could undo his plea."

Admittedly, in my spare time, which usually meant the middle of the night, I had been researching overturned murder convictions, and well, they were no walk in the park. I stumbled onto the Innocence Project website, and even with all their successes of getting innocent people out of jail, it often took nine, ten, fifteen years to do so. It could be that, on the off chance Darren was innocent, it could take his entire twenty-five-year sentence to prove it and to actually get him out of prison. But I had to try. "Are you okay with me asking around, talking to Leslie and the forensics team? I won't be at the station in an official capacity."

"I think you'll find people will cooperate with you because you're one of us. So, of course, we'll cooperate."

"I appreciate that." And then stared down at the floor, processing all the information. What was I about to dive into? Would I learn all the dirty details of my brother's life? Likely I'd find things I didn't want to know, things I always assumed but didn't have evidence to back up. He had told me himself he had done really bad things. That was when he claimed to be innocent, only changing to a guilty plea later.

Well, if it was a simple open-and-shut case and he was guilty, it shouldn't take me long to prove it, and then I could move on, and hopefully so could my mom. And if they did everything by the book, there was nothing to worry about. But like Hirsch said, if there was a hole at any step of the way in prosecuting my brother, I would find it. But I did take to heart Hirsch's concern. Would I be able to look the other way if he hadn't gotten a fair deal, if the plea agreement was rushed because they knew they didn't have a solid case? Could I let that go? It wasn't even a question. I couldn't, *and I wouldn't.*

5

CANDACE

SIX MONTHS EARLIER

STARING down at the gold band on my finger, I never wanted to take it off. I could still remember when Travis slid it on my finger on our wedding day. He was so handsome in his black tuxedo with a lavender pocket square and a white Calla lily pinned to his lapel. The sun shone down, and his brown eyes glittered like chocolate diamonds. He had a tear in his eye as he slipped the ring on my finger, promising to love me until death do us part. He had fulfilled his promise, mostly anyhow.

I had been to enough support group meetings to have heard the same story over and over again. Most of the members of the group claimed they couldn't quite pinpoint the day that everything changed, the moment it all fell apart. But I could. It was vivid, and it played through my brain so many times I wished I could erase it. I wished I couldn't remember, but I did.

It was the day of his accident.

Travis had been driving home from work. He had called me before he left the fire station to tell me he'd be home in thirty minutes. I promised to have dinner ready since I was off that day. One of the perks of being a nurse: I had several days off during the week. On those days, I could play house, make dinner, and open a bottle of wine. I was excited because we had just decided to start trying for our first child.

When he didn't arrive, I grew concerned, and when I finally received a call from his cell phone, I was all fired up and about to rip him a new one. But the voice on the other end wasn't Travis. It was a police officer telling me my husband had been in a terrible accident and that he was at Mount Diablo Medical Center in the intensive care unit.

That was the moment everything changed.

Later, I learned that the accident was caused by Travis avoiding a deer in the road. That was just like Travis, always caring about others, creatures big and small. It was hard to hold a grudge against wildlife. I also learned when I arrived at the hospital, with my sister, that he was in surgery. They weren't sure if he was going to make it, and a few hours later, they told me he would live but they weren't sure if he was ever going to walk again. The doctor explained he had been lucky and could have been killed. I was grateful, but when Travis woke the next day and heard the news, he was devastated.

He was a firefighter who could no longer walk. Or fight fires.

After the accident, he wasn't sure what he would do. He fell into a deep depression, but then he turned those dark thoughts into anger, and then miraculously that anger turned into determination. He worked hard at physical therapy, and he walked again, but he was still in a lot of pain.

Everyone kept telling me it was a miracle he could walk and that the pain would subside, but it was excruciating, and he still couldn't work. Our finances had been strained, living off my nurse's income, but eventually, he started to seem better, less in pain. I thought the nightmare was finally coming to an end, and we decided it was time to start trying for a baby again.

And we did.

We tried and tried, and a few months later, it happened. We were going to have a baby. Travis was ecstatic, and I was over the moon. I was about to have everything I had ever wanted.

But then, Travis started acting strange. At first, I thought it was because he wasn't so sure about the baby after all, even though we had always said we both wanted children. He was just angrier, saying he was in pain, and then he would be fine. It was frustrating, and I blamed myself when I didn't see the signs sooner.

I should've seen them sooner.

But in my blissful pregnant brain, I didn't let myself think about that. Think about how he was miraculously better one minute and the next he wasn't.

It wasn't until the check to the mortgage company bounced that I took a closer look at our finances. Money was being withdrawn from our account on a regular basis.

"What is this money for?" I had asked Travis.

"Medical supplies," is what he told me at first, but there weren't any new medical supplies that I could find.

We argued.

And we made up.

And I let it go.

I wanted my happy family. I wanted Travis happy. I wanted to be happy and for our new baby to come into the world with loving parents who didn't fight all the time.

As a last resort, I asked my parents for money. He made me lie. I couldn't tell them Travis had been taking money out of our account and refusing to own up to it.

"Let me see the medical supplies," I finally demanded.

"I don't have to show you anything," he said with venom and dilated pupils.

I knew it then—it was drugs.

All the signs had been there.

When I confronted him, he refused to admit it. Pleading with him, I promised I would support him as he sought help. He just got angrier, and one day he left, took nearly the remainder of our bank account, and didn't come back for twenty-four hours.

Terror seized me as all the thoughts of where he could be and what he could be doing took hold.

But he returned, and when he did, he was high as a kite. The latest stunt forced me to go back to my parents and ask for more money and to open an account that Travis didn't know about, to make sure we still had a house and electricity.

When the money ran out, that's when things got really bad. He finally confessed he'd been buying fentanyl—apparently it was the cheapest and most effective pain killer. But his body was building up a tolerance and he needed higher doses. I knew we couldn't continue on the way we were. I begged him to get help, and he finally relented. He went to exactly one meeting and then refused to go back, saying he wasn't an addict, that it was the doctor's fault he needed pain medication. And that if the drugs were so bad, why had the doctor prescribed it?

Excuses.

It was the accident's fault. It was the doctor's fault. It was everyone else's fault. Maybe. But it was Travis's fault he refused to get help.

The day he died, we'd had an awful argument about his drug use, about our finances, about our home, and about our family. I threatened to leave him unless he got help. He stormed out.

I never saw him alive again.

He was found in his car, dead from an overdose. He'd taken too much. They weren't able to determine if it was accidental or on purpose.

I nearly fell apart, wondering how I would raise our baby on my own. How could I continue on without my partner? But then, the spotting and cramping started. And in what seemed like a flash, I no longer had a husband or a child. All my hopes and dreams were gone. I almost had it all—a husband, a child—both ripped from me because of drugs.

It had been a year since I had lost absolutely everything, and it didn't seem right. Drugs killed my husband, and the people who sold them, knowing he was an addict—they were to blame. They took him. They took her. They had to pay.

I had nothing left, except for my job. And even my supervisor could feel my grief and see the lack of energy. After a leave of absence, they transferred me to a "less intense" area of the hospital. The only thing that kept me going was knowing I had a new purpose.

I would find the person who sold Travis drugs, and he would pay for what he did to my husband, to my baby—a baby who never had the chance to meet her father, or live, or breathe a single breath. That drug dealer took everything, and I was going to take everything from him.

6

MARTINA

With confidence, I approached the records clerk. We had only met a few times, but I recalled he had been on the force for fifteen years, and after suffering a gunshot wound to the hip, he could no longer work active cases and chose to wait for his retirement in the records department. Most officers would be pretty unhappy about the change, but he insisted working in the records department enabled him to keep up with his old buddies and meet new ones. "Martina, how's it going? What can I help you with?" Roger asked.

With a nervous smile, I said, "I need a recently closed case."

He pushed forward a clipboard and said, "OK, just go ahead and sign in here and provide all the details, and I'll get that right to you."

I stared down at the paper, realizing I was about to write down the case file number—the case file in which my brother pled guilty to the murder of an innocent man. He claimed he killed him and that I had to let it go, but something wasn't feeling right to me, and I wouldn't let it go until I had all the evidence and facts in hand. I would prove to my mother, and myself, what my brother had done.

With a lopsided grin, the records officer headed back into the stacks, and I paced, wondering how many members of law enforcement checked out murder files that included their family members. Probably not that many, although during my time with the Cold Case Squad we had discovered a few bad apples within the CoCo County Sheriff's Department.

Pacing, I tried to think of what the investigation might tell me about my brother. Things I could never un-know. Would my mom want to know every single detail of what her son had done? Would I also find bad acts my other brother, Clark, did? Sometimes ignorance was bliss, and I was about to shatter that bliss into pieces.

"Martina, is that you?"

Turning toward the familiar voice, I froze and said, "Oh. Hey, Leslie, how's it going?"

"Good. What are you doing down here?"

"I'm taking a look at my brother's case."

Her dark brows knitted together. "Oh?"

"My mother won't let go of the idea he's innocent, even though he's still claiming he's not. I'm just trying to find as much information as I can to explain it to her. So maybe she can move on."

Detective Leslie, the arresting officer and the person to have built the case against my brother, and I had been colleagues. We worked together for a few years on the Cold Case Squad. It had been years since we actually worked together, but I knew she was good at her job. I didn't think I would uncover anything unsavory about how the case was handled. I just... I didn't know what I was hoping for.

"Well, let me know if I can answer any questions for you. I know something like this can be hard to let go. Especially for a mother."

"I appreciate that."

Roger returned with the file and placed it on the counter before glancing up at Detective Leslie and saying, "Well, if it isn't one of my favorite detectives. What can I help you with?"

I quickly thanked the clerk and waved at Leslie as I clutched my brother's case file and hurried out.

DESPITE THE WILLINGNESS of Hirsch and the rest of the CoCo County detectives to help, I opted to bring the case file back to my office at Drakos Monroe. It didn't feel right to review my brother's case at the sheriff's department because in a sense I was investigating the CoCo County detectives. Secluded in my private space, I took a deep breath and read the file.

An hour later, I leaned back and shook my head.

The victim's name was Toby June, a known drug dealer. The victim had been shot at close range, once in the head with a .22 caliber weapon, killing him instantly. The gun was never found. Therefore, they couldn't actually tie it to Darren. The only physical evidence pointing to Darren was the plastic bag filled with fentanyl tablets in the victim's pocket that had Darren's fingerprints all over them. There was no refuting that, but that didn't prove Darren killed him. The motive was listed as rivalry.

Toby June was a rival drug dealer encroaching on Darren's territory. It wasn't unusual for one set of dealers to take out another if they were encroaching on their territory. It was a solid motive. The evidence certainly pointed to Darren, but it didn't without a reasonable doubt prove he was the shooter. And I couldn't shake the fact the only thing pointing to Darren as the shooter was the eyewitness testimony and the fingerprints on a bag of drugs. There could have been a number of reasons for Toby to have a bag of drugs from my brother. Darren was a drug dealer. It didn't mean he was also a killer.

One eyewitness wouldn't be enough to prosecute, especially with no physical evidence like gunshot residue on Darren's hands or the actual murder weapon to corroborate the crime. The case didn't go to trial because Darren had confessed and signed a plea deal. If he had gone to trial, would he be a free man?

The single eyewitness, Candace Mason, had been pivotal in putting my brother in jail. As a civilian, that must've felt really strange. To think your testimony, along with the corroborating fingerprints on the drugs in Toby's pocket, put a man in prison for twenty-five years. I wondered if it had changed her somehow or if she was happy to help. If I witnessed someone kill another person, I would be eager to help.

The circumstantial evidence certainly pointed to Darren, but it didn't without a reasonable doubt prove he was the shooter.

And who was Toby June? There were not many details about him, his life, or his drug affiliations. All the report said was that he was a "rival drug dealer." What organization was he with? There were so many different drug gangs and organizations in the Bay Area. I would've expected for the homicide detective to have consulted with the narcotics team to capture those details. Maybe Detective Leslie had, but it just wasn't in the report. Why wasn't it in the report?

And what drug organization was Darren involved with? That wasn't in the report either. So, how did they know Darren and Toby were rivals?

And why would Darren leave the drugs behind? If he was smart enough to get rid of the gun, why leave the drugs with his fingerprints all over them? And why not take the twenty-dollar bill jammed in Toby's pocket?

I leaned back in my chair and scratched my chin. Why would Darren leave the drugs? Why would he kill some low-level drug dealer like Toby June? Surely a warning would've kept him from selling on his turf. Perhaps those were all questions for my big brother. I sighed and thought, *Looks I'll be visiting Darren after all.*

7

MARTINA

My brother agreed to put me on his visitors' list. It hadn't been difficult. He wanted me to visit, and so did my mother. Of course, I didn't explain why I was visiting or that I would be by myself. It was a little sneaky, but my instincts told me he wouldn't see me if he knew my true intentions.

I'm not a fan of trickery, but I needed Darren's account of what happened, and I wanted to match it up with what the eyewitness had put in her statement. If there were any discrepancies in his story, or hers, I'd find it. Or I'd corroborate the chain of events and explain to my mother that there was no doubt her son was a killer.

I really didn't want to have to deliver that news. My story to anyone who asked was that I was trying to help my mother move on, but of course Hirsch saw right through me, knowing it was me who had a flicker of doubt about my brother's guilt.

Darren and I had practically been strangers since we were in our teens, but I remembered him from when we were little. He wasn't always on the wrong side of the law. But he did have a penchant for trouble, but that didn't necessarily make him bad or evil. Having known my brother in early life, I knew he wasn't the kind of kid who pulled legs off spiders or tortured animals. He was a normal boy who had liked playing baseball and riding bikes. It wasn't until drugs entered the picture that he changed. Sure, he'd always been an annoying older brother who teased me because I was the only girl in the family, but nothing in my memory from our childhood pointed to him being rotten at the core.

Growing up wasn't easy for him, or for me, or for Clark. Our dad left us before I could even remember. We were poor, our mother was an alcoholic, and we lived in a trailer. It wasn't exactly a recipe for greatness. Truthfully, drugs and a life in the shadows was the most likely route for all of us. But while Darren and Clark used harder stuff, I chose alcohol. Addiction was in our DNA and wasn't something any of us could escape.

Guilt seeped inside me.

Maybe I should've shown them more grace. Instead, I thought I was better than they were. After entering the Army, my life had turned around, and I met Jared and had Zoey. I didn't want anything or anyone to hurt my family, and I chose to do everything I could to protect them, even turn my back on my mother and brothers. But I wasn't better than them.

Who was I to judge?

We had all come from the same place. And I couldn't deny they were a part of me, whether they were in my life or not.

Even with that realization, I couldn't bring myself to ask my mother about Clark, to see if he'd want to meet Zoey. It was natural she'd want to know her uncles, but I wasn't ready. Conflicted, I recalled how my mother and I had reconciled several years earlier after she got sober and found me in a hospital bed. If Mom and I could be clean and reconnect, maybe Zoey was right. We were all capable of redemption. That included Darren and Clark.

The door opened, and my brother was escorted into the

room. He had a black eye that was turning gruesome colors, and he had lost weight since I'd last seen him. He sat down, looked me dead in the eyes, and said, "Little sister, how are you?"

"I'm doing well. How are you holding up?"

He shrugged. "Where's Mom?"

Time to come clean. "It's just me today. There are some things I wanted to talk to you about without Mom here."

Darren nodded slowly and leaned back in his chair. "Why are you here, Martina?"

He was annoyed, but he had to know I was going to ask eventually. Didn't he realize how his blasé attitude was affecting his family? "Do you know that you're killing Mom? The fact that you're here, that you're insisting that you're guilty?" Why did I say that? It wasn't my plan to attack him. But I was so angry at the situation, and something about his demeanor fired me up. Indifference. That was what it was. And he didn't get to be indifferent.

He fidgeted in his seat. "That's because I am. I don't know why she can't accept that."

"Because she's your mother, and as a mother myself, I don't know if I could ever accept it either. But I'm trying to help her. I want her to move on. I want her to accept that you're guilty and that you'll be in here for the next twenty-five years."

"Less if I keep up my good behavior."

His statement gave me pause. "Look, I want to help Mom. I want to be able to definitively prove what happened. I think it's important for her healing."

He glanced around the room before he said, "What do you want to know?"

"I want you to tell me what happened that day. Where you were, who was there, how the drugs ended up in his pocket, what happened to the gun—everything."

He let out a breath, glanced over at the door before saying,

"It was late in the day, and I was meeting Toby. He said he needed to score."

But he was a drug dealer. A *rival* drug dealer. Why would Darren give Toby some of his supply? I kept that to myself, wanting Darren to keep going.

"I knew he'd been dealing in my territory, so I agreed to meet, and we did our transaction. I gave him the bag of fentanyl, he gave me his money, afterward I told him he was done, and I shot him in the head."

He said it monotonously, no emotion, no remorse. Indifferent. "What did you do with the gun?"

"Tossed it in the bay."

"When did you toss it?"

"Right after I shot him. I got in my car, drove down to the marina in Bay Point, and tossed it."

"And what kind of gun was it?"

"A .22."

His story was plausible. "Why did you leave the drugs?"

Darren remained silent.

"You gave him drugs. You had a transaction, you just described it to me. Why didn't you take them back? Why would you leave perfectly good drugs behind when you could sell them to someone else?"

He shifted in his seat. "Well, after I shot him, I just wanted to get out of there, you know, before there were any witnesses."

My head cocked, and he looked stunned, not sure why I was reacting to what he said. "But there was a witness."

"Oh, I... I didn't see the witness, but I heard there was one. That was my mistake."

He hadn't seen the eyewitness. It didn't make sense. How could the eyewitness see the entire thing but still be invisible to Darren? "You don't remember seeing a witness?"

"No. But there were a lot of people at the park. You know,

it's a place known for dealing, and usually, when someone gets capped, everyone just looks the other way. No one talks to the police."

Then why was this witness different? Who was Candace Mason, and if she was there buying and selling drugs, why would she talk to the police?

"So, you dealt at that park regularly?"

Darren nodded.

"What organization are you with?"

"Organization?"

"Come on. This isn't my first day on the job. Where do you get your supply?"

He looked up to the corner of the room and said, "You know, it's been a while. I don't remember."

He was stonewalling me. He wasn't going to give up his supplier, which most likely led to a much bigger dealer, a drug kingpin. He wasn't going to rat them out.

"You know I can find out, right?" I asked him.

He wasn't giving anybody up, which was probably smart, considering they could probably get to him in prison. I continued, "Anything else you can tell me about that day that could help me prove to Mom what you're saying is true, that you're guilty?"

"Look, Martina, I appreciate the visit, but you need to take my word for it. I just told you he was selling on my turf. I agreed to meet, gave him the drugs. I told him, 'This is what you get for dealing on my turf,' and I shot him, then I ran so that nobody could ID me."

I could tell Darren was getting frustrated with me and my questions. "If he was a rival dealer, why would he think he could buy drugs from you?"

Darren's amber eyes widened, and he looked away. He was lying or avoiding my question. Why?

My pulse quickened. "Darren, if you didn't do this, I can help you."

He turned back and said, "You need to drop it. I'm guilty. I killed him. Let me do my time in peace, and if you're only going to come here to interrogate me, don't come back." With that, he shoved his chair away and stormed out. The guard got to him quickly, considering they weren't supposed to be shoving or kicking furniture around.

Darren didn't like my questions, but why? He had already pled guilty. Was it because there was a huge hole in his story, unless he was higher up in the drug organization, and there was another reason why he killed Toby June. And that was what I needed to find out. Who was Toby June, and who else had a motive to kill him? And what was that motive? If he had no drugs to sell, he wasn't at the park dealing.

Something wasn't adding up, and I was going to find out why.

8

MARTINA

The name on the caller ID made me anxious, but I answered anyway. "Hi, Mom."

"Hi, Martina. I just talked to Darren. He said you visited. That's so great, honey. I'm so happy."

Why was she so happy? Did she know what we talked about? "Well, I'm not sure it went all that well."

"He says you were asking about the case, that you're looking into it."

"I am. I've got the case file, and I'm trying to corroborate everything that the police found against him."

"I just know he's innocent. Thank you so much. I know you're going to prove it, honey. I'm so proud of you."

Mom was far too enthusiastic, too sure her son was innocent. "Thanks for the confidence, Mom, but did Darren tell you anything useful? He didn't seem to want to answer my questions." At least not the ones that could actually shed light on what really happened.

"No, and of course, he said he's guilty and that I had to accept it, and he was going to do his best to be a model prisoner and get out as soon as he can. But Martina, I can feel it. I feel it in all my motherly instincts. He didn't do this," she said, with a bit too much glee in her voice.

Admittedly, what I found so far didn't seem to add up, but it was still possible Darren killed Toby. It may just not be for the reason that was stated in the report. He swore he killed Toby June for dealing on his turf. But what rival dealer would meet up for a drug deal? The story didn't make sense, which most likely meant it wasn't true. It meant that Darren was hiding the real reason Toby June was killed. This meant he knew what really happened, but that didn't mean Darren was innocent. In fact, I began to suspect something bigger than two rival dealers was the reason for Toby's death. What I needed was to talk to the witness to find out what she really saw, a play-by-play.

"Mom, I don't want you to get your hopes up too high. I'm going to prove what happened, but that doesn't mean Darren is innocent. You have to understand that."

"I hear you. But where do you think you got all that gut instinct from? Me. It's women's intuition. You have it, and I have it, and honey, I'm telling you, your brother didn't do this."

"Mom, I'm going to level with you. There are things Darren will not talk to me about. He's not telling me the truth and he's not telling me everything. Why would he do that?" I didn't want to hurt my mom, knowing she was as fragile as she was over the whole situation, but she had to come down to earth. Her son was a criminal. No amount of digging into the past would disprove that fact. The burning question was which crimes he'd committed.

"I don't know, honey, but I know you'll figure it out. I'm just so worried about him in there. I think they've been roughing him up."

It wasn't uncommon. There were a lot of fights in prison. "Unfortunately, that's life in prison. Do you have another reason to believe he might be in danger?"

"No, but I've seen a few injuries. When I ask about it, he says it's nothing and changes the subject."

Typical prison code. "I'll do what I can. I'm going to prove the facts of the case, but I can't promise you anything else, OK?"

In a condescending tone, she said, "OK, Martina. I hear you. You're going to prove the facts. Excellent."

I rolled my eyes. Was she having some sort of mental break? Had Darren's murder conviction pushed her too far? She'd been sober for almost a decade. She had a new husband who was sweet and loving, a good partner. Could this be the thing that pushed her over the edge, her manic belief that her son was innocent, despite his guilty plea?

Maybe I should tread lighter with my mother. I didn't want to push her off the final step of that ledge. How could I keep her expectations realistic? In the past week, I'd had enough of failing others. Eliza's family had been devastated when we delivered the news. And I didn't want to disappoint any more grieving mothers.

"Mom, take care. I'm going to keep working."

"OK, dear. Are you and Zoey still coming over for dinner on Sunday?"

"Of course."

We said our goodbyes, and I hoped I wouldn't break my mother's heart even further, but she had to know the truth, as painful as that might be. I glanced down at the witness statements. Candace Mason, the eyewitness, Jack Jefferson, who arrived after the shooting, and Mark Flowers, the man who called 911 and gave his account of what was happening at the time he arrived on the scene.

Considering my brother wasn't talking to me, I would interview all three of them. And I'd like to find that gun. The case file didn't include the ballistics report to determine if the gun had been used in other crimes. I took a mental note to add a phone call into the ballistics department to my list of things to do.

Not wasting any time, I picked up the receiver, ignored the nagging feeling inside of me that I was about to crush my mother *or* the CoCo County Sheriff's Department—both of which I held dear, and dialed the number to the ballistics expert I had worked with in the past. A female voice answered, "Ballistics."

"May I please speak with Ms. Pinkerton?"

"This is she. Who is this?"

"Hi, this is Martina Monroe."

"Oh, hi, Martina. How have you been? It's been a while."

"Doing very well, thank you very much. And yourself?"

"Not too shabby, just working for the weekend. What can I do for you?"

"I'm working on a closed murder case for Toby June, and there was a firearm used that was never recovered. The bullet from the body should have been submitted. Do you know if that bullet was run through ballistics to see if the gun was connected to any other crimes?"

"What's your case number?"

I rattled off the case number and waited patiently as she clicked away on the keys of her keyboard. If the gun had been used before, we could tie it to a different shooter, or I would learn my brother had killed before. Maybe that was what he was trying to hide. Twenty-five years was a lot less than twenty-five years plus another life sentence, meaning he would never get out of jail.

"OK, I see it here, and we definitely did run it through to see if it matched with any other bullets found at any other crime scenes, and there was not a match."

"Thank you," I said with exasperation.

It was a dead end.

"Sorry I couldn't help you out."

"I appreciate your quick response."

"All right, say hi to Hirsch for me."

I promised to do so and hung up. The gun hadn't been used in other crimes; it was clean. Which was consistent if they were going to execute someone: a clean gun, tossed, not connected to any other place, records, or crimes, solved or unsolved.

Perhaps Toby June really was a victim of a hit, but it seemed awfully sophisticated for Darren. But what did I really know about my brother? I needed to know who his supplier was, who he was working with, as well as the details for the victim Toby June. It was important to know everything I could about my brother and the victim. My gut said it may lead to more questions. But I needed answers, and I knew exactly who I could get them from.

9

CANDACE

SIX MONTHS EARLIER

THE FIRST TIME I followed Travis, which was shortly before he died, I felt an immense sense of guilt. Guilt for not trusting my husband, the man I had vowed to be with for the rest of my life. This guilt turned to heartbreak when I saw him pull into the parking lot of a park on the other side of town.

He walked up to a man wearing baggy jeans, with floppy brown hair and a scar on his neck. They both looked around cautiously. I ducked down in my car, so they couldn't see me. When I popped back up, Travis was handing the man something, and he stepped away. A few minutes later, another man, tall and slender, with dark brown hair and an oversized coat, handed him something I couldn't see. Travis hurried back into his car.

While Travis was focused on his new acquisition, I sped out of the parking lot and drove home with tears streaming down my face. I knew he had a drug problem. I shouldn't say I knew, but I suspected it. The signs were there, but this proved it. I had been married to a drug addict, one who didn't want my help.

The second time I followed him was after a big argument we had, where he denied everything. That time, I was more cautious and knew where he was going, so I was prepared and knew where to park so I wouldn't be seen.

Quietly, I climbed out of my car and made my way to the edge of the park and watched from behind a hedge. The park wasn't huge, and I could see the cement paths lining the grass leading to a playground and what look like a set of restrooms. It was there behind the bushes I could get a better look at how it all went down. He would give money to the man with a scar on his neck and then the tall man would hurry over and hand over the baggy of drugs to my husband. With each moment that passed, a chip of my heart broke off as I wondered if Travis and I could overcome this. I knew his painkillers could only heal his physical pain but not his mental anguish. He hadn't been himself since the accident and the drugs. By the end, we had become strangers instead of the loving couple we had once been.

Even so, when I received the call he was dead, I broke in half.

They found Travis dead in his SUV in the parking of a local grocery store. They didn't show me any pictures, but I could still see it vividly in my head. It was like a photograph in my brain, and it stayed there, refusing to be shoved to the back with all the other bad memories.

Having intimate knowledge of how the deals would go down and a plan in my mind, I entered the parking lot of that godforsaken park.

With the car off, I stepped out wearing clothes I'd found in an old box labeled "donation." My hair hadn't been brushed and makeup had been left in the drawer.

The park had a half a dozen people milling about. Thankfully there were no children. Sure of myself, I made my way toward the money guy. He was right on the left—it must have been his usual spot. I approached him cautiously and said, "Hey, how's it going?"

"What's up? What are you looking for?"

Same neck scar. It was one of Travis's killers. I glanced around and whispered, "Got any pills? Fentanyl."

He looked me up and down. "A gram will cost you two hundred."

I hesitated. "I don't have that much cash on me."

"No money, no product."

"I didn't realize how much it was going to cost. I thought it was more like twenty. I need them for my husband." It was no wonder Travis had managed to drain our bank account.

"Who is your husband?" he asked, evaluating me.

"His name is Travis. He's a firefighter."

He extended his hand. "Oh yeah, good guy. I'm June Bug."

"Crystal," I lied. He didn't need to know my real name.

"How's he doing? Haven't seen him around."

Who knew drug dealers were so friendly? Was Travis actually friends with these people? "He was doing really good, but he took a fall, and he's in a lot of pain, so I offered to come get him some stuff."

"He's lucky to have you."

He was, but he didn't see it that way. He chose drugs over our baby and me. "I'll come back with the cash."

"For sure. Tell Travis I said hey."

"Thanks," I said, turning away.

He didn't know that one of his best customers, my husband, would no longer be buying from him. It had been a year since he had died, you'd think he would've figured it out. But then again, maybe he wasn't friends with Travis and he didn't pay attention to who he sold to. Before I could head back to my vehicle, another man approached, with amber eyes and olive skin. He was the tall man who handed over the goods. The two killers' faces were etched in my brain.

"Got a problem here?" he asked.

I shook my head. "No, nothing's wrong. I'll be back."

The man with the amber eyes looked at the other one and then asked me, "You a cop?"

I shook my head and laughed at the ridiculousness of the idea. "Not even close. Just trying to get something for my husband to make him feel better."

"She's Travis's wife," June Bug, the man with the scar on his neck, interjected. "She didn't know it cost so much. He's in pain."

Amber eyes nodded. "Here." He pulled a baggy out of his pocket and handed me a tiny pill. "This will help until you can come back with more cash."

If Travis were alive and I really was there to help, I might have seen this gesture as kind. But that wasn't the case. They were trying to keep him hooked.

What they didn't know was my husband's life was over and had been for a year. These two men would soon realize that and would pay for their crimes. When I returned, I would ruin their lives like they had ruined mine.

But how? I hadn't quite figured out that part yet. Should I film them and call the cops? Or did I need to think bigger?

10

MARTINA

Approaching my favorite narcotics officer's cubicle, I said, "Knock, knock."

Kiva looked up at me with his big brown eyes. "Martina Monroe, how's it going?"

Kiva and Rourke were part of our narcotics team when we were hunting down a criminal organization masquerading as a commune. They had been extremely helpful in solving the case. The duo certainly had my respect, and I hoped the feeling was mutual *and* they would give me the information I needed.

"Things are going pretty well," I replied.

"How's Zoey doing?"

Kiva and Rourke had met my girl at a few of the BBQs Hirsch had held throughout the years. Zoey left an impression. "A little too eager to go off to college for my taste."

"It must be crazy having your baby leave the nest."

"It is, and I don't love it." Was it as crazy as the fact that I was trying to prove my brother was guilty of murder?

Kiva smiled and said, "I'm guessing you need something."

"Guilty. I'm looking into a case. A murder from six months ago. A drug dealer named Toby June was shot."

"Ah, June Bug," Rourke said from the other side of the cubicle. He hopped up and said, "Hey, Martina, thought I heard your voice. What do you want to know about June Bug?"

Rourke came over to Kiva's desk, taking a seat on the edge.

"Hey, Rourke. Well, I'm hoping to find out more about his death."

"I'm not sure how much we can help. One of our CIs said that he got capped by another dealer. After the CI told us, we updated our file."

"Homicide didn't come and talk to you?"

Rourke and Kiva exchanged glances. "No."

"Wouldn't that be typical? I've reviewed the case file, and it says the motive for the killing was over turf. That a rival gang took him out for selling on their territory. But if Homicide didn't talk to you, how would they know that? It wasn't anywhere in the files."

"Who was the arresting officer?"

"Leslie from homicide."

"Oh, she's good police. It's odd she didn't come talk to us."

Indeed. How would they have gotten the theory that it was a rival gang that killed Toby if they didn't even know what gang he was part of? I would have to follow up with Leslie to get her side of the story. This was one more piece that was not fitting into the picture that had been painted. "Okay, so aside from not being consulted during the homicide investigation, what can you tell me about June Bug?"

"He was a low-level dealer and a pretty good guy in general, as far as dealers go. But he started to get high on his own supply. It's a big no-no. Word on the street is he owed money to the boss."

"Who's the boss?"

"Jaime Ragnar of the 98Mob."

"I'm guessing he's a bad guy?"

Kiva and Rourke nodded in unison. "Oh yeah. They're not a huge organization, but we think they're buying their supply from Mexican cartels. They're not part of the cartel, but the leader of 98Mob, Jaime Ragnar, is rumored to be aspiring to be the next big drug kingpin in the Bay Area. Kind of a young guy, early thirties, real ambitious, smart too, considering he's avoided arrest. The 98Mob operates mostly in the Tracy, Brentwood, and Oakley areas, but rumor is Jaime wants to expand."

If Toby owed money to the big boss, that was a motive for murder. But so was turf.

"Good to know. What can you tell me about Darren Kolze?"

"Darren Kolze? Heard he was locked up. Killed someone." He let that linger for a moment. "Wait, are you saying Darren took out June Bug?"

"He confessed to the murder."

"That doesn't make sense," Kiva said.

"Why?"

"Darren is with the 98Mob. But it could make sense. Maybe the boss asked Darren to take out June Bug because of his bad debts."

That was a more plausible explanation for Darren killing Toby than a rival gang, considering they weren't rivals. Shaking my head back and forth, I said, "That's odd. Homicide's report says June Bug was killed for selling in Darren's territory."

"No, that's not right. They worked together, same team. Both are 98Mob. If Darren took out Toby, it's because it was ordered by the boss. Both were pretty low-level, not big-time."

"Was Darren known to do the boss's dirty work?" Was Toby Darren's first kill or simply the only one he'd been caught for?

"No. But everyone's got a first time."

Was that the real reason why Darren wouldn't talk to me about it, because he was protecting his boss? That actually made sense. If he was protecting the boss, he wouldn't want me to investigate and uncover a conspiracy to commit murder scheme that would implicate Jaime Ragnar. If Darren ratted on Ragnar, my guess was he'd be pretty upset and possibly take out Darren to silence him. It explained how adamant Darren was about being guilty and for me to let it go. Ragnar may have even threatened Darren's family. My mom. Me. Zoey.

"This isn't lining up, huh?" Kiva asked.

"No, it's really not. I spoke to Darren. He confirmed the motive—said he took out Toby because he was dealing in his territory."

"Why, if you don't mind us asking, are you looking into this case?"

My latest least favorite thing to explain. I used to think it was telling people that my husband was dead and I was a widow, but saying that your brother is a convicted murderer was a whole different ball game. "Darren is my brother."

"Oh, shoot, seriously?"

"Yeah, he swears he's guilty. My mom is having a hard time reconciling her child killed someone. I'm just dotting Is, crossing Ts, making sure nothing was missed, and hopefully trying to explain to her that this is how it is, and she has to accept it."

"I'm so sorry, Martina. I had no idea. That's tough."

"It is, but I guess I don't understand why they would've closed out the investigation without the actual motive. Their motive is wrong. That's strange, right?"

Had Leslie thought the case was a slam dunk because of the eyewitness account of the crime and didn't bother to check the facts of the case?

"It is, and it's a little odd Homicide didn't come and talk to us. It's not like Leslie."

It really wasn't. Leslie had been on the force for decades and was a solid detective.

"How did they catch him?" Rourke asked.

"An eyewitness saw Darren shoot Toby. There was a bag of drugs in Toby's pocket with Darren's fingerprints on it. They gave him a deal—twenty-five years."

"Seems kind of weak. Did they find the gun?"

"No."

"So, there's no physical evidence actually tying Darren to the shooting?"

My gut stirred. If Kiva and Rourke thought this was unusual, it wasn't all in my head. Something was very off about the case. Should I go straight to Leslie? Or should I go to Hirsch first? I looked at my watch; I was going to be late.

"Look, you've been really helpful, but unfortunately, this has created more questions than answers."

"I hear you. Talk to Leslie, and try to get this straightened out. I'm sure there's a simple explanation for all of this."

I stared straight into Rourke's eyes and gave him a look that said something was fishy and I wasn't so sure. He gave me a slight head nod like he understood.

"We'll see. I need to head out, but thank you."

"Good luck, Martina. Anything we can do to help, we will."

I gave them a sheepish grin and headed toward the rehabilitation center. It was time to try to inspire addicts that sobriety was achievable and sustainable over the long term. With a quiet prayer for them and me, I hurried out of the station trying not to think of the holes I had found in Darren's case.

11

MARTINA

Entering the rehabilitation center, I tried to erase the conversation with the narcotics team from my mind because I needed to focus on the task at hand. But I was having trouble with it. Instead of simple answers regarding Darren and Toby's drug affiliations, the facts only led to more questions. Not only questions about Darren and his motive but about the investigating detective's motive too. She was someone I had trusted. Darren's false statement made perfect sense if the 98Mob boss ordered him to kill Toby. It was self-preservation. But what I couldn't wrap my head around was why Detective Leslie took Darren's statement of motive at face value without corroborating it with the narcotics department. Leslie closed the case when the facts of the case were wrong. What else did she miss?

Shaking my head, I opened the door and stepped inside, waved at the center's receptionists and headed back toward the colorful counseling rooms where my workstation was situated. The program coordinator was standing near my desk.

"Good evening, Martina."

"Hi, Lisa, How's it going?"

"Good. We have a couple of new members who I think would be inspired by your story."

Could I be inspirational while crumbling on the inside? Had Hirsch been right? Was I already falling down a rabbit hole with the inconsistencies I had uncovered? Where else could I go? I couldn't ignore what I had found. They didn't have motive —not at all. For a solid prosecution, you needed means, motive, and opportunity. It sounded like Darren had opportunity, maybe even means, but he didn't have motive, at least not one that was documented in the case file.

"Everything okay?" Lisa asked.

"Sorry. Yes. Work has been a little nuts."

"I can only imagine with a job like yours."

The job was only half of it. The other half was worrying about uncovering police misconduct. How would that play out? Shaking the thoughts away, I said, "Yes, but I'm okay. What's the plan for tonight?"

"After the group sessions, there is a couple of people I want you to meet one-on-one. Is that something you're up for? I know it's late, and I'm sure you had a long day, but I think there is one in particular who could really benefit from hearing your story."

"Sure, sounds great."

It sounded like a distraction, and I was all for it. Focusing on other people's problems instead of my own was a specialty of mine.

AFTER THE LAST SESSION, I was walking toward my desk with thoughts of packing up and going home. Lisa stood next to my chair with a man with an olive complexion and haunted brown eyes. "Hey, Martina. I was just speaking with one of the new members. Do you have a minute to meet him before you head out?"

I had completely forgotten she had wanted me to do a one-on-one with a new member. "Sure."

Lisa turned to the man and said, "This is Martina. She's been sober for nine years. It's remarkable. Martina, why don't you tell him how your journey started and what keeps you on a straight path."

Was that all? At least it would save me from my thoughts drifting back to my brother's case. Meeting his gaze, I said, "Hi, and yeah, so like Lisa was saying, I've been sober for nine years. It hasn't been easy. I entered AA a little over nine years ago, after I nearly killed myself in a drunk driving incident. My boss said, 'get sober or find another job.' Well, it was a wake-up call for sure. But it was the kick in the seat I needed to take my drinking seriously." I leaned up against my desk. "After ninety days, I went back on the job. My job is stressful and raising my daughter by myself was a true test but also the reason I keep up with meetings, and stay in contact with my sponsor. I think we're all capable of sobriety with a strong support system." How was that for inspirational and all under a minute?

Lisa said, "Tell him what you do."

I nodded. "I am part-owner of a security and private investigations firm. And I also contract with the CoCo County Sheriff to solve cold cases."

"Martina's been on the news. She and her partner have solved some really tough and famous cases," she said with pride.

"We do a lot of good, but it takes its toll. I have had suspects come after my partner, my daughter, and me. My sobriety is tested daily, but my sponsor Rocco is on speed dial. Plus I've got my friends, and my mother is also a sponsor. She's a recovering alcoholic, ten years sober. She has a whole year on me. She and my teenage daughter inspire me every day," I said with a smile.

He said, "That's incredible. Plus you're a single mom."

I nodded. "Yeah, Zoey is about to head off to college. My husband died when she was six years old, and I've been raising her ever since. I've had a lot of help from our nanny and my mom. But soon it'll be just me and Barney, our fluffy Yorkie mix."

The man looked at me with a twinkle in his eye. "It sounds like you are truly one of the success stories."

"If you want it bad enough, you can do it. What's your story?"

He gave a lopsided grin. "I've been an addict, off and on, for years. First heroin, and I beat that for a whole year, and then I turned to alcohol, thinking it was going to ruin my life *less*. That didn't work out, so again, I tried to get sober and was successful for about six months. But it's been really hard. I slipped up, and now I've decided I really need to be here and get sober or it'll be my end. I haven't seen my sixteen-year-old daughter in three years, and I want to be there for her. Even if she hates me, which I hope she doesn't because I really want to get better for her and for me. Her mom is an alcoholic too, and I just hate myself sometimes for what I've done to her."

Tears were forming in this man's eyes, and it hit me that I didn't even know his name. We had completely skipped an actual introduction, but there was something about him that made me want to know more about him.

Maybe it was because we both had teenage daughters and were alcoholics. It sounded like he didn't have the support system I had, and maybe I could be part of his new one. "I'm sure she doesn't hate you. Kids have a way of forgiving their parents, even when we mess up really bad. What do you do for work?"

"I'm a writer. I used to write for newspapers, but I've been working on a novel, and I need to stay sober, or I'm going to lose my contract with my publisher."

"That's incredible. What kind of stories do you write?"

He began to tell me about his book and the short stories he had written. I somehow felt a strong connection to this man. It was weird and alarming, and something was happening inside me I couldn't put my finger on.

"I'm sorry I'm talking your ear off. That's a writer for you. Ask us about our stories and you'll never get a moment's peace."

"It's okay, really. It's a nice distraction. It's been a day, to be honest," I said with a reassuring smile, and he smiled back. And something stirred inside me again. It was unnerving, and I became flustered.

Looking for an exit, I glanced down at my watch. "It's getting late. You know, I'm here once a week. I hope we can meet again and talk."

Lisa gave me a knowing look and I chose to ignore it. My phone alarmed, and I glanced down at the screen. *Thank you.* "That's my partner. I've got to go. So great to meet you." I hurried away without having learned his name. Instead, I answered, "Hirsch, what's up?"

"Where are you?"

"I'm still at the rehab center. I'm leaving now," I said as I hurried out of the building into the warm, late-summer air, unsure what had just happened in there. I had never felt like that after meeting someone. My stomach grumbled, and I realized I'd skipped my protein-bar dinner. That explained the weird feelings. It was probably just low blood sugar.

To gain privacy, I unlocked my car and hopped in. Hirsch said, "I was talking to Kiva. He told me what you found."

Oh, that's why he's calling. "It's weird, Hirsch. The facts of the case are wrong. The motive is wrong. None of the facts were checked. They're not rival drug dealers. They're on the same team. How could Leslie make that mistake?"

"I don't know, but I'm calling because I need you to be sensitive in the event something bigger is going on. We need to keep this quiet."

Seriously? "So I shouldn't ask Leslie about it?"

"Not yet. Let me do a little digging, and I'll let you know."

"What are you thinking, Hirsch?"

"This is not like Leslie, that's what I'm thinking. And I want to give her the benefit of the doubt, and figure out why the investigation was not done properly. Can you give me a few days?"

"Of course, Hirsch, anything. I was just... I was surprised."

"So am I."

With that, more questions swirled in my mind. Had Leslie intentionally changed the facts of the case? Or at a minimum, did she not investigate according to protocol? If so, why? I may not be able to talk to Leslie to sort it out, *but* I could reinterview the witnesses.

12

MARTINA

THANKFULLY, Candace Mason had agreed to meet with me to discuss Toby June's murder investigation. The other two witnesses, according to the responding officers' statements, had shown up after the shooting occurred. One tried to save Toby, and the other called 911. Unfortunately, the contact information for the witnesses no longer worked, or maybe it never did. Considering where they were during the crime, chances were they didn't want to be known to the police. Perhaps the witnesses had families that didn't know they were drug users, or maybe they were dealers themselves. It was possible the names in the statements weren't even real.

What struck me about the statement from the man who had called 911 was that he said Candace Mason had collapsed at the scene, and he caught her right before she hit the ground. He suspected she was in shock from the horror of seeing a man die. It was understandable from the looks of the crime scene photos. A gunshot to the head resulted in a gruesome scene.

For a civilian, it would be a shock, but Candace was a registered nurse. I would've thought she could've handled seeing the gore with more decorum, but you never know how you're going to react when you see somebody's life extinguished right before your eyes. It must've been a terrible thing to see.

Keeping my promise to Hirsch, I wasn't planning to question Leslie about all the inconsistencies in her reports, her conclusions, and how she presented it to the district attorney for a prosecution. I wasn't convinced Darren was innocent, but I *was* convinced something was off with the investigation. And whatever it was, I planned to figure it out.

By speaking with Candace, I hoped to glean some insight into what happened during the shooting that wasn't captured in the report. Like if there was a conversation between Darren and Toby before the shooting. The record simply stated a tall man with dark hair walked up to Toby and fired his weapon, and said, "This is the end," before running off, which didn't match what Darren told me.

Inside Mount Diablo Medical Center, I shivered at the over air-conditioning and planted myself near a bank of chairs and a reception desk and called Candace to let her know I had arrived. She had agreed to speak with me in a public spot inside the hospital. Hopefully, the shock hadn't changed her recollection, or erased it, or hidden it away to protect her. It was a known fact that stress and trauma could impair memory.

Ten minutes later, a woman of thirty-five, wearing pink scrubs with her blonde hair pulled up into a messy bun, approached me. "Are you Martina Monroe?"

"I am. You must be Candace."

She nodded.

"Let's have a seat."

I preferred to be able to see somebody face to face, but side by side would have to do. Sitting, I pivoted toward Candace.

She had a sadness to her, like all the life had drained out. Maybe witnessing a murder did that to her, but who knew what her story was before she witnessed it. Why was she at the park that day? Was she an addict? She looked tired but not strung out. Hospital staff was tested for drug use, so that couldn't be it, unless she was a former user and had gotten clean since the shooting. But I didn't get that vibe from her, just an overwhelming lack of hope.

"I was surprised to get your call. I was under the impression the man was in jail and the case was closed."

I nodded, indicating what she said was true. "It is, but from time to time, we double-check the facts of the case." Like when an investigation was not done properly.

"And you're with the sheriff's department?"

"I do contract work with the sheriff's department, but I'm actually a private investigator myself." I handed her my card, and she stared at it for longer than what seemed necessary. Perhaps she was surprised. Truthfully, I hadn't been exactly honest with my affiliation. Yes, I work for the sheriff's department, but I wasn't there on behalf of them.

"I was hoping you could tell me what happened the day Toby June died. In your own words, just to make sure we have all the facts straight."

She hesitated before glancing at the floor. "It was awful. I was standing by the bushes, and I saw this tall man with dark hair. He walked up to June Bug and said, 'This is the end,' raised his arm, and fired straight into his head. June Bug fell to the ground, and the tall man ran off."

It certainly could describe Darren, but a lot of men were tall with dark hair. "Do you remember what he was wearing?"

"No."

"Was 'This is the end' the only thing the tall man said before he ran off?" It was a strange thing to say.

"Nothing else." It matched the statement she had given the police, which I would usually conclude that the match meant it was likely accurate.

"What did the gun look like?"

Candace scrunched up her face. "It was black. A handgun."

That was consistent with a weapon that utilized 0.22 caliber bullets. "And how were you able to identify the shooter?"

She cocked her head and looked at me. "What do you mean?"

"Did you know the shooter? You said it was a tall man with dark hair. Did you pick him out of a lineup?"

She nodded as if she understood what I was asking. "After the paramedics took me to the hospital for evaluation—I had fallen from shock, I believe, at the whole situation. Thankfully, there was somebody there to pick me up before I hit my head on the concrete. Anyhow, a police officer came to pick me up at the hospital and drove me to the station to take my statement."

"Did you speak with anyone else about what happened before the officer picked you up at the hospital?"

She shook her head, indicating she hadn't.

"You didn't speak with a family member or spouse?"

Her faced paled. "No, I don't have a husband and I didn't want to concern my family."

Didn't want to concern her family? "How long after the shooting did the officer pick you up at the hospital?"

"I don't know, four or five hours later. Detective Leslie was really nice."

"Yes, she is. She's a great person and police officer. Was she the only one present when she took your statement?"

"Yes."

"Can you walk me through what happened when you were at the station?"

Candace relaxed her shoulders. "I gave her my statement, and then she showed me some pictures of suspects."

"Do you remember how many photographs she showed you?"

"There were six."

How had Detective Leslie known to show my brother as one of the six photos in the array if she didn't know his drug affiliation? "How long after you gave your statement did you see the photographs?"

"It was, I don't know, maybe five minutes?"

Five minutes? How could Leslie have identified six possible suspects after only five minutes with such a vague description? "Did the six men in the photographs look similar?"

Candace cocked her head, as if trying to remember. "Most of them were Hispanic. But the shooter was Caucasian, I think."

It was procedure for photo lineups to have all potential suspects look similar so that no one stood out over the others. Had it been intentional? "Did the officer tell you that the suspect may not be one of the six men?"

Candace tilted her head as if trying to remember. "I don't think so."

Another failure to follow procedure. Usually the officer told a witness the suspect may not be in the lineup to avoid undue pressure on the witness and to avoid misidentification. It was well documented that a witness was more likely to pick someone in a lineup that most resembled the suspect, and not the actual suspect, if they believed one of the people in the lineup was, in fact, the offender.

"And then what happened after you looked at the photographs?"

She returned her focus to the floor. "I pointed out the suspect, and the detective thanked me for my help and offered me a ride back to my car."

"Did you have to do any follow-ups, like a live lineup?"

"Yes, the next day. She asked me if I could take a look, and I did, and I pointed him out. It was the same one from the photograph. It was the tall man with the amber eyes."

Detective Leslie had fallen short on the proper procedure for identifying suspects, but the fact Candace pointed him out twice was compelling. "Had you seen the shooter before?"

"No, never. Why? You don't think he's innocent, do you?"

Her question surprised me. "I don't know. I'm just checking the facts of the case."

"I heard they were both killers and deserved what they got. I don't know why the sheriff's department cares so much. As far as I'm concerned, they are both right where they belong."

Where did that come from? "I thought you didn't know Toby June or the shooter."

She shook her head and stood up. "No, I don't. But I heard later they were drug dealers, and well, drug dealers kill innocent people every day with their drugs and their violence. I'm sorry, Miss Monroe. I really have to go back to work. I hope I've given you what you need."

"Just one more thing. Why were you at the park that day?"

Terror washed over her face. "I, uh, don't remember. I have to go." And with that she jogged back into the depths of the hospital without another word.

She didn't remember? A chill went down my spine, and I wasn't sure if it was the hospital's chilled air or the odd ending to our conversation.

13

CANDACE

THE SOUND of the front door shutting echoed throughout my empty home. After Travis died, I contemplated selling our house along with the dream we once had to raise a family, maybe get a dog. The dream was shattered, and along with it, my sense of self. If I wasn't his wife and her mother, what was I? A nurse. A lonely, heartbroken woman. I had this delusional idea if I gained a new purpose, everything would be better.

My goal of seeking revenge was at the forefront of my thoughts. My rationale for ruining the drug dealer's lives was noble—to save the next wife and the next mother from having to go through the pain I had. I contemplated for quite a while how I would actually get revenge. Across all my thoughts, never had I considered killing them.

Unsure what to do, I decided to learn more about them. To know who their families were, where they went, and what was important to them. It was necessary in order to teach them a lesson. What I learned was that they didn't have much. No kids, no spouses. They slept on mattresses on floors, played video games during the day, and met with shady folks at night before hitting the park to sell their death. Upon learning of their sad existences, I was more unsure than before how I could actually ruin their lives. They certainly didn't have ones that I envied.

Instead, I wondered how they landed in a life like that. Maybe they were once good, like Travis. Maybe they had an accident, and something altered their paths. Nobody was born an addict and drug dealer. What happened to them?

The only way to make their lives worse was to send them to jail. Plus, if they were in jail, they couldn't sell drugs to innocent people anymore. That was the plan, anyhow. But I hadn't figured out how I was going to pull it off. It wasn't like there were a lot of ways for me to film their activities and then call the cops without them noticing. As it was, I had blown through several hundred in cash trying to get closer to them and didn't want to continue to drain my savings or have them too familiar with me.

When June Bug was shot, I thought my luck had turned around, that God had stepped in. Fate. He had taken my husband and now somebody had taken him.

I should've known better than to think it was luck.

I flipped on the light switch, and the kitchen illuminated. It was spic and span clean. When Travis was still alive, he was messy, didn't like to do the dishes, and left out cutting boards with crusty knives on top of them, as if he would use them again that day but never did. But without Travis, the home was clean, never messy. What I would give to see his wet towel on the bathroom floor.

Nothing about my life had been lucky. Why did I think his dealer's death was a sign that my luck had turned around? And who was this Martina Monroe, and why was she checking the facts of the case? The case was closed. At first, I thought maybe she was working with the detective on Toby's murder. But it seemed like she was checking on the detective's work. Why?

What was she hoping to find, and did I have anything to worry about?

From the freezer, I pulled out a frozen dinner. Food resembling meatloaf and mashed potatoes again—it was a grim meal. It was fitting. My days hadn't been bright, even with June Bug dead and Darren Kolze in prison. The sun hadn't shone upon me since the day I found out I was pregnant.

With Travis and my baby gone, I was an empty shell. The purpose I once had to get justice for them seemed hollow. The two dealers who killed my husband were taken care of, one permanently and one in prison for twenty-five years. Why didn't I feel better? Why hadn't I felt like I could move on? And I didn't feel victorious or like I had made a difference. I felt even more broken than before. If my luck had changed due to the demise of those two dealers, I was beginning to fear it was for the worse.

After having the last bit of watery, grainy, mashed-potato-like substance, I rinsed the plastic microwavable dish in the sink and threw it in the recycling bin.

Who was Martina Monroe, really, and did I need to worry? I walked over to the computer desk and sat down, firing up the old desktop. The Internet was full of information. Surely there would be something on Martina Monroe, considering her name was on the letterhead of her company.

With the search engine open, I typed in her name. My eyes widened as I saw the long list of responses that returned. I clicked on the first. There was a photo showing her standing next to some tall, rather handsome man with sandy blond hair and blue eyes. As I read the article, I learned the man was Sergeant August Hirsch of the CoCo County Sheriff's Department, and they had just solved a nearly impossible case of a missing girl who had disappeared five years earlier. The reporter made a comment that the two were known for finding the deepest, darkest secrets, exposing them, and bringing loved ones justice, and even finding the missing and bringing them home.

A shiver went down my body as I read the very last line of the article. "If there are facts buried, Martina and Hirsch will no doubt uncover them." There were several other articles with similar accolades. This didn't bode well for me. Or maybe I was being paranoid. The case was closed. But if I was simply paranoid, why had Martina been assigned to check the facts of the case? Did Sergeant Hirsch question my testimony?

Should I call Detective Leslie and ask what was going on? No, I couldn't. I didn't dare do that or anything else that might bring suspicion to myself or anyone else. And I meant what I said: both June Bug and Darren were where they belonged. The only thing left was to banish the sinking feeling inside of me that told me the nightmare was far from over.

14

MARTINA

As I APPROACHED Hirsch's office, I wished my Friday night and weekend included exciting plans. But it didn't. Zoey was going to a party and my love life was DOA when Wilder and I split. My world was quickly evolving into work, volunteering, and cuddles with Barney on the sofa. Maybe it wouldn't always be that way.

Why did I think that? Was it because of the man I met at the rehabilitation center who stirred something inside of me? I barely knew him, but he made me see how quickly and easily I could connect with someone new. I would like to meet someone special. It had been more than six months since Wilder and I broke up. He had texted recently, letting me know he was doing great. After I had wished him well, I let him stay in the past.

Never one to feel lonely, but with Zoey leaving, I worried about what it would be like to rattle around in my house all alone. It was becoming more apparent to me that I would like a partner, not just one to help me solve murders. At least I had the case to keep me preoccupied, instead of the thoughts of my impending loneliness and empty house.

Hirsch waved as he set the receiver of his phone back onto the base. "Hey, Martina."

I shut the door behind me and took a seat across from him. "How are you doing?"

He let out an exasperated sigh. "You know, there are never really days off with this job, are there?"

"That's not news."

"No. But the thing with Leslie—it's really got me bothered."

Of course it did. Hirsch was a straight arrow who thrived on following the rules. "Me too. Have you talked to her to find out why she skipped protocol?"

"Not yet."

Why not? That wasn't like Hirsch. I added, "I spoke with the eyewitness yesterday and something's weird there, Hirsch."

"What do you mean?"

"Well, first of all, I asked her how she identified Darren. She said she gave a vague description of the man who shot Toby, and then just a few minutes later, Leslie came back with a six-pack of suspects. How could she figure out my brother could be a suspect that quickly?"

"She couldn't have."

"And that's not all. The eyewitness, Candace, said that five of the six photos were of Hispanic men. Darren is fair skinned with amber eyes and dark hair. I don't think anyone has ever mistaken him for Hispanic. I also asked Candace if Leslie had told her it was possible the suspect wasn't in the array. She said no."

His face paled. "She broke protocol."

"That's just the beginning of her missteps, Hirsch."

He glanced around his small office before stating, "But she picked Darren out of a live lineup, right?"

Did that matter? She could have been simply matching up the photo to the actual person. *Or he's guilty.* "Yes."

He raked his fingers through his golden hair. "I don't know what to make of this. Most of law enforcement understands eyewitness testimony is highly unreliable, especially with that new report out stating around seventy percent of wrongful convictions, overturned with DNA evidence, were due to mistaken eyewitness testimony. They shouldn't have been able to prosecute Darren without physical evidence corroborating the testimony. This is quite the predicament."

At least Hirsch could tell the case was a stinker. "Exactly, and they worked for the same organization, so it could've easily been the drugs in his pocket were a resupply. It's possible Darren was nowhere near Toby when he was shot."

Hirsch cocked his head. "Except the one thing you can't ignore, Martina, is that Darren confessed. If he was still claiming his innocence, I would say, yeah, something's not right here, so let's take a second look and see what we find. I can see that Leslie didn't follow protocol, she didn't follow up with the narcotics team, and there wasn't physical evidence proving without a doubt that Darren shot Toby. But he confessed and there's the eyewitness."

I shook my head, not accepting Hirsch's explanation or the implication that I should give up simply because Darren confessed. "But what about the phone call? And what about the fact you can't actually corroborate that Darren was the shooter? You wouldn't take a suspect's word at face value. You have to verify what they say is true. There was no verification."

"Look, I don't know what to tell you. Yes, something went wrong with this investigation, but that doesn't mean Darren is innocent. I've been quietly asking around about Leslie. Asking if anyone has seen anything she's done that's not by the book. I've gone through a few of her recent homicide investigations to see if there were any inconsistencies in how the investigations were performed. I didn't find anything."

"Then why this one?"

"I don't know."

He clearly wasn't convinced there was something bigger going on, like I was. "And another thing. When I questioned the eyewitness about what she was doing at the park that day, she didn't answer. She just ran off. I think there's more to this than we're seeing."

Hirsch stood up and walked over to the second visitor's chair next to mine and said, "Martina, I'll do anything I can to help you, but I think you're heading down that rabbit hole I was worried about."

My heart rate sped up and fury filled me. I couldn't believe what I was hearing. Hirsch always had my back, and I felt like he was trying to silence me. Something was wrong with this case, so why was he trying to shut down my investigation? "I know what you're saying, but I'm telling you, this is different. The witness is lying, and Detective Leslie did not follow protocol, for the first time since we've known her. Something else is going on here, and if you won't help me, I will find out, and I'll expose whatever needs to be exposed, even if that means misconduct by the CoCo County Sheriff's Department."

Hirsch looked stricken.

I couldn't remember the last time he and I disagreed about something. Perhaps it was when Vincent and I worked for the sheriff's department all those years ago, and we got in trouble for leaking some damaging information to the press. We were suspended and Vincent nearly fired.

"What do you think you're going to find, Martina? Do you really think Darren is innocent?"

"I don't know, but I know the facts of the case are wrong. Protocol wasn't followed, and the eyewitness who pointed to Darren is lying. Your case doesn't hold up," I said with a raised voice.

"What is she lying about?"

I threw my hands in the air and said, "I don't know, but she's not telling the truth. You know me, you know that I'm not just trying to find holes. Something is off with her. The interview was going as expected, but in the middle of it, her demeanor changed, and she asked if I thought Darren was innocent. I said I didn't know, and she exclaimed Toby and Darren were both killers and got what they deserved. It's pretty clear there's more to the story, and even if Darren is guilty, lying to the police and not following protocol is not acceptable."

He exhaled, as if he couldn't believe what I was saying or that I was wasting his time. "Point taken, but unless you have something concrete other than your gut saying you think the witness is lying, I'll handle the issue with Detective Leslie. Stay away from her until I can figure this out. That's the best I can do."

I shook my head in disbelief. Was my best friend really turning his back on me, no longer trusting me after we'd worked together for so long? After we had saved each other's lives on numerous occasions? Or was he toeing the company line? I knew Sheriff Baldwin, and as much as he was a straight shooter, he wouldn't necessarily want me broadcasting the news that one of their homicide detectives hadn't followed procedure or checked the facts of the case before sending a man to prison for murder.

But Hirsch was right.

The fact that Darren pleaded guilty wouldn't help the situation or garner any sympathy from the sheriff or the public. They would likely turn a blind eye to the shoddy police work, figuring Darren was a dirty, rotten, murdering drug dealer nobody cared about, so why reopen the case? But he was a person, and every person deserved a fair trial. If we didn't have that, then what did we have? Why did we do this job if not to bring justice for families?

I shot up from my seat and said, "Fine, you deal with Detective Leslie and figure out why she didn't do her job, and I will figure out why that eyewitness is lying and what she's lying about."

Without another word, I opened the door and stormed out of Hirsch's office. I didn't know what was going on with Hirsch, but I didn't like it, and I wasn't going to let the sleeping dog lie. I would find the truth, even if it meant going up against Hirsch and the CoCo County Sheriff's Department.

15

MARTINA

Pacing my office, I wouldn't have been surprised if there was actual steam coming out of my ears. I didn't know how many traffic laws I broke on the way from the Sheriff's station to my office, but there were at least a few, and I had been lucky to not be pulled over.

My mind was in shock and wasn't able to come to terms with the fact Hirsch was turning his back on my investigation. Was he covering up for Leslie or was there something more?

Or was I overreacting?

Hirsch had never given me a reason to believe he wasn't completely on my side or on the up and up, until now. The only time he had ever kept anything from me was because he had to. Maybe he was investigating Leslie but couldn't tell me due to department procedure.

Maybe I should have given him the benefit of the doubt.

My heart sank. Was I diving down a rabbit hole? Was my judgement clouded because I was too close to the case? It was pretty standard procedure to not work on a case you were personally attached to. It was why when we were investigating

Hirsch's brother's murder he wasn't allowed to work it. If it was personal, you lost clarity.

Dang it.

Glancing at the clock on the wall, I wondered if it was too late to call Hirsch and apologize. Thinking I needed more time to cool off, I opted to give it a night.

Maybe the real problem was that the investigation and my life changes were all becoming too much for me. There was a lot of pressure from my mom and my brother opposing it. And Zoey leaving for college. And Hirsch was probably mad at me, thinking I'd finally lost it.

I plopped down into my desk chair and buried my head in my hands, and I cried. Perhaps I had taken on too much. I should let it go. My brother insisted he was guilty and was going to stay in jail, and Mom would have to get used to it. Maybe this was the one time I had to let it go, if not for anyone else, then for my own sanity. I had been pushed to my limit. Maybe all the holes I dug up in the investigation didn't mean anything at all. It wasn't my job to make sure investigators did their job, unless I was investigating a case, and nobody asked me to look into it, except for my mom.

My confidence crumbled as I started to doubt myself. What had happened to me? This wasn't who I was. I pulled a tissue from atop my desk and cleaned up my face.

The sound of a knock on the door grabbed my attention. I glanced up and quickly threw away the tissue into the wastebasket. "Hey, Vincent."

He was tanned and looked happy, but his expression changed to concern when his eyes met mine. "Is everything OK?"

After a shrug, I shook my head. Was everything OK? I didn't know. It seemed like everything was falling apart. It was me, that dog with a bone who wouldn't let it go. Why couldn't I let it go?

"I'll be OK. The case is just getting to me."

"You're working on your brother's case?"

"I am, and I got into an argument with Hirsch. I stormed out of his office."

"That doesn't sound like you and Hirsch at all. What's going on, if you don't mind me asking?"

Vincent had proven himself to be a worthy investigator, friend, and confidant. I motioned to the desk chair in front of mine. He stepped inside, shutting the door behind him, and took a seat. "Tell me what's going on. Maybe I can help."

With nothing to lose, I said, "I've been checking the facts of Darren's case..." I explained everything I had learned, including how Leslie hadn't followed protocol, the strange vibe I got from the eyewitness, and how Hirsch told me to stay away from Leslie, claiming he would handle it.

Vincent nodded and said, "Maybe Hirsch is already investigating. Or Internal Affairs is and he can't tell you."

Vincent was probably right. "Maybe."

"Permission to speak freely?"

I had a feeling Vincent was about to give me the honest, brutal truth. "Of course."

"It sounds like you're just verifying facts of what the original investigators did."

Right. "That's exactly what I did."

"Is that how you would normally start a new investigation?"

I sat up straight and said, "No, that's not how I investigate a case."

"Exactly. You start the investigation as if it's day one. Maybe by just checking facts, you're missing something. It's just like opening a cold case. If you really want to know the truth about how Toby June was killed, treat it like it's day one.

Maybe by not following your own protocol, it's making it difficult for you to make sense of it. Also, maybe what's rubbing Hirsch the wrong way is that you're basically double-checking his detectives' work as opposed to launching your own investigation."

What Vincent said was absolutely correct. How had he become so wise?

Because the case involved my family, I let my emotions get away from me and went off book. I needed to treat Toby June's murder like any other case. But I needed a team. And I knew there was one person who would be perfect to help me. "You're absolutely right. I think I was blinded by my own feelings about the case and trying to help my mom, so I didn't follow my own process, getting me all jumbled up."

"You should definitely investigate the Martina Way. Martina finds the truth," he said with a smile.

"True, but I also usually have a pretty good team with me."

"Hey, I just closed out a case. You've got me, as much as you need me. You don't even have to pay me anything. Whatever you need, Martina, you got it."

My emotions were now on overload. A friend reaching out, giving me a hand to help, which I desperately needed, was a true blessing. "I appreciate that, but I already talked to Stavros. This is on the books. You'll get paid."

"Excellent. The missus prefers I bring home a paycheck."

That made me smile. Vincent and Amanda were blissfully happy newlyweds. It was wonderful to see. "How is Mrs. Teller?"

"She's great, and we had a great time on our honeymoon."

"Looks like you spent some time in the sunshine."

"Yep, seven days of fun in the sun. I think I could live in Hawaii, Martina."

He definitely had a glow. "It suits you."

"Perhaps we'll just have to take a honeymoon every year we're married."

"I think that's a great idea."

My cell phone buzzed with an unknown caller. My smile faded as I answered, "Hello?"

A female voice said, "Please stop. I was wrong. Just make it stop, or it'll get worse."

The call ended, and I immediately tried to call back. The phone rang three times before I said, "It was the caller."

"The one who said your brother was innocent?"

I nodded. "But they're not answering. It's gone to voicemail."

"Well, guess where we are? In the office of the best researchers in the world. Let's go trace it."

Without another word, we rushed out of my office and headed toward the tech suite. Thank goodness for friends who were incredibly talented and willing to help at a moment's notice.

16

MARTINA

Hovering over Vincent's shoulder as he tapped away on the keyboard, I said a small prayer that we'd actually be able to find the location or the identity of the caller. The caller obviously knew intimate details of Toby June's murder to have claimed they knew Darren was innocent and then turning around trying to convince me to let it go. Neither call provided a useful explanation why.

Three minutes earlier, I had considered dropping my brother's case. But with the second call, there was no way I could. There were too many unanswered questions. Questions that could be answered by my brother. The brother who also told me to quit looking into the case. Maybe I could talk to my mom and ask her to convince him to tell me the truth, including why Toby was killed.

Vincent exclaimed, "Aha! Right there!"

My heart rate shot up as I saw a blinking dot on the screen.

Vincent said, "We've got them. They're in Bay Point, and they're on the move."

With a quick glance at my watch, I said, "It will take about forty minutes without traffic to get down there. Vincent, stay here and keep tracking. I'll head over and try to get a face-to-face with the caller."

The blinking disappeared, and my heart sank. "It's gone."

Vincent turned and looked at me. "Either they turned it off or they tossed it." He pointed to the screen and said, "They're at the marina. I think it's gone."

I should've known it wouldn't have been that easy. Sometimes, a lucky break is all you need to solve a case. But it didn't look like we'd get one of those.

Leaning back on the desk, I said, "Well, we at least know the person doesn't want to be found. And is savvy enough to dump their cell phone. Which gets us exactly nowhere."

"Not necessarily. It means someone isn't happy we're looking into the case, which means you're on to something. Could be big. What do you say we start working on a murder board?"

He's right. Again. This is getting embarrassing. "It's awfully late."

"Oh, do you have plans?"

Of course not. "No, but I figured you might have plans."

"I'll call Amanda and let her know I'll be late. What about Zoey?"

"She has a party tonight, and Barney's at Mom and Ted's."

Vincent grinned. "Well, then. It sounds like you and I have a date with a murder board."

I nodded and was grateful Vincent had pulled me back to a place of sanity and clear thinking.

We entered a conference room with a whiteboard, and Vincent said, "I'll get our structure started, but as I go, fill in all the information behind me, okay?"

With a small grin, I said, "You got it, boss."

He turned to me and smiled before picking up a dry erase marker and starting in on the board.

As I filled in the victim details, I realized the error of my ways. I could've learned a lot if I'd questioned the victim's family. It was usually the first thing we did in an investigation—cold or hot, it didn't matter. You could learn a lot by asking the questions, "How was the victim acting? Were they afraid of something? Was there a change in his routine? Who do you suspect might have wanted to harm him?" If the family didn't know, then we'd get a list of friends, girlfriends, or coworkers. Learn who he may have confided in.

It was all so obvious, like right in front of my face, that I felt like a fool. All I knew about Toby June was he had been a drug dealer, wasn't married, and didn't have any children, at least not that were on the record. As for the crime scene, I had an address and I had photos, but I hadn't even walked it. I couldn't even picture it. I had done this all wrong. Thank goodness for Vincent.

An hour later, Vincent and I stood side-by-side, staring at the Toby June murder board.

"Looks like there are a lot of unknowns, Martina," Vince remarked.

"True. I think I need to talk to the family. Can we pull records to get a list of known relatives in the area?"

"You got it, boss," he said with a wink.

"And I definitely need to go to the scene of the crime, walk around, see what's around there, not just looking at Google Earth."

"It's kind of a rough place, and I know you can handle yourself better than most, but if you want some company, I don't have any solid plans tomorrow."

"I'd appreciate it. We might be able to meet some of Toby and Darren's associates as well as find somebody who witnessed the murder other than Candace."

"That could tell us a lot."

"Yeah, I think so. I'd also like to find anybody who may have seen Candace, the eyewitness, before the murder. I think she could be the key to all of this." Actually, I would really like to know if Darren had seen her before or knew her. They were both withholding information, but I couldn't understand why. The only thing that potentially made sense was that Darren killed Toby on behalf of the 98Mob boss. But then why would Candace withhold information if she wasn't involved in the organization? Was Candace somehow tied up with 98Mob?

"Typical Martina case," Vincent teased.

Unfortunately, I thought it might just be.

Normally, after interviewing the victim's family and friends, I would interview suspects. In this case, one suspect was my brother. And I realized I didn't really know much about Darren and the details of his life over the last twenty years. Did he have a girlfriend or close friends? Were he and Toby friends? So many questions. I needed answers.

There had been no statements from family and friends in the case file. Was that why I hadn't thought to reinterview them like I had the witnesses—because they'd never been interviewed in the first place to be *reinterviewed*? The only interviews conducted were of the three witnesses at the scene. That should have been my first clue the investigation was off kilter.

The only thing I knew was there was more to Toby June's murder than we understood. And I was going to find out exactly what it was, with or without Hirsch's help, although I was feeling guilty over how I acted at Hirsch's office. It was late and calling him was out of the question. When he and I first started working together, he didn't have much of a life, and he was always available for a call. But that had changed. Time changed things. Maybe he wasn't the same Hirsch I always knew, but I couldn't believe he would look the other way, knowing Leslie didn't follow procedure. Maybe Vincent was right; he was investigating on his own before he could share any information with me.

Vincent said, "What's wrong?"

"I feel stupid that I missed all of this," I admitted.

"Nonsense. You were simply looking into your brother's case, and you were doing it alone. What do I always say? Two minds are better than one. We'll figure this out, Martina, together. Plus, I'm not your only friend. I'm sure others would be more than happy to help if we need them."

"Glad you said that because there's one thing we don't have a grip on, and that's any real information about 98Mob. I only spoke briefly with Kiva and Rourke. Under normal circumstances, they'd help, but since things are tense between Hirsch and me, I'm not sure we can go back to them. But I guess your friends at the FBI might know more about the 98Mob, to see if this is somehow connected to the boss and to understand how they normally operate."

"Good thinking. I'll reach out on Monday. I'm sure our pals in organized crime will be able to help."

"All right, sounds like we have a plan now."

"Yep, I'll get right on finding all known family members and friends of Toby June. We can start interviewing them tomorrow, if we can find them."

With a pat on the shoulder, I smiled at Vincent, knowing the path was clear. With my friends by my side, I would learn the truth. Even if that truth broke my mother's heart and maybe a little of mine.

17

CANDACE

Scrubbing the bathroom tile, I wondered if I was trying to clean the floor or my soul. Admittedly, I had upped my cleaning game since Travis died. At first, I thought it was that I finally got to have a clean house because my messy husband was gone. But since June Bug's murder, it had gone to extreme levels: cleaning the floors every day, even after working a shift. Windows sparkled, tile glistened. Truthfully, I felt guilty. I didn't want to feel that way, but I did. When I became a nurse, it was because I wanted to help others. Boy, had I taken a detour.

I thought I was better than Travis. I hadn't lied or ruined our lives with drugs, but I wasn't better. And my guilt didn't just extend to Toby's death but also to Travis's. I should've pushed harder to get help for him. I should've enlisted his family, friends, anything to get him better, to keep him with me, to have the family we always dreamed about. Now, my world was empty and sterile.

My phone rang, and I wondered who was calling. My friends had tried to be there for me after Travis's death, but I pushed them all away. The only one who refused to let me wallow in my misery was my older sister. I took off the rubber gloves, stood up, and picked up my phone from the counter.

"Hello?"

"Candace, is that you?" a somewhat familiar voice asked.

Peculiar. It was not my sister. "Yes."

"This is Detective Leslie. Do you remember me?"

Why was she calling? "Of course."

"I just wanted to let you know there's an investigator looking into Toby June's murder. I don't want you to worry."

Not to worry? Detective Leslie was behind the eight ball on this one. That woman, Martina Monroe, had already come to see me. She tripped me up and asked me questions that Detective Leslie hadn't, like why I was at the park that day. I didn't have a good explanation, only one that made me look guilty and deranged. Had I become both of those things?

"I know. Martina Monroe came to talk to me."

"She did?" Detective Leslie sounded surprised.

Did she not know? "Yes, I agreed to meet with her. She told me she works for the CoCo County Sheriff's Department. I assumed she worked with you."

Detective Leslie didn't respond, and after a few moments, I couldn't take it.

"Detective Leslie, are you still there?"

"Yes, I'm still here. I'm just surprised she's already talked to you. And yes, we do work together occasionally, and she does work with the sheriff's department on cold cases. But that's not why she's looking into the case."

"It's not?" I asked, startled.

"No, this is her own private investigation. You see, her brother is Darren Kolze. I think she's trying to prove he's innocent."

The news hit me like a Mack truck. "She's Darren's sister?"

"Yes, and she's a great investigator and a good person. But

on this one, I think maybe she's taking it too personally, not thinking clearly. Just stick to your statement, and you'll be fine. How did the conversation with her go?"

I didn't think it went very well, and I wasn't sure if Detective Leslie wanted to hear that. Maybe I owed her that much since she had put the killer behind bars.

Martina Monroe was Darren's sister? That hadn't come up in my internet search. And I couldn't believe I was talking to the killer's sister. She seemed so nice, so normal, so clean. Detective Leslie said she was a good person. How could that be? "I think it went OK. I didn't change any of the details. I told her exactly what I told you."

"Everything went smoothly? She didn't seem puzzled or ask you questions you weren't comfortable with?"

"Well, she asked me a couple of questions that flustered me. And I was at work, so I ran off without... I was just busy, and I hadn't thought about that time for so long. Then it came back, and I kind of... I kind of wobbled a bit, and I just told her I had to go."

I could hear Detective Leslie breathing on the other end, but she didn't respond. Had I messed everything up? "I'm so sorry, but I think she gave me a look, and I just knew I had to get out of there."

"Was the statement you gave me accurate?"

One day I would look back on that moment and realize it had defined my moral compass. "What I told you was correct."

"OK then, there shouldn't be anything to worry about. You have a good night. You can call me if you have any questions."

"Thank you, Detective Leslie."

The call ended, and I had to wonder, if Detective Leslie was calling me, who would call me next? If Martina Monroe really was Darren Kolze's sister, and she had a sparkling record for solving cases and finding the truth, was I in trouble?

Would I be the one who spent my life behind bars? My body shook, and I tried to ignore the thoughts in my head. With determination, I slipped my rubber gloves back on and returned to my task of cleaning the grout on my bathroom floor. It needed to be clean. *I needed to be clean.*

18

MARTINA

Vincent and I had called ahead to schedule a time to speak with Toby June's mother. She seemed more than willing and actually happy we wanted to know more about Toby. Detective Leslie should've been the one to talk to her, to interview her, and to learn all about her son, but she hadn't.

We explained on the telephone we both worked with the CoCo County Sheriff's Department, not elaborating or explaining that the affiliation wasn't the reason for the visit. It was a little deceptive, and I didn't feel great about it, but I needed to know the truth. Vincent agreed.

Standing on the porch of the June home, which could use a new paint job and someone to pull the weeds from the uncared for yard, I knocked three times. Footsteps sounded before the door cracked open.

"Hello," said the woman who answered. She had dark hair with silver roots and weathered skin. I was guessing she was Toby June's mother.

"I'm Martina Monroe, and this is my associate Vincent Teller. We spoke on the phone." I handed her my card.

She glanced at it and said, "Drakos Monroe Security & Investigations?"

"Yes. We're investigators. But we also take on cases for CoCo County."

"Oh, OK. I'm Kat. Please come in."

We entered, and she brought us over to a well-worn sofa and offered us coffee. After declining her offer, we sat, and she took the lounger across from us. "I admit I was surprised when I got your call."

"It's a bit unusual. My colleague Vincent and I have been reviewing the file, and we saw that nobody had interviewed you after Toby's death."

"Nobody asked me a single question about him. Just got a call from some officer, saying my boy died, and I went down to the morgue to identify his body. That was it. No follow-up. No condolences. It's all so strange."

I wasn't sure what she was referring to as strange. The police hadn't talked to her, and that was odd, but was it something more? "We're hoping to learn more about Toby, about what happened shortly before his death. Like if he seemed afraid of something or someone? Acting different? Different routine?" According to records, Toby lived at home with his mother, so she would know.

Mrs. June let out a breath. "I'm not going to lie. My boy had his demons. But he had a good heart and was usually a big help around here. But right before he died, he was using drugs pretty heavily. As long as he got his fix, he was pretty OK, but he was stealing from me, I think, to pay for more drugs."

"When did Toby's drug problem start?"

"His late teens, in high school. He started dealing, and then he started using. The fact he was stealing made me think that he was in trouble."

"How so?" I already knew from our narcotics team that he

was in deep to his employer, the head of the 98Mob, getting high on his own supply and not paying for it.

"He said he owed people money. That's never good in his line of work. To be honest, I wasn't super surprised they killed him."

"Did you know his friends, people from that world?"

"Only Darren, which is just the weirdest thing. I can't believe it was Darren who shot him. Of all Toby's friends, Darren was the nicest one, almost normal. You know, he had a sadness about him. I figured he got in so deep that he could never get out, but he was good on the inside, or so I thought."

Stunned by the revelation, I glanced over at Vincent.

Vincent then asked, "So, you knew Darren?"

Mrs. June nodded. "Yeah, he'd come by the house. He'd stayed with us a few times. He and his girlfriend stopped by. I made them dinner a few times. She was nice, and they were a good couple. It seemed like both had their demons, of course, but they were polite. She even offered to do the dishes."

Darren had a girlfriend. Who was she? "Do you remember Darren's girlfriend's name?"

"I don't. It was something unusual. I can't remember. I only met her a few times."

"How long before Toby's death did you last see Darren and his girlfriend?"

"Just the week before."

Would Darren really kill his friend? "Did Toby have a girlfriend or other friends or family in his life? Does he speak with his father?" I asked.

Mrs. June shook her head. "Toby's father ran off when he and his sister were still in diapers. I always blamed Toby's problems on his father running off. Toby didn't have any good role models. I wish I could've done more for him. I can't believe he's gone." Tears fell from Mrs. June's eyes. She wiped them with the back of her hands and said, "I'm sorry, but you know, he wasn't a bad boy. He was always so sweet, even though I know what he did was wrong, dealing drugs and using. That wasn't who he really was. He was kind, generous, and loving. He always had been. The drugs changed him a bit, especially when he couldn't get his fix, but I still see that little boy, that smile, his love of Tonka trucks when he was a kid. I miss him, you know. I don't miss the thieving and the erratic behavior, but most of the time, he was nice to have around, and he'd get groceries for me if I didn't have time to go out. You're not supposed to outlive your children."

Indeed.

Had I been guilty, just like the others, of assuming Toby was merely a drug dealer with no wife or kids? He was a person, a child. His mother was heartbroken over his death.

"When did you hear about Darren's involvement?"

"The police officer called to tell me, and I just couldn't believe it. They were friends, you know. I just can't believe Darren would do it."

"Do you remember the name of the officer you spoke to?"

"I think it was a detective. Not someone I'd ever talked to before."

"Do you have any idea why Darren would've turned on Toby?"

"I assumed it was on behalf of his boss, to be honest. I shouldn't be saying that around here, but that's the only thing that made any sense. They were friends. Darren didn't seem the type to do that kind of thing, you know? Not all those dealers are rotten. I think my boy and Darren were doing the best they could, considering. Have you talked to him about the case?"

Vincent and I exchanged glances. I still hadn't revealed my connection with Darren. "He says he did it but doesn't want to give me any details." At least not any that were accurate.

"That makes sense. The boss would probably come after him if he did, right? They're not supposed to talk to police."

"True."

Not that we were police—I was his sister.

Mrs. June frowned. "Well, it's a tragedy all around. I can only imagine how Darren's mother is feeling."

"Did you know her?" I asked, a little surprised by Mrs. June's concern for her son's killer's mother.

She shook her head. "No, but he talked about her. Said she was sober for a long time and that she was married to a retired police sergeant. Can you believe that?"

"I can actually." Sucking in my pride, I said, "I have to admit, I have a personal interest in the case. Darren's my brother."

"Oh." She tipped her head toward me. "What are you hoping to find? Do you think Darren didn't do it?"

"I don't know if he did it or not, but like you mentioned, my mom is having a really hard time accepting that he would've done something like this. I'm just trying to understand the facts of the case."

"I get it. I have a hard time believing it too. And I thank you for asking about Toby."

"It sounds like he was very loved."

"I didn't always do a great job as his mother, but I did love him."

And sometimes, as a parent, that's all we can do.

We said our goodbyes and stepped outside. Vincent was the first to speak. "We need to find Darren's girlfriend."

Agreed. "Maybe we'll find her down at the park."

"Well, let's go ask around. Find out who she was. Maybe she saw what happened."

It struck me. "Maybe she's the anonymous caller."

At that point, anything was possible.

Mixed emotions swirled around in my mind. Part of me felt we were on the path to finding the truth, perhaps why there were inconsistencies in the homicide report. The other emotion was guilt. I knew so very little about my brother. Like the fact he had a girlfriend and close friends. I had no idea what his life had been like over the last two decades. As much as I thought I should know from a sister's perspective, I had a feeling from an investigator's perspective, I needed to know even more.

19

MARTINA

Driving through the neighborhood surrounding the park where Toby June lost his life, I better understood the environment that fostered a crime scene. Vincent said what I was thinking, "I see why property values are lower out here."

"Yep." Lawns weren't cared for, cars, mostly older, some without tires, were littered around the homes. It wasn't an affluent area. In fact, it was one of the lesser expensive places in the Bay Area, where crime rates were higher and property values lower.

Chain-link fences blocked off some of the more kept-up yards and homes. The residents must have known if they wanted to keep their lots nice, they needed to keep out the bad element.

Blinker on, I turned left into the small parking lot next to the park. There were a few cars, old and banged up, scattered across a dozen parking stalls. The park wasn't large. It had grass, trees, a small playground, and a walking path that disappeared behind the homes. When the area was built, it was likely thought that the residents would take a nice stroll along the path, admiring the hills around it, and that it would be a great place for the kids to play.

Parked, we exited the car, and I surveyed the scene. Vincent walked up next to me, looked at a crime scene photo, and pointed. "Over there, along the hedges. That's where he was found." It wasn't deep into the park. Anyone in the parking lot would've had a full view of the murder, which made it even stranger. It happened in broad daylight and there was only one eyewitness.

Standing about where the shooter must've been, I surveyed all around. To the right were the playground, a thicket of trees, and picnic benches, along with a restroom. "Darren said he didn't see the witness. She must've been near the bushes or hiding, for him not to see her. Otherwise, it's pretty open."

"She could've been in a car," he ventured.

"True." The original statement didn't say exactly where Candace had been when she witnessed the murder, but it did say she was in the park, as opposed to parked in her car. I definitely needed to learn more about Candace and to get her to open up to me about that day. Why she was there, where exactly she was when she witnessed the crime—all things that should've been handled by the detective investigating the shooting.

A few men and a woman with a small child were near the play structure, not together but near one another. The woman with dark flowing hair was pushing the child on a swing. I nodded over there and said, "Let's go see if they know Darren, Toby, or Candace."

"You got it, boss."

The woman didn't pay us much attention, but the two men looked our way suspiciously. I waved, trying to act friendly, but their stares remained fixed on Vincent and me, no smile in sight.

"Hi, my name is Martina, and this is my partner, Vincent," I introduced.

"You cops?" the taller man asked.

"No, nothing like that. I'm actually a friend of a man who was killed here, June Bug," I explained.

"If you ain't cops, what's he to you?" he asked, sounding a bit confused.

"We're private investigators. I'm working with the family to try to understand what happened the day June Bug died. Did you know him?"

"Heard he got killed," the large man in the black jogging suit responded.

"Were you here that day?"

"We might've been, sometimes I bring the kids to play in the park," he said nonchalantly.

I glanced over at the young woman who had focused her attention on us before she picked up her baby from the swing and started heading away from the playground. I glanced at Vincent, and he nodded, following her casually.

"All we're trying to find out is who was here that day. I'm not here to bust anybody," I said, trying to reassure them.

"Why does the family want to know what happened? They got the guy who did it. He's in jail," he said.

"True, but we only had one eyewitness, and she's not answering my questions. I'm just seeing if there's anybody else who might've been here."

"Nah, we weren't here that day," he said firmly.

Really? Because two minutes ago, you said you weren't sure. I pulled out a picture of Candace and showed it to them. "Have you seen her around before?"

They shook their heads, neither being particularly helpful. I thanked them for their time and headed toward Vincent but kept my eye on the two men who were likely there to deal.

Members of 98Mob? If they were, they surely wouldn't tell me.

As a couple of women strolled up the walking path, I thought maybe I'd get lucky. I waved and greeted. "Hey."

They gave me the cold shoulder and kept on walking, but I caught up with them and said, "Hi, my name is Martina. I'm looking for anybody who is a friend of Darren Kolze or June Bug."

One of the women stopped, crumpled up her face, and asked, "Who are you?"

Realizing that being an investigator or part of the CoCo County Sheriff's Department wouldn't help me, I decided being Darren's sister just might. "I'm Martina. I'm Darren's sister, and I'm looking into Toby's death."

The woman, wearing rather large hoop earrings, said, "You do kinda look like Darren. Same eyes."

"Yes, a gift from our mother. I'm looking into June Bug's death."

"You don't think Darren did it?" she asked.

"I'm not sure. I'm just trying to find the truth—for my mom and for the family. Were you here the day Toby got shot?"

The other woman, with cat eye makeup, replied, "I was here, but I didn't see it go down."

That was something. "Did you know Candace too?"

"Candace?"

I showed her the photograph of Candace.

"Oh. Her. Seen her a few times down here. Why?"

"Well, I'm trying to figure out why she was here that day."

"Do you think she's involved?"

I hadn't considered it. "She said she witnessed the whole thing." Typically, I wouldn't divulge the identity of an eyewitness, but it was public record.

Hoops said, "Interesting."

"Do you know why she was at the park?"

"I heard she came down to buy for her husband."

Candace had a husband? She didn't wear a ring. "Who did you hear that from?"

"Darren."

"Oh, you're a friend?"

"More like acquaintances."

The women were likely dealers too. "Do you know his girlfriend?"

"Yeah. Izzy's cool."

"Does she hangout down here?"

"She used to, but since Darren got locked up, she stopped coming down here. But she works at the pizza place over on Third."

"I appreciate it."

"If you're Darren's sister, how come you're not asking him all this?"

"He's not thrilled I'm looking into the case and doesn't want to talk about it, but my mom is pretty broken up about it. Since I'm a private investigator, she's pressuring me to look into it. She swears he's not capable, even though he pled guilty."

Hoops said, "I get it. Darren's cool, not the kind to take someone out. Especially June Bug. Well, if you see Darren, tell him Tracy and Ally say hey and to hang in there."

"Do you know why he might've done it?"

She shrugged and said, "No, sorry."

I doubted that but thanked them and met up with Vincent, who was standing near the entrance to the parking lot.

"Learn anything?" I asked.

"Yeah," he said, his eyes wide.

"What did you learn?"

"One, the single mom is friends with Darren's girlfriend,

Izzy. Two, Candace has been here a few times, said she was buying for her husband."

All the folks we had met at the park likely knew Darren and Toby, despite claims by the two unhelpful guys. "That's what my new friends Tracy and Ally said too. Did your new friend say anything about Izzy?"

"No, just said that she was a friend of hers but wouldn't give me a last name. Said she told me too much already."

"Well, those helpful ladies didn't give me a last name either but did tell me Izzy works at the pizza place down on Third."

Vincent checked his wristwatch. "It's a bit early for lunch, but I can always eat a slice."

"A slice it is."

If only I had visited the scene of the crime earlier. In the span of thirty minutes, we had learned Darren's girlfriend's name, where she worked, and that Candace frequented the park to buy drugs for her husband.

Who was Candace's husband, and where was he? She said she wasn't married and didn't have any kids. It sounded like we needed to learn a heck of a lot more about Candace and to have a conversation with Darren's girlfriend. She may be the only one close enough to him to be able to explain why Darren wouldn't talk to me, *and* why he may have killed Toby.

20

MARTINA

Vincent and I had struck out at the pizza parlor, only learning Izzy was off that day and they wouldn't give us her contact information. We opted to divide and conquer. Vincent would perform a background check on Candace, figuring out everything we could about her. Meanwhile, I would question my mother, since I had Sunday dinner plans at her house, to see if she knew anything about Darren's girlfriend and his life over the last twenty years.

"Mom, you seem a million miles away. What's going on?"

I put the car in park in front of my mother's house, and said, "Sorry. I've had the case on my mind."

"Uncle Darren's case?"

Turning to Zoey, I said, "Yeah, it's more complicated than I originally thought."

"And you think he could be innocent?" Zoey asked with hope-filled eyes.

"I don't know, but I've got a feeling people aren't telling me the truth, including your uncle Darren."

"That must be frustrating. Maybe Grandma knows something."

That was exactly what I was hoping for. "I hope so."

"I'll put the leash on Barney."

"Great, thanks."

Outside the car, I walked up the path to Mom and Ted's two-story Mediterranean style home. Moments later, Zoey and Barney bounced up the walkway next to me. Barney loved going to Mom and Ted's. They had offered to watch him during the day while I worked, which was really handy since the little pup didn't like to be by himself. He was a people dog and needed lots of play and love. Thinking about that, I supposed humans really weren't that different.

Before I could even knock, Mom had the door open. "My favorite women in the whole world!"

After a hug from my mother, she went after Zoey, and, of course, knelt down to give Barney scratches as he licked her face. Zoey let him off his leash, and he bounded into the house.

Mom let us inside and shut the door behind us.

"Smells great in here."

"I made a new recipe: Chipotle meatballs with basmati rice and baked delicata squash."

"Sounds great."

"What dessert did you make, Grandma?"

"Oh, you know me too well, Zoey. I made a lemon meringue tart for dessert, but I'll need some help with toasting the top. There's fire involved," she said with zeal.

"Boy, do I miss having you at our house, Mom."

"You know you're welcome over here anytime."

We approached the kitchen with its white cabinets topped with marble countertops, and I waved at Ted, who was mixing a pitcher of iced tea.

"Hey, Martina! Hey, Zoey!" His eyes diverted to the little bouncing pup. "I'm guessing you missed me too, Barney." He gave him scratches before returning to his task. "Talk to Hirsch lately?" Ted asked.

I still had to muster the courage to call Hirsch and apologize for overreacting. "Not yet, but I owe him a call. I saw him on Friday, and well, things got a little heated."

"Oh?"

Mom hurried over. "Is it about Darren's case?"

I had hoped to have my first sip of iced tea before getting into work talk, but the cat was out of the bag. "Yes, we're having a bit of a disagreement on how to proceed. It's looking like maybe things weren't handled like they should have been."

Ted raised his brows. "That's not something Hirsch usually tolerates."

"No, which is why it's a little strange, but I don't want to get into it. And—"

"Well, I'd like to get into it. It affects all of us, Martina, don't you think?" Mom asked with a furrowed brow.

"It does, I suppose. I just don't want to get your hopes up, that's all."

"Martina, I am your mother, and my son is sitting in prison for a crime he didn't commit. *Murder*. I think I deserve to know every single detail. My hope is my own."

Zoey gritted her teeth, looking like she was glad she wasn't in my position. Ted poured a glass of iced tea and handed it to me. I took a sip and said, "It's great, thanks."

"You're stalling, Martina."

Geez, she really wasn't going to let this go. For better or worse, I explained the disagreement I'd had with Hirsch, the inconsistencies I'd found in the reports, the lack of proper procedure being followed, and the unreliable eyewitness.

"Oh, Martina, I knew it. Something is not right with this case."

"Well, then I need your help, Mom, because Darren won't

talk to me. He told me he's going to take me off the visitors' log if I ask him any more questions about it. He swears up and down he's guilty."

"I'll talk to Darren. I'll get him to tell you what you need to know. I just don't know why he's saying he's guilty. I know he's not."

"He could be protecting himself, and you, and me, and this whole family. If one theory is correct—that he was ordered to take out Toby June for the boss—he's protecting the boss. The boss could come after Darren and his family—us—so we have to tread carefully with the information. What I just told you, we have to keep between us."

"That's a tricky situation," Ted offered.

"Vincent is helping me out by doing background checks on Candace, the eyewitness, and we're hoping to meet Darren's girlfriend. I don't know if they're still together."

"Darren has a girlfriend?" my mother asked, surprised.

"Yeah. When I spoke with Toby's mother, she said they'd come over for dinner and that she was really nice, even offering to do the dishes. I have a feeling she might be able to help. Maybe you could talk to her, Mom."

"Oh, my. Do you have her number?"

"No, but I know where she works. Vincent and I went there yesterday, but she wasn't on shift. We're hoping that someone who cared about Darren as much as we do will talk to us."

"OK, but you'll try to find her?"

"That's the plan."

"Once you find her, I'll offer to have her over for dinner, or we can meet her somewhere, whatever is easiest for her. And I'll talk to your brother. He needs to tell us more information."

"Or you could surprise him," Zoey suggested.

"Surprise him?"

"Well, if you go in together, you and Grandma, then maybe

he'll be more willing to talk to you. With Grandma there, it's his mom, so he has to do what she says."

My mother chuckled and said, "I don't know if Darren has ever done what I've asked him to do. But Zoey's right, it might help if I'm there. It breaks my heart that the two of you are practically strangers at this point in your life, but I understand."

"Have you talked to Uncle Clark about meeting me yet?"

The look on my mother's face was one of shock and then accusation as she turned to me. "What is Zoey talking about?"

"Mom, you did ask Grandma about meeting Clark, right?"

With their gaze burning into me, I said, "Sorry, honey, I've been really busy, and I haven't had a chance to talk to Grandma about it."

Under her breath, my mother muttered, "Ha, sure," like she didn't believe a word of it, and said to Zoey, "Do you want to meet your Uncle Clark?"

"I do. I want to meet Darren, too. I want to know all my family."

Ted and I locked eyes, and I could see he understood my concern but knew better than to go up against his wife on this one. "I'm just concerned about the life Clark leads. Speaking of which, Mom, I need you to tell me everything you know about Darren. It could help the case."

She nodded. "He didn't usually tell me much about what was going on. I didn't even know he had a girlfriend or that he was such good friends with Toby that he would go to this mother's house for dinner."

Part of me was glad Mom didn't know more, but the other part was disappointed to not have learned anything new. "Well, if you can get me a meeting with Darren, I can ask him myself." My expectations for that happening were low. And with that, I hoped it was the end of work talk.

Mom said, "I'll do what I can. Zoey do you want to help me finish off the tarts before dinner?"

Zoey cheerfully said, "Sure."

With Mom and Zoey fussing over the finishing touches on the lemon meringue tarts, I eyed Ted, and we met up in the dining room. He said, "Sounds like it could be a really dangerous situation, Martina."

Thankfully, Ted, a former sergeant and colleague, understood what I was up against. "That's what I'm afraid of. I want Darren to tell me the truth, but at the same time, if the theory is correct and he was acting on orders of the boss, then he's not going to tell us out of fear for his life and maybe ours."

Ted nodded like he understood. "I'll talk to your mother. Maybe I can get her to understand the dangers of pushing Darren."

"I'd appreciate it. I decided a long time ago no case was worth dying over."

"Exactly. I'm surprised Hirsch isn't helping out though?"

"Vincent and I have a theory he is working on it, but he can't tell me the details." I sighed, recalling how I had stormed out of his office without a word.

Ted smirked and said, "I'm sure he is looking into the case. If one of his investigators didn't follow the rules, he will find out why. It might take him some time, maybe give him some space. The two of you have something special, a true friendship. One storming out or one argument isn't going to end that."

"Thanks, Ted."

"But be careful. Maybe have some extra members of your team help out if they can. The 98Mob's dangerous."

"We're reaching out to some FBI buddies to see what we can learn."

"That's wise, but like I said, be careful."

"Thanks."

He patted me on the shoulder in a very fatherly-like gesture. Ted had been a great sergeant, and he was a great stepfather. At first, I was a little apprehensive about Mom dating my sergeant, but they were a great couple and balanced each other out. He was good to me, Zoey, and little Barney too.

I was about to get up when I felt the vibration of my phone in my pocket. A quick glance at the screen told me it was another unknown caller. I gave Ted a look, then lifted my finger to my lips, signaling for silence. "Hello?"

"Stop asking around. I'm serious."

"Is this Izzy?"

The call ended, and I let out a breath. I knew better than to call Vincent and try to get him to trace the call. He wouldn't be able to.

Ted asked, "What was that?"

I hesitated. "I've been getting anonymous calls, telling me to stop investigating. It's a female voice. I didn't tell Mom, but I'm thinking it might be Darren's girlfriend. The first call I got said he wasn't guilty, and this is the second call telling me to let it go."

"You're getting to them. This could be dangerous. Maybe you and Zoey should stay here for a while."

"You think it's that serious?"

"It could be. They have your personal cell phone number. They may know where you live too."

Ted had me worried. If he was suggesting I stay with him and my mother, maybe it was more dangerous than I thought. Or maybe he was being overprotective because earlier in the year, someone shot at my house, and Zoey and I had been put in a safe house. Either way, no case was worth dying over, and I was going to tread carefully, even more so than before.

21

CANDACE

Talia insisted on coming over, as she usually did. Although she was only two years older than me, I often referred to her as my pushy older sister, who didn't take "no" for an answer. I watched as she shuffled around my kitchen, looking for baking supplies. I was glad she'd come over; I could use a distraction from all the thoughts about June Bug's murder, the calls from Detective Leslie, and Martina Monroe questioning me about what happened that day. I didn't—I couldn't—take any more thoughts of what would happen if they knew the truth. If I was found out, what would they do? How much trouble would I be in?

Talia shut the last cupboard quietly and turned around. "You weren't kidding. You hardly have any supplies. You used to always have brown sugar, white sugar, flour, chocolate chips, baking powder, baking soda. What happened to all of it?"

After reading an article that claimed sugar triggers your brain similarly to the way cocaine does, I decided it was a drug too and threw everything away. It was a bit hasty, but I wanted nothing to do with anything that was drug-like. As if sugar could ruin our lives more than it already had. "I threw them all out. Sugar is bad for you."

She cocked her head and said, "What are you talking about? You love to bake, or at least you used to. Come on, let's go to the grocery store. Maybe it'll make you feel better."

"I don't know. I mean..."

"Seriously, Candace, we've got to get you living again. You seem almost... I don't know, worse. I know that it's been rough, with Travis gone and then you witnessing that terrible murder. I just think it's time we took you out. We can go out to dinner, go out to a nightclub, hey." She swung her hips around and snapped her fingers as if she was dancing.

"I don't know about that, but I guess we could bake something. I mean, we could try one of those low sugar recipes with protein powder."

Talia stuck her tongue out as if the idea made her gag. "Look, I've known you since you were born. I was there. I saw you. And I've known you every day since. Travis wouldn't want you to be unhappy. He would want you to move on. I know everybody grieves at their own pace, but it seems like you're sliding backwards, and I'm really worried about you. What can I do to help?"

Talia made an excellent point. She knew me better than anyone. Would she hate me if she knew the truth? "You're right. It's just, there's been an investigator asking about the murder I witnessed, and the detective called me. It is bringing up all these memories, and I'm not sleeping. I called in sick to work, and now they're putting me on leave."

Talia's face fell. "I'm so sorry, Candace. Why didn't you tell me? You know I can stay with you for a while, or you can come stay with me at my house. You shouldn't have to be alone. This house doesn't seem to be a good place for you anymore. It's like..." Her thoughts drifted off.

She was trying to handle me delicately, so I figured I'd throw her a bone. "Sterile, lifeless."

She nodded. "Please, let me help. You're my only sister. I can't—I can't imagine losing you. Please, let me help."

I nodded and wondered if I should tell her the whole sordid story of what had happened to Travis. My family didn't know he died of an overdose or that he had become an addict. I'd lied about it to my parents and to my sister. I said it was a complication from one of his surgeries. I'm not 100% sure they ever believed me, but they didn't question me either. If I was going to get through this, I had to come clean.

Wasn't that what I wanted from Travis? For him to come clean, to get clean, to be his old self again? In the aftermath, I had become just as toxic. Instead of propelling me forward, my need for revenge and a purpose had pushed me backward.

Talia was right, I needed to get out of this house, for good. Put it up for sale. It was my original plan, but then I got stuck, and then the shooting. I had to make an effort. I had to go back to the counselor. This wasn't who I was or at least it wasn't who I wanted to be. "You're right. I don't want to be like this anymore."

My sister hurried over and wrapped her arms around me as my body rocked and I cried about what I'd become and how I needed to not be that person anymore. I wanted to be the old Candace, the one who had hopes and dreams and wanted to help people. That desire had been the reason why I became a nurse. But I had been put on desk duty and then put on leave. They said they could tell I needed a break and told me when I was ready, I could return. It was the final sign pointing to the fact I couldn't hide from myself anymore.

Talia stepped back and said, "We're going to get you back. We are. I'm going to be with you every step of the way."

"Thank you, but there's something you should know."

Before I could finish and spill everything, there was a knock on the door.

"Are you expecting someone?"

I shook my head, and fear rushed through my body.

Talia said, "What's the matter?"

The fear must have shown on my face. "Oh, nothing. I'll get the door." I hurried and stared through the peephole. All I could see was the top of a dark-haired head. Truthfully, I didn't want to see more.

With Talia right behind me, I said, "I don't think I should answer it."

"Why?"

"I can't see his face."

A second pounding on the door echoed. "Candace, I know you're in there."

Talia whispered, "Should I call the police?"

I shook my head and opened the door, and my jaw dropped open. Fear took hold of me and held me in place.

"Hi, Candace. Hello, Miss," he said in a sickly sweet voice. "I only need a moment of your time. Do you mind if I come in?"

Frozen with fear, I couldn't move. There I was again, fight, flight, or freeze, and I was frozen. But I managed to lift up my hand as if to invite the man inside my house. The man was inside my house. How had he found me? He closed the door behind him but didn't lock it.

Thank goodness; we needed to be able to run if we needed to, if we could.

"Candace, I can tell you're surprised to see me. What I came to say won't take long." He paused and stared at me since I couldn't speak, then said, "That's OK. I'll do all the talking." He smiled creepily at Talia and turned back to me. "I'm here to make sure you understand that we need you to keep your testimony as it was. There can be no changes—not a single one—in your statement. Am I making myself clear?"

I nodded quickly, grateful I was able to move.

"Because if you don't keep your statement exactly as it is, I'm gonna have to come back, and from the looks of things, you don't seem to want me to come back. Don't even want me here right now. I get it, I understand. I'll be going now, as long as we're clear." He paused and tipped his head at me.

Nodding quickly, I just wanted him to leave.

"Excellent. You two have a great day." With that, he walked toward the door and let himself out.

Talia rushed over to the door and locked it. She turned to me with widened eyes. "What was that all about?"

Filled with dread, I said, "There's something I have to tell you."

22

MARTINA

Agreeing to let my mother drive to San Quentin seemed like a good idea at the time. My reasoning had been that I could have a call with Vincent to discuss what he found on Candace Mason. But Mom was a nervous driver, putting me on edge too. Maybe I would offer to drive on the way back.

"You're still OK with me taking a call, Mom?" I asked to ensure my conversation wouldn't distract her driving. It wasn't worth a wreck.

"Of course."

After a few buttons pushed, I put the phone up to my ear and stared out at the deep, blue bay waters that lined the highway.

"Hey, Martina."

"Hey, what did you find on Candace?" I realized I had skipped over all niceties and the usual "how are you doing," but Vincent knew how eager I was to finish up this case. It was getting more peculiar and dangerous with each new development.

"After I did a full background on Candace Mason, maiden name Candace Marie Davis, I learned she was married to a

Travis Mason, who died a year and a half ago from a drug overdose. Manner of death undetermined. Could have been an accident or intentional."

That explained the sadness that oozed off her. "That confirms what the witnesses at the park said about her, that she had a husband who was an addict."

"But there's a twist! At the time of Toby's shooting, Candace's husband had been dead for over a year. So, why was she at the park that day?"

That may be *the* question. "Any signs she could be a user herself?" After all, she could have lied to the dealers saying the drugs were for her husband, but they were really for her.

"Well, I may have called her employer and asked a few questions. Not completely copacetic."

And that was why I could never be in law enforcement, because sometimes you need to work in the gray area to get to the truth. "And?"

"I found out that she is currently on leave."

"As of when?"

"As of last Friday."

"The day after I talked to her at the hospital. A coincidence?"

Not a believer of coincidences, I wondered if I had triggered her. Candace was likely still grieving the loss of her husband, and then I reminded her of the awful memory of watching a man get murdered. Had I pushed her to the edge? Maybe. But that didn't explain why she was at the park the day of Toby June's shooting. "You didn't happen to find out if she was forced on leave, or took it herself, or is on medical leave, like having to go to rehab?"

"They said they wouldn't discuss it, but I did ask if she had taken much leave before this last Friday. They said no, only a short time after her husband passed away. I deduced the timing based on the dates they gave me."

"How did you get them to tell you all this information?"

"I said she was applying for a new home loan, and they gave me the facts of salary, time of leave, and employment dates."

"It doesn't prove she's a drug user, but it doesn't rule it out either. I don't know, Vincent. I feel like I have even more questions."

"You and me both. Since you're on your way to visit your brother, do you want me to go talk to her again?"

"Yeah, give it a shot. Maybe bump into her casually somewhere, like a grocery store, to see if she's really strung out, or poke around the hospital and ask around to see if she's been using drugs or suspected of it."

"My hat, glasses, and fake mustache are ready for the mission. I can also run by the pizza place to see if I can find Darren's girlfriend."

I assumed the fake mustache was a joke, but I couldn't be certain. It *was* Vincent I was talking to. "I'd prefer to go with you to the pizza parlor if that's okay."

"No problem."

"All right, thanks for the update, Vincent. Good luck. Stay safe."

"You too, boss."

I hung up the phone, and Mom immediately asked me what was going on. All I told her was that we were looking into one of the witnesses trying to corroborate a story. In an effort to deflect away from the conversation, I started telling her about volunteering at the rehabilitation center.

"Sounds like you really like it," she observed.

"I do. I'm meeting some interesting people."

Mom side-eyed me. "Oh?"

"Yeah, I just... I don't know. I was talking to this one man the other day, and he's a writer. He said he was a heroin addict and then turned into an alcoholic. Now he's trying to get clean, once and for all. He knows it's now or never, life or death."

"That's usually how it goes."

My thoughts drifted back to my conversation with the man at the rehab center. There was something about his eyes, his energy. It gave me a feeling that I could stay up all night talking to him. A real connection. It was weird and unexpected, and I found myself looking forward to seeing him again during my next shift.

Was I losing my mind, or had I really made a connection with someone I had one small conversation with?

We finally arrived at San Quentin, and Mom parked. "You ready for this?"

Knocked out of my thoughts, I refocused. "I am."

"Don't go too hard on your brother," she cautioned.

"All I'm after is information to help us find out what really happened."

She agreed to support the effort, and we made our way through the security checks and finally into the visitors' room. Mom and I sat nervously waiting, not speaking.

Finally, the door opened, and a guard brought in my brother. He looked pale and even thinner than before, if that was possible.

"Hi, honey, how are you holding up?" Mom said.

"I'm doing okay, Mom. Hi, little sister. Are you here to interrogate me?"

"No, not really."

He sat down, and I realized I needed to start the conversation with a little sugar as opposed to vinegar. "How are they treating you in there?"

"Like a prisoner," he said with a sheepish smile.

Mom frowned. "I wish they'd let me bring you some food in

here, but you received the money I put in your commissary, right?"

"I did, thanks, Mom. How is Zoey doing?" Darren asked me.

It was almost like the start of a normal conversation between siblings, if we hadn't been in a maximum security prison. "She's doing really well. She's starting to decide what she's going to take to college next month."

"I can't believe I have a niece going to college, and I've never even met her."

Mom cut in. "She really wants to meet you, though. We had them over for dinner last night, and Zoey wants to meet you and Clark too."

He nodded slowly and then gave me an earnest look. "I understand why you didn't want us around, Martina. I don't blame you for that. If I were you, I wouldn't want my kid around dealers and addicts. I'm glad that your life turned around and you have a great daughter. I heard your husband was really cool too. I have no hard feelings. I'm glad Mom and you got clean and are living healthy."

I tried to keep a cool demeanor, but I wasn't known for my poker face, and I worried shock was written all over me. "Thank you for that, Darren."

"Maybe one day, I'll be out of here, and we can start over. Be a real family."

Near speechless, I couldn't respond. Mom said, "Oh, honey, I'd love that. I know change is hard, and I've been amazed at how much you've progressed since you've been in here."

Progressed? What did I miss? After I picked up my jaw from the floor, I said, "You know, these past few weeks have made me realize how little I know about you and your life over the last twenty years."

"Well, I haven't exactly been leading a life to be described in an annual Christmas letter. As I'm sure you know, I've been dealing and using drugs. It's not something I'm proud of. But I have to say, once you're in it, it's really hard to get out. Not that I tried very hard. I was just sort of existing. But being in here has changed my perspective and my health. Who knew you could get clean in jail? Not that I couldn't get drugs if I wanted," he said with a smirk. "But there are actually resources to get me sober and I've started going to church."

I glanced over at my mother, who had tears in her eyes, and she nodded like it was all true. No wonder she was pushing so hard to get him out. Even so, if God had a plan for Darren, maybe prison was exactly where he was meant to be. I liked to think we all had free will, but if he hadn't confessed to murder, he wouldn't be trying to turn his life around, albeit behind bars, and he'd be there for twenty-five years.

It was incredible how some events that appeared to be a massive failure could actually turn your whole world around and force you to become the best version of yourself. Was that what happened to Darren? Had his conviction been a blessing in disguise, a chance to get him off the streets, off the drugs? Could our family be put back together again?

"That's awesome, Darren."

"Yeah, it's weird. Getting arrested that day was the last thing I wanted, to be locked up in a cage like an animal. But lately, I've been seeing how maybe this is my time to really reflect. Start anew. Don't really have much else to do while I'm in here," he said with a sad smile.

"I'm really happy to hear that." I wanted to ask him about Candace and about his girlfriend, but I felt like I'd really break this family moment. My mom might get mad at me, or more likely I'd be kicking myself.

"I have to confess. I've been asking around about what happened..." But before I could finish, he shook his head.

"I'm telling you, Martina, you need to let that go. Leave it. This is okay. You heard me, I'm doing okay. I'm where I'm supposed to be."

"I know, I just... I keep getting anonymous phone calls, and someone told me that you had a girlfriend. I just..."

"The Lord says we should forgive, so I'm going to forgive you for coming here under false pretenses to question me more about that case."

Oh boy, that felt like a gut punch.

"I'm only going to say it one more time, Martina."

Before he could finish, Mom said, "Don't be so hard on her, Darren. She's only trying to do what's right, after I begged her to."

With a stern voice, he said, "Then I need both of you to listen to me carefully. Please, drop this. I'm here. I'm gonna be here for the next two decades. I'm okay. This has been good for me. I'm begging you to leave it alone."

I wasn't sure I could. But a part of me wondered what would happen if I didn't. Would it put all of us in danger?

My mom said, "We'll never give up on you, Darren."

"I'm not asking you to give up on me, Mom. I'm asking you to let me do my time. When I get out, we can all have dinner. I can finally meet Zoey."

Darren wouldn't cooperate. That was obvious. But I had already opened up that can of worms, and they were wiggling all over the place.

23

MARTINA

With an extra-large coffee in my hand, I took a sip and knew I would need all the caffeine I could get. The long drive home with Mom had been an emotional one, and I was still recovering. She told me about Darren's sobriety and how he had found God, claiming he was a changed man. My pessimistic side told me it was possible he could be faking it, but I couldn't come up with a motive to do so. If on the other hand, he was screaming he was innocent and begging for help to clear his name and get him out of jail, it would be a different story. But he was saying he found God and he was guilty and to *stop* investigating.

Conflicted, I didn't know what to do next. Since he pleaded with me to stop investigating the case and to let it go, I wondered if I could. His stance made me question his guilt more than ever before. But should I let it go? What if my theory was correct and he was simply protecting himself and our family? Despite what Darren asked of my mother, she still wanted me to dig into the case and prove he was innocent. She swore she knew in her heart her son didn't belong in prison.

Undecided if I would continue investigating, I figured I had already put out feelers so learning the fruits of those efforts wouldn't hurt, right? If I did continue, we would have to be quieter about it. Maybe Vincent's idea of a funny disguise wasn't so funny after all. I spotted Vincent over by the coffee machine and made my way toward him.

"Good afternoon."

"Hey, Martina."

"Fueling up?"

"Yeah, it was a long night, but I did find some interesting things. Very covertly, I might add," he said, pausing and leaning up against the counter as the coffee machine dripped heavenly brew into his mug. "I went to Candace's house. She wasn't there. Peeked around in the windows, but no one was home. Car not in the garage. I stayed there all day, all night. She never returned."

No wonder he was drinking coffee late into the afternoon. "Maybe she's on vacation or visiting family." Perhaps that was the reason for her leave of absence at her job.

"It's possible. Her parents live a few hours away. But her sister lives in Pleasanton, so I went by the sister's house and poked around. No signs of life."

"Did you try calling her cell phone?"

"Nine times. Goes straight to voicemail."

"Did you trace it?"

We really weren't supposed to do that, and you had to go through back channels to find that kind of information. It wasn't on the up-and-up.

"I did. Don't tell anyone, OK?" he said, wiggling his brows.

It was one of the great things about working where we did and the fact I was one of the bosses, so I could look the other way or pretend like it never happened. It wasn't like we were trying to hurt anybody with the information, but technically, one of our computer specialists had hacked into the system, which was highly illegal. Of course, we had safeguards to make sure it didn't come back to us.

"My lips are sealed."

"OK, well, either the battery's dead, she took out the SIM card, or she threw it in the bay."

"So she's untraceable."

"Exactly."

I was about to ask if he checked the credit cards or bank statements from Candace Mason, when he shook his head. "Checked credit card and bank info. No movement. Nothing."

"That's a little concerning. Did you see signs of a struggle at her or her sister's house?"

"No. But I put in a call to the FBI to see what they know about the 98Mob and to find out if they know Candace. Maybe she's involved in the gang. I'm still waiting to hear back."

Thank goodness for Vincent. I didn't know how many times I thought that recently, but it was quite a few. He had saved me on multiple occasions, with great ideas and his willingness to help with my brother's case. "So right now, we've got nothing on Candace. She's disappeared, and we have no way of finding her."

"I couldn't have put it better myself," he said as he picked up his mug and led me toward the conference room containing our murder board.

The room was small with only a tiny window on the door and a motivational poster featuring a cat on the far wall. Inside, I shut the door behind me and took another gulp of my coffee. "I was suspicious of Candace before, but now I'm concerned."

"Me too. How did your meeting with Darren go?"

I shrugged. "He's begging us not to look into the case anymore. Says he's found God and he's clean, and I tend to believe him because he has no reason to lie about it."

"That's great news, but I guess that means he didn't give you any information."

"He did not, and he said that he forgave me for visiting under false pretenses."

Vincent gritted his teeth. "Yikes. What did Betty have to say about that?"

"Mom wants me to prove he's innocent and get him out of jail."

"A tall order. So, what do you want to do?"

Ted really got the idea in my head that the 98Mob could be coming after the entire family if we continued on, but maybe playing offense would stop them from coming after me and anyone else. "If the 98Mob is as dangerous as we suspect, they may come after my family whether we stop or not." Had I just made my decision? I said a silent prayer that it wasn't the wrong one.

"True. The case stinks, and I think it's bigger than your brother."

My gut said the same thing. "I don't disagree, but I think we have to be very, very quiet moving forward."

"All right, well, the only thing we were going to do today was go to the pizza parlor and try to find Izzy."

"I shouldn't go. I've already told a few people I'm Darren's sister. Maybe somebody else from the team could go and ask around for us."

"That's a good idea, although—"

"I'll check around the office to see who can go."

He cracked a smile. "Or we can just call."

Was I losing it? Too close to it to think like I normally would? Obviously, we could just make a phone call and ask if Izzy was there. If she was, we could send someone down to talk to her. "Smart."

"I'll go grab one of our untraceable phones and give the pizza parlor a call, ask if she's working."

Feeling antsy about the whole situation, I was glad I wasn't alone. Vincent was a great partner and had a great relationship with our friends at the FBI which could really help us.

Vincent rushed back in, phone in hand. He dialed the number, and I watched him. He nodded when there was an answer. "Yeah, hi, may I please speak with Izzy? No? Oh, OK, I must have the wrong number. Thanks, bye."

He sat the phone down on the table and said, "They say nobody by that name works there."

"Did she quit?"

Vincent shrugged.

Had we just hit two dead ends? Candace was in the wind, and Izzy didn't work at the pizza place anymore—or ever? *Now what?*

"Sounds like we need to wait to hear back from the FBI."

Vincent raised his brows. "Or we could look into visiting records..."

Breaking into a federal database was not something we liked to do. The firm could get in big trouble for doing so. We blurred the lines, but there were some hard ones we didn't cross. "Too risky for the firm."

"Or if we could find someone in law enforcement to help us out. Have you talked to Hirsch yet?"

"I left a message earlier, asking him to call me back, but he hasn't."

"Maybe he's got something?"

"Or he's too mad at me to call back."

"I don't think so. My spidey senses are saying he's onto something. Have faith, Martina."

Hirsch had never failed me before. But if he had found something, why hadn't he called?

24

MARTINA

After a day of admin work at the firm, I was looking forward to my shift at the rehab center. Hirsch still hadn't called me back, and neither had the FBI. I didn't want to push my luck and start asking around the park again. Vincent and I couldn't be seen investigating. A gut was telling me it could be dangerous if people found out, so I was going to have to be patient, which was not my strong suit. I preferred answers immediately. Considering the number of times my mother had called to ask for updates, I understood who I inherited that trait from.

I waved to the receptionist sitting behind her desk and headed back toward my workstation among a sea of low cubicles. Butterflies swarmed my insides as I spotted the man, the writer, in the hallway chatting with one of the other volunteers. I waved and smiled. If I didn't know better, I'd say his eyes lit up as he waved back. What were these feelings? I had met him exactly *once*.

The writer finished up his conversation and headed straight for me. "Hi, how's it going? It's good to see you again."

"Oh, you too." Mildly flustered by my nerves, I said, "How was your week?"

"Sober, and I did some writing, so for me, at this point, that's a big win."

Was I still smiling? *Oh. No.* It was a crush. How did I not see this coming? At my desk, I said, "Do you want to have a seat?"

"Absolutely." He sat down in the visitor's chair, and I sat in mine.

Trying with all my might to squash the butterflies, I said, "So, what kind of challenges did you have this week?"

"There's been a few. It was a good week, but there's always something in the back of my mind I can't shake—the guilt."

Guilt was something that could eat you up, starting small and growing throughout your body, eventually taking over. "Do you want to talk about it?"

His smile faded and sadness took its place. "It's my daughter. I've wronged her. I did harm. I left her to be with an addict —my ex-wife. Not that she can't handle herself, she's incredible. When she was little, I could barely believe she was mine. So smart. Even with her high IQ and independent nature, I know every kid needs a mom and a dad to love them, to be the ones to take care of them. Not the other way around."

It was how I thought of Zoey. Since the day she was born, I wondered how that girl could have come from me. "It sounds like you're worried about her."

"The last time I spoke to her, her mom, my ex, had some creepy guys coming around. She's an exceptionally bright girl, but smarts aren't always enough. And she often thinks she knows what's best and has a penchant for telling people exactly what she thinks. It worries me that she might cross the wrong person and get hurt."

Like one of her mother's boyfriends. It was a valid concern. "I understand. She sounds like my daughter. Zoey's seventeen and going off to college next month. She's really bright but sometimes she thinks she knows better than me and, well, just about everyone. Even with high intelligence, you're right, they need an adult, someone guiding them, showing them the way." That realization was why I had to stay sober. I couldn't leave Zoey to fend for herself.

"I feel like I can't give that to her because I'm still finding my own way, you know?"

With empathy, I said, "I do."

"Still working on that tough case?"

He remembered. "Yeah, this one's personal, so I brought in some help. We don't typically allow our team to work on cases when they have a relative or friend involved. But I'm kind of the boss, and I get to decide."

Do as I say and not as I do?

"Has it tempted you to drink?"

"Not really. Thankfully, I have my sponsor I talk to about the stressful things going on, and that helps. Honestly, I probably should just get a therapist and not bother him so much, but it helps me stay on the right path."

"I'm learning that too. Like meeting you last week, I thought about our conversation and how easy it was and how much better I felt afterwards."

I tried to suppress the smile. He felt it too. He was handsome in a medium-height, dark, and handsome kind of way. As my heart fluttered, I could tell feelings were growing.

That was *not* part of my plan.

You are *not* supposed to fall for addicts, especially in their first year, as it could be problematic. Why couldn't I shake this guy? This guy whose name I didn't even know.

My phone rang, and I nearly jumped out of my chair. It was my mother. "I'm sorry, I have to take this."

He nodded me on.

"Hi, Mom, what's going on?"

"Martina."

I could barely understand what she was saying. She was sobbing. I could barely understand the words. I sat up, growing increasingly more concerned. "Mom, has something happened?"

Sounds of static followed by Ted's voice emanated from the speaker. "Martina, this is Ted."

"What's wrong?"

"Darren was attacked earlier today. They don't know if he's going to make it."

A chill went down my body, and I feared the worst. Darren had warned us to let it go, and we didn't, and he had paid the price. Would my brother's death be on my hands? "What do you mean they're not sure? When will they know? Where is he?"

"They rushed him to a local trauma center. He was stabbed several times in the abdomen. They think they nicked the liver. There is internal bleeding. He's just out of surgery. They will be monitoring him very closely."

I shook my head in disbelief. "Is he allowed visitors?"

"Yes, he is. I'm about to drive your mother. He's at Marin County Hospital."

"Okay, I'll pack up and meet you at the hospital." I could call Zoey and let her know what was happening on the way there.

"Be safe, Martina."

"I'll see you soon." I ended the call and looked over at the man. "I'm so sorry, I have to leave."

"Is everything all right?"

"I'm not sure. I'll see you next week. Have a good night." I rushed out of the rehab center and hoped I made it to the hospital before Darren was gone forever.

25

CANDACE

WITH THE LAST SIP, I peered over at my sister and said, "This is exactly what I needed. Thank you." After I confessed everything and had a mini breakdown, Talia insisted that everything would be fine and decided the two of us needed a break.

"Of course. We were well overdue for a girls' trip."

What better place than Napa Valley? Scenic vineyards with rolling hills offering belly-warming beverages. *Yes, please.* We had wine tasted and pampered ourselves with massages at the spa. It was exactly what my soul needed: a place to recuperate, clear my mind, and start my journey of getting back to me. Back to a person who didn't seek revenge, or get mixed up with drug dealers, or hide things from my family because I was too ashamed to tell them the truth. I should've known I could trust Talia with anything. If nothing else, this awful experience brought us closer together. All I had left to do was avoid scary men coming to my house threatening me, and all would be okay.

It was Talia's brilliant idea to go off the grid.

We shut off our phones to avoid any outside distractions or triggers that might send me spiraling. Of course, eventually, I had to go back to the real world, back to work, back to what I was supposed to be doing with my life before I was swallowed up by my grief.

But I had made a few decisions while sipping cabernet and chardonnay. I was definitely going to sell the house. It was no longer part of my current life and had become a sad reminder of all the things I had lost. I needed to move forward and start over, find that new normal my sister kept talking about. For the first time in a long time, I was feeling optimistic about the future.

"You know we could stay longer if you want. I could call work, let them know I'll be out a few more days," Talia offered.

Staring out at the golden hills and perfectly neat rows of grapevines, I said, "No, I think I'm ready. With time off from work, I can pack up the house and start calling real estate agents."

"I have the perfect realtor for you. I'll give you her number."

"Cool. Once the house is ready, I can start looking for a new one or a townhouse, a place with a small yard. I could have a garden. And of course I need to decide what city I want to live in."

"Well, we've got some great places in Pleasanton. And you'd be closer to me." She paused and set down her empty wine glass. "Actually, great idea! If you want, while the house is up for sale, you can stay with me. I've got an extra room. What do you say?"

It was a nice idea. If I did that, I wouldn't have to rush any decisions about my new place. Definitely wished I would've talked to Talia earlier. I could have avoided a lot of the extra grief I had experienced over the last six months.

With a bright smile, I said, "I accept."

Talia practically leaped out of her seat as she clasped her hands together. "I can't wait! We'll be roomies. Of course, until you decide you're ready to find a new place, but no rush."

"Thank you so much. For everything. For understanding and not judging me."

"I'm not going to say I agree with everything you've done, but I think putting it all behind you is the right thing to do. And once it's in the rear view, never look back."

"That's exactly what I intend to do."

BACK AT TALIA'S, I switched on my cell phone and realized it was actually dead, not just off. I plugged it into the charger on the kitchen counter and let it boot up.

"Ready for real life and living with me?" she asked.

"Absolutely."

The iPhone, plugged into the outlet, rang, and I saw a familiar number go across the screen. I quickly picked it up, still attached to the cord, and answered. "Hello?"

"Candace?"

The calm I had been feeling faded fast. "Yes."

"This is Detective Leslie."

"Is there something I can do for you, Detective?"

Talia stopped fussing with her suitcase and hurried over to where I was standing in the kitchen, watching.

"I'm calling because I wanted to let you know the sheriff's department may be reopening the case. I need you to be careful about what you tell people. Definitely don't talk to Martina Monroe, and make sure you lock your doors and windows."

Just moments before, I was feeling lighter. It was replaced with a heaviness pressing down on me. "Somebody came to visit me. Did you know that?"

"No, who was it?"

If that wasn't why she cautioned me to keep my doors and windows locked, why had she said that? Could I really trust

Detective Leslie? "He didn't say his name, but he was tall, had dark hair, and he told me he would come back for me if I changed my statement."

"Do you plan to change your statement?"

"No, definitely not." Darren Kolze was not worth dying over. I was one hundred percent ready to move on and forget about that chapter in my life.

"Good. So, the reason why, to be honest with you, is that the shooter, Darren Kolze, was attacked in prison. He's in critical condition, and we don't know if he's going to make it yet. We think it was an intentional act to silence him, to ensure he doesn't take back his plea."

"Do you think they'll try to silence me?" I asked with a shaking voice.

Talia placed her hand on my shoulder, and I stared at her, trying to convey the situation had gone from bad to worse.

"We don't think so. Since you've already had a visit, and if you don't change your testimony, you're likely okay."

"Are you sure? If they went after Darren, why wouldn't they go after me?"

"They might find you less of a liability," she said, rather unconvincingly.

After the visit from the scary man, I would surely lock up the house. I didn't need the detective to tell me that. But maybe it was like she said—I was less of a liability. If they wanted to kill me, the man could have done it when he showed up at my house. Maybe Detective Leslie was right. Maybe I wasn't in danger. Or maybe I was wrong for trusting her. "Is there anything else I should know?"

"That's it. You can call me anytime if anything seems out of place or you're worried."

"Okay, thanks." I shook my head and ended the call, placing the phone back on the countertop.

Talia said, "What was that about?"

After I explained what the detective had told me, Talia said, "You are definitely staying here with me. You don't want to be alone. Now, if they come for you, they're coming for both of us. We'll have a security system installed *immediately*."

"You don't have to do that for me."

"I will do that for you, and for me. I told you, we're going to get through this together. You're not alone in this. I'll do everything I can to protect you, okay?"

I nodded, knowing better than to argue with my pushy older sister. But she was right. I definitely felt safer with her, in her house with a security system, than alone in my empty house where that man knew where I lived.

26

MARTINA

My footsteps echoed down the empty hallway as I hurried toward Ted who stood outside Darren's hospital room. After a quick hello hug, I said, "How is Mom holding up?"

His expression was somber. "She's a wreck, Martina. I've never seen her like this. I don't know what she'll do if he doesn't make it."

That explained why he was worried. A stressed-out alcoholic, even one sober for a decade, was a reason for concern. "Well, she has you and me. We'll help her through. What's the latest?"

"The doctor said the surgery was a success. They were able to stop the bleeding. They think he might pull through. Your mom hasn't left his side since they wheeled him into the room."

After a prayer for Darren and my mother, I said, "Any idea who did this to him and why?" Not that I didn't have my own theories. But Ted had been in law enforcement for more than thirty years before he retired, I was sure he had some old friends who could provide information.

"I made a call over to the warden. It sounds like they suspect it's a member of the 98Mob."

As expected. "Is anyone being held accountable?"

Ted pursed his lips and shook his head, frustration evident in his eyes. "No, it's the same old 'nobody saw anything' story. You don't snitch in prison, but word around the block is that it was, in fact, the 98Mob."

"Does the warden have a theory as to why they went after him?" It wasn't common for a gang to take out one of their own unless they snitched or double-crossed them.

"You're not going to like this, Martina."

I shut my eyes and braced myself for what was coming.

"It was because of the investigation. Somebody found out. They wanted to make sure the case remained closed. That's much easier with Darren dead. Considering the sheriff's department is a lot less likely to spend time opening a closed case with a signed confession from the suspect. If he were alive and wrongfully convicted, and there was another suspect, that's a different story. They would have good reason to put resources into proving his innocence."

We knew the 98Mob could potentially hurt Darren and the rest of our family based on the calls I received to stop my investigation. "Did they say how they figured out I'm looking into the case?"

"Nothing specific. But word around the block is that some people are getting nervous that someone with your track record for solving cases is digging into their business. You've ruffled some feathers. And the working theory is they're tying up loose ends."

That wasn't anything new in my world. I was a feather ruffler if there ever was one. But this was the first time the crime involved a member of my family.

"But why do they care?" I said, still struggling to believe the entire scenario.

"No one's talking about the 'why,' just that they don't want anyone opening up the investigation."

That didn't sit right with me. "Thanks, Ted. Have you told my mom any of this?"

"I did."

"And what did she say?" Did she still want us to keep moving forward with Darren's life at risk? And maybe even Candace's, the eyewitness's, life at risk too?

He looked toward the entrance to the room as Mom walked out, her eyes red and puffy. I rushed to her and wrapped my arms around her. After a moment, I released her, and she said in a voice choked with emotion, "He's still asleep, but he looks so pale. I just hate all of this, Martina. I feel so helpless."

Before I could reassure her, convince her I wouldn't stop looking and that I'd make sure Darren had protective custody while he was in the hospital, footsteps approached. I looked over my shoulder and did a double-take.

It had been a long time since I'd seen him, but there was no mistaking it. Six foot two, built, with dark hair graying at the temples, and those amber eyes. *Clark.* His and Darren's resemblance was unmistakable. He gave me a quick glance before rushing over to our mother.

"Clark, I'm so glad you're here," Mom exclaimed, relief evident in her voice.

His eyes drifted over to me.

"Hi, Clark," I said, trying to mask the surprise in my voice.

"Hey, little sister," he replied, a hint of warmth in his tone.

"Hi, Clark," Ted interjected, likely to fill the silence.

"Ted, how's it going?" Clark asked, as he shook his hand. "So, do you know what happened? Who did this?"

Ted said, "The police are still looking into it."

With my focus on Darren and his gang affiliation, it hadn't

occurred to me to investigate Clark too. But it would make sense that if Darren was dealing for the 98Mob, Clark was too. What did he know about Toby June's murder? And more pressing, what did he know about the attempt on Darren's life?

"Maybe you can tell us what happened. You're closer to the streets than we are," I suggested cautiously.

My mother glared at me and said sternly, "Martina."

I looked away, but I knew I was right to ask. I wasn't naïve to what my brothers were up to. Clark stared at me, looked me directly in the eyes, and said, "They're not telling me anything. If I knew, I'd say."

A wave of emotion ran through me. Clark seemed sincere, like he would really tell us if he knew who had hurt Darren. Was it possible that Clark was turning his life around too? His dilated pupils suggested otherwise. Gangs, or organized crime, typically made the members be loyal to them over all else. He wasn't likely to be much help, but I had to try.

"Are we allowed to go in and see him?" I asked, changing the subject.

"They said just for a minute, but I had to see him, Martina. You should too," Mom urged.

"I'd like to." With that, I walked past Clark, giving him a look that was intended to convey I was keeping an eye on him.

Inside, Darren lay pale and looked near death, surrounded by tubes and blinking lights. In that moment, I knew I had to stop these people from going after Darren, after Clark, after my mother, and after anybody else's family.

Clark walked in and stopped at the edge of the bed. He lowered his head and murmured something I couldn't decipher. He moved a few steps closer. "He doesn't look good, does he?"

I shook my head. "No, but Ted says they think he'll pull through. The surgery went well."

"Hey, Martina," Clark said softly, "I just wanted to say I think it's cool what you're doing, looking into this. But if you don't stop, they'll come after all of us. You. Your daughter. Mom. I can't even be seen talking to you." He glanced around before completing his message. "There are seriously bad people involved, Martina."

"Why did they do this? Did Darren really kill Toby?"

He lowered his gaze. "I can't say any more. I've already said too much. As it is, being here is risky."

If Clark was involved in the 98Mob, I understood the risks he took to see Darren and to talk to us. My heart ached to think my brother could lose his life for talking to me. "I understand. Are you safe?"

"For now. Are you doing okay? Mom says Zoey's going off to college and wants to meet me."

A wave of emotion washed over me. It was strange how my brothers and I had spent so much time away from each other, our paths taking us in opposite directions, yet at the core, it didn't matter. We were family and my love for them could never be extinguished. And I could never stop wishing the best for them and, despite my better judgement, maintained a sliver of hope that one day we could be a real family again. "Overall, things are good. And yes, since Darren's case, Zoey has been curious about her uncles."

"I get it if you don't want her around us. If I were you, I wouldn't either—especially now."

"If you need help getting out, I have resources. And you have people who love you and will help."

He shook his head. "Not with these people, Martina. You need to be careful, really careful." He patted me on the shoulder and walked out.

I heard him exchange a few words with Mom and Ted, then

the faint sounds of his footsteps moving farther and farther away. My gaze fell back on Darren, who'd attempted to change his life and almost lost it. My other brother was unable to get out of that life. That didn't change the fact there was love there. And I knew, in my heart, Clark risked his own safety to come to the hospital to warn me of the dangers if I forged ahead.

27

MARTINA

After a squeeze of Darren's hand, I left his bedside and rejoined Mom and Ted in the hallway. A set of nurses walked past before Mom said, "Did Clark say anything to you?" With a note of concern in her voice.

"He told me to be careful."

Ted's eyes met mine, conveying a mutual understanding. Clark visited the hospital to deliver a message and it was received loud and clear. How could I move forward without triggering a dangerous attack on my family?

"But you have to see it now, Martina. He doesn't deserve to be in jail," Mom insisted, her voice filled with conviction.

"That may be, Mom, but this is really dangerous. They could come after us, after you."

If only I had more help looking into the case. Like law enforcement help.

"Have you heard from Hirsch?" Ted asked, breaking into my thoughts.

"No." But I sure would have been grateful to hear from him. "What can we do to make sure that Darren is protected while he's here? They're likely to make a second attempt on him."

"The warden said there isn't much. He's not a state's witness. He's just a prisoner."

Really? Did we only care about a prisoner's safety if it was beneficial to the state? "But someone tried to kill him. He can't get his own cell or something? Take him out of general population?"

"Usually high-risk prisoners like former law enforcement will get solitary, or be housed in special units, but there's still a risk."

"There's no one you can call in a favor to?" Mom asked.

"Well, as long as he's in his current condition, he'll stay in this hospital, and there'll be a guard here, obviously, since he's a prisoner."

But that guard could be compromised. I wasn't naïve to the idea of dirty corrections officers. The 98Mob likely had far-reaching tentacles and could easily pay off a guard to look the other way while one of their gang members finished what they started. Without other options, I said, "I'll get someone from the firm to stand guard. My people will ensure nobody messes with him."

"Good, that gives you more time to find the truth, Martina, to get him out of jail and out of harm's way," Mom said, hope and determination flickering in her eyes.

"I'm not sure how I'm going to do that. I don't want them coming after Zoey or you. Or Clark."

"We can't just let them kill him, can we? He's my baby, Martina."

Sacrifice your entire family for just one? Would I do the same if I were in her position? "I don't know what to do."

Ted, the ever-knowing voice of reason, suggested, "It's been a long day. Why don't we just take this one day at a time? Martina, you and Zoey are more than welcome to stay with us while we figure this out."

Before I could answer, I felt the vibration of my phone in my pocket. Pulling it out, a sense of relief washed over me. I answered after one ring and stepped away. "Hirsch."

"Hi, Martina. I heard about Darren. How's he doing?"

"He's out of surgery. They think he'll make it." Walking a little farther away, I said, "I'm at the hospital now. But I worry they'll come after him again."

"You're probably right."

Did Hirsch know something? "I want to apologize for the other day. I..."

He cut me off. "We're good. I just had to look into some things, and I think I have something for you."

I knew he wouldn't let me down. "What is it?"

"Come down to the station tomorrow. Leslie will explain everything."

My heart raced. "Really?"

"Yes. Is there anything I can do to help with Darren?"

"I'm going to get someone from the firm to watch him in the hospital, but after that, he has no protection. Mom's begging Ted to call in some favors."

"Hopefully he can. It's late. Let's talk more tomorrow."

"Okay, thanks, Hirsch."

"Stay safe."

We said our goodbyes, and I glanced over at Ted, giving him a quick head nod. I didn't know what Hirsch had found, but I had a feeling it was important. I only hoped it would be enough to save my brother's life and keep our family out of danger.

Walking back to Mom and Ted, I said, "I'm going to get someone out here to watch over his room, and then I'll head back to be with Zoey."

Ted pulled a key with a green fob from his pocket and said, "Here's a key to the house. Call to let us know you made it, okay?"

Ted's obvious concern did nothing to ease my nerves.

28

MARTINA

With Zoey safely at Mom and Ted's, I rose early and with travel mug in hand, left the house to meet Hirsch. It was a little strange and unsettling to be in my mother's guest room with Ted and her not far. But their home was fortified with a security system, and Ted, a trained officer, was an added bonus. It was reassuring to know there was someone to rely on should our perimeter be breached. Despite missing the comfort of my own bed, for the time being, I would endure.

Upon reaching the reception of CoCo County Sheriff's, I waved to a familiar face.

"Martina, how are you doing? I don't think I've seen you since you and Hirsch closed the Eliza Mitchell case."

"I've been working on another case. It's good to see you," I said to the receptionist before I continued on to Hirsch's office. Surprisingly, he was alone, despite telling me Leslie would be there. He motioned for me to come in. "Hey, Hirsch."

"Hey, Martina, how's your brother?"

"Well, he made it through the night. The doctors say it's a good sign. Mom and Ted are hosting Zoey, Barney, and me."

"Ted's that worried, huh?"

"We all are."

"Hopefully, Leslie can shed some light on all of this."

"What did she tell you?"

"I'll let you interview her. She can explain everything."

Glancing around his tidy office, I said, "Where is she?"

"She's going to meet us in the conference room, with her union rep by her side."

Union rep. It confirmed what Vincent and I suspected. Hirsch was investigating Leslie but couldn't disclose it to me, and probably having involved Internal Affairs. I was about to learn everything Leslie had done wrong and why. I prayed it would give us what we needed to end this madness, to return to our regular lives, where my family wasn't under attack, and I wasn't visiting prisons and hospitals to see my brother. "Can I ask her anything I want?"

"She's agreed to answer any and all questions you have. She promised to be truthful. Her continued employment is contingent upon it."

Yikes. Hirsch was taking this very seriously. I should not have doubted him.

He stood up, and I followed him to the conference room. On the way, he said, "If you and Zoey need anything, you let me know."

"Thanks," I replied, knowing he meant it.

We reached the room where Detective Leslie awaited. Her face was long and covered with shame. Beside her sat a woman in an ill-fitting suit, presumably the union rep, which was confirmed by her visitor's badge.

Hirsch introduced us. "Ms. Daniels, this is Martina Monroe. She's a consultant here at CoCo County and an owner at Drakos Monroe Security & Investigations."

We exchanged handshakes, and I handed her my business

card. "Nice to meet you," I said, my tone tinged with curiosity. "Hi, Detective Leslie."

With an earnest look in her eyes, she answered, "Hi, Martina."

Hirsch, sitting next to me, began. "As everyone in this room knows, we're here to discuss the shooting of Toby June. Martina has been investigating the murder because her brother, Darren Kolze, pled guilty to the shooting. She's been verifying the facts of the case and found inconsistencies and procedures that weren't followed. I'm now opening the floor to Martina to ask Detective Leslie questions about the case."

Nods of agreement circled the room. "Martina, you have the floor."

Leslie sat up straighter in her chair.

Here goes. "First of all, thank you for meeting with me. This case is personal since it involves my brother. I hadn't seen or spoken to him in twenty years until his arrest. As you know, Darren originally claimed innocence and asked for my help. But I was shocked when, after resolving another case I was working, he had pled guilty and accepted a twenty-five-year sentence."

Heads tipped around the room, letting me know everyone was on the same page. I continued, "My mother asked me to look into the case. When I reviewed the file, it was thinner than I would have expected, and soon I understood why. The first inconsistency I found was regarding the motive for the shooting. The claim was that it was a turf war between two sets of drug dealers, but when I spoke with narcotics agents Rourke and Kiva, they said not only were Darren and Toby both dealers for the 98Mob but that Detective Leslie never consulted them. There was nothing corroborating the motive. The second inconsistency I found was when I interviewed Candace Mason, the only eyewitness, and she described how she identified the suspect from a lineup, and it was clear procedure wasn't followed. I'd like to ask Detective Leslie to explain these two inconsistencies and breach in protocol."

Detective Leslie nodded. "Before I explain that, I have to give you some background. I have a son, Ethan. He's twenty-three years old. A few years ago, he started using drugs—prescription pills, at first. I put him into rehab, but he relapsed repeatedly. About a year ago, he went missing. He'd been gone two days which was unusual. I went searching for him, and I found him high at a park, surrounded by users and dealers. They were holding him because he owed money. That day I met his dealer and paid off his debts and took him home. That dealer became a confidential informant for me. He's a member of the 98Mob."

I knew there had to be a reason for Leslie to break protocol.

She paused, then said, "On the day Toby June was shot, I received a phone call from the CI. He claimed to know who shot Toby, saw the whole thing. He told me he saw Darren Kolze shoot Toby. That's how I ended up with the mugshots—one of Darren Kolze and five other known Hispanic gang members. The CI told me to make it obvious it was a white man, Darren specifically."

"How did the eyewitness respond to the six-pack? Did you explain to her that the suspect may not be included in the photos?"

"No, I didn't tell her that. I didn't want to risk her not picking Darren. It only took her about ten seconds to finger him," Leslie recounted, her voice laced with relief. "I felt uneasy about using a not-so-anonymous tip and breaking procedure, but she identified him immediately."

That didn't bode well for Darren unless Candace was somehow connected to the 98Mob. "And the motive? How did you come up with that?"

"The CI called again, providing the motive. He instructed

me not to confirm it with narcotics or discuss the case with anyone else and not to question any more witnesses. They said they would take care of the rest."

"And you just went along with it?" I asked, noticing tears leaking from Leslie's eyes.

"Not at first," Leslie admitted, her voice breaking. "They put my son on the phone. They had him, and they threatened to kill him. I caved. I brought in Darren. As you remember, I allowed you to speak with him. Then he confessed, and I thought everything was resolved. I didn't follow protocol. I should have interviewed the victim's family, canvassed the park where he was killed, and spoken to narcotics to confirm the motive. I'm so sorry."

"Did Darren shoot Toby June?"

"Honestly, I don't know," Leslie admitted. "I assumed he did when the eyewitness picked him from the photo array and my CI identified him. Then, a few days after his arrest, he pled guilty. The CI's instructions were odd, but I hadn't considered it could be a set up or anything other than the truth."

She trusted the person who had kidnapped her son and threatened to kill him? "What made you eventually think the CI wasn't being truthful?"

"You," Leslie said. "Narcotics approached me, questioning why they hadn't been consulted and told me the motive was flawed. Toby and Darren were both in the 98Mob. The CI lied to me about the motive. So, I started to wonder what else he lied about. And the eyewitness seemed credible enough, but honestly, I just don't know."

"But you know the only physical evidence that Darren was even near Toby was the drugs in his pocket. And now that we know they worked together, those drugs could've come from any other day. You haven't found the weapon, and there's zero physical evidence linking my brother to the murder itself. Plus, you only had one eyewitness. You know how unreliable they can be." Incredulity laced my tone. "You didn't think to question it?"

"I did," Leslie acknowledged, her voice heavy with regret. "But like I said, Martina, it all lined up at the time. The CI said it was Darren, the eyewitness identified Darren, and Darren himself confessed. If they hadn't threatened my son, I would have dug deeper, crossed every T. You know the drill. But they did threaten him. I felt like I only had one option, or I could lose my son."

It never made sense Leslie would run a dirty homicide investigation, but considering they threatened her son, her actions fit. But she had other options. She could have gone to Hirsch. "I need to learn more about the 98Mob. They're the ones who pointed to Darren. Why would they rat out one of their own?"

Her story raised even more questions about Darren's guilt.

Leslie shrugged. "I honestly don't know."

Hirsch, who had been listening intently, tipped his head and said, "Martina, you're right, it doesn't make sense. We're reopening the case."

My eyes met his and he gave me a reassuring nod. "What does that mean for Darren's confession?"

"Well, like you said, we can't corroborate he was the actual shooter with physical evidence. We need to talk to the kidnapping, blackmailing CI and the eyewitness again. We start at day one."

My hope well refilled. I had my partner back. I should never have doubted him. If anyone was a purveyor of truth and justice, it was Hirsch. And the two of us—strike that—the three of us including Vincent, would find the truth.

29

MARTINA

Before I could launch into questions about Candace Mason and the informant's identity, I told Hirsch I needed a moment and stepped outside the room to call Vincent. My mind was reeling from the revelations disclosed by Detective Leslie, but we couldn't proceed without Vincent. He was a crucial member of our team. His insights and unconventional thinking were essential in asking the right questions, and I wanted him to hear Leslie's story firsthand. With my cell phone up to my ear, I anxiously waited for Vincent to pick up.

"Hey, boss, what's up?"

"Well, quite a bit," I replied, my voice tinged with the weight of the morning's events. I proceeded to detail everything I had learned from Detective Leslie, including the unexpected news that Hirsch was reopening the case.

"Boy, you've had quite the morning."

"No kidding. Can you come down here for the rest of the interview?"

"Yes, ma'am. Give me fifteen minutes."

Ma'am. That's a new one. "See you when you get here," I said, ending the call. I took a deep breath, gathering my thoughts before glancing back at the door. The situation was peculiar, not because I hadn't encountered officers in the sheriff's department hiding things before, but because this involved a friend. Someone I would have never suspected to be capable of turning a blind eye to a potential homicide cover-up *and* a kidnapping scheme.

Unsure about Darren's innocence, I saw that several pieces were starting to fit together, but there were also more questions than ever. For instance, why would a member of his own team rat him out? And why would Darren kill someone who was not only on his team, but also a friend?

BACK IN THE conference room with Vincent by my side, we exchanged introductions and greetings. Vincent broke the ice by addressing a crucial point. "Martina told me what happened, and I guess one thing I haven't heard is the identity of the CI and where we can find him—like STAT."

He was right. The CI, the one who had started it all, would be our focus. Leslie responded, "They call him Ace."

Because he always had one up his sleeve? "What's his real name?"

"Anthony Hernandez. He has a record. You can look him up."

"Where does he hang out?" Vincent inquired further.

"One of the parks in Bay Point. He used to hang at the park where Toby was killed but changed locations when he got promoted. I can give you the address of his territory."

"Promoted, like, within the 98Mob organization?"

"Yeah."

How big was the 98Mob organization? "What else do you know about him?"

"That's about it. I only know about the promotion because he was bragging about it when he called and told me to come pick up my son."

Ace seemed like a real winner. Drug dealer. Kidnapper. Blackmailer. Sounded like he needed to have his rear end behind bars. Turning to Hirsch, I said, "We should have some uniforms pick up Ace and bring him in for questioning."

Before Hirsch could answer, Leslie said, "I'm obviously going to help in any way I can, but I am concerned about you going in guns blazing."

"What concerns do you have?" I asked.

"Not just about my son, Ethan, but also about my safety and yours, Martina, and your family's. I know they went after Darren."

At that point, we didn't know if Leslie was being truthful and telling us the whole story or if her concern for her son's safety was driving her to desperate measures. But her concern seemed legitimate. "What about Candace Mason, the eyewitness? Are you concerned for her?"

Leslie looked away and said, "I don't know. If she really saw Darren shoot Toby, she should be okay."

Why couldn't she look me in the eye? "Do you have reason to believe she didn't?"

"Other than this whole mess? No."

Eyeing Hirsch, I said, "Where is your son now?"

"Ethan should be at home. He's still using. I wish I could get him clean but it seems near impossible."

"He's a witness. He knows Ace, and he may know other things too. Maybe bringing him in will keep him safe, and we can find out what he knows about the drug dealers."

"I'd appreciate that, Martina," Leslie said, relief evident in her voice.

Hirsch stood up. "I'll have uniforms pick up Ace. It's likely there are plenty of reasons to haul him down here. I'll go and put out the order to pick up Ace and Ethan."

"Can I call him, so he knows you're coming?" Leslie asked with concern in her voice.

Hirsch hesitated before replying, "I don't think that's a good idea, Leslie."

"You're right. I was just worried it would scare him. But if anybody knew I was warning him, they might go after him," Leslie conceded.

"Exactly," Hirsch affirmed. "I'll be in my office," he said, then exited the room.

If we could get Ace into custody and get him to talk, it could break the case wide open.

Fingers crossed.

With the door shut, Vincent asked Leslie to retell him everything she had told us up to that point. It was a tactic to find inconsistencies in her statement and see if she could provide any new information.

After she confirmed her original story, I said, "Do you know anything else about the shooting of Toby June? Any hint of why they actually killed him? Why they would rat out Darren and then try to take him out?"

"That's all I know. Ace threatened my son and forced my hand. He told me what to do, and I didn't ask questions. I regret that. I really do," Leslie said with a hint of remorse in her voice.

"And what do you know about Candace Mason?" Vincent probed.

Detective Leslie said, "Not much. I know I should have done a background. The first time I met her was when I picked her up at the hospital the day of the shooting. I made small talk about how she was feeling since she was pretty shaken up, but once we were at the station, I interviewed her about what she saw, nothing more, nothing less. She told me she saw the shooter point the gun at Toby and take one shot."

"You didn't ask her why she was at the park that day?" Vincent asked.

"No, by the time I picked her up, I was rattled and so was she. I wanted to get the whole thing over with. Close the case and get my son back."

Leslie was acting under duress.

"Did you know that Candace..." As I was about to divulge more information, I paused, censoring myself. I was on the verge of explaining that we knew Candace Mason's husband was a drug user and that Toby was his dealer. However, I also didn't want to reveal that we couldn't locate Candace. Given the uncertainty surrounding Leslie's allegiance, it was important to be cautious. "Have you followed up with Candace since the day of the shooting?"

Leslie shifted her gaze to the floor.

What was that? "Leslie?"

She looked right at me. "A few times."

"What were the nature of the follow-ups?"

"I asked her to come down for the live lineup, let her know the case was closed, and told her that she wouldn't need to testify in court."

"When was the last time you spoke with her?"

"The day before yesterday."

That didn't make sense. The case had been closed for six months. And it also meant Candace wasn't missing. "Why did you talk to her?"

"After I found out Darren had been attacked, I called to warn her to be careful."

"Why? I thought you said if she really saw Darren shoot Toby, she would be fine." Was Leslie telling us everything or just bits and pieces?

"In the event the 98Mob would come after her too."

Something wasn't adding up. "How did she react to that?"

"She said someone already approached her. Told her not to change her testimony or he'd be back."

Was Leslie not going to tell us about this? What else *wasn't* she telling us? "Did she know who it was?"

"She didn't. Just that he was tall with dark hair."

Like her description of Toby's shooter? Something was fishy about Candace's involvement. If she really saw Darren shoot Toby, why would someone be concerned she may change her testimony? We needed to get Candace down to the station and reinterview her. "I don't have any more questions for Detective Leslie. What about you, Vincent?" I asked, turning to him, hoping he had one of his "aha" moments.

"I'm guessing there aren't any more details about the CI, his motive, or his associates that you can tell us?" Vincent asked.

Leslie lowered her head. "No. I thought the less I knew, the better."

"In that case, I'd say we're done here," Vincent concluded.

30

MARTINA

Outside the conference room, I said, "What do you make of that?"

Vincent scrunched up his face. "I hate to say it, but I'm not sure she's telling us everything. Like the fact she called the eyewitness, and she learned the eyewitness had been threatened but didn't tell us until we specifically asked her about her last conversation with Candace. I didn't like that one bit."

"You and me both."

"We need to get Candace in for an interview. I have a feeling she's also not telling the whole story."

I thought, *Can someone please start telling us the whole truth?*

"Do you think she's involved with the 98Mob or is being threatened by them?"

"No idea. But I'm suspicious."

"Yeah. Let's go talk to Hirsch and tell him we need to bring her in and find out if Ace has been picked up yet."

"Good plan, boss."

Boss was better than ma'am.

We headed toward Hirsch's office, but before we could reach it, we caught sight of him deep in conversation with Rourke and Kiva. The expression on Hirsch's face as he glanced our way was far from reassuring. It certainly didn't convey the sense he was about to be the bearer of good news. He gestured for us to join them.

"Do you want the good news or the bad news?" Hirsch asked, his tone indicating the situation was serious.

I didn't like the sound of that. "What is it?"

"I was updating Rourke and Kiva on the case," Hirsch began, explaining that he had informed them about our decision to deploy uniforms to apprehend Ace. "They told me there's no need. They know exactly where he is. That's the good news."

"He's already in custody?" The question escaped my lips, hoping that was the second half of the good news.

Hirsch let out a weary breath. "No. He's dead."

And that was the bad news.

Ace was dead.

Darren was lying unconscious in a hospital bed.

Darren's girlfriend's whereabouts were unknown.

What could we learn from Candace and Leslie's son, Ethan? Or would they both go missing before we could talk to them too?

"When did he die?"

Kiva said, "His body was found thirty minutes ago. Jayda is assigned the case. She called us after inferring from a witness that he was with the 98Mob."

"Any witnesses? Any idea who killed him?"

"Jayda says no one is saying anything useful."

I glanced over at Hirsch and Vincent. "Something's really rotten about this case," I said, feeling a growing sense of unease. "Everyone connected to Toby June's murder is either dead or unconscious. The eyewitness is our only live lead."

Hirsch said, "But weren't there two other witnesses at the Toby June crime scene when the first responders showed up?"

"Yeah, but they said they didn't see the shooting. And both witnesses gave fake numbers. Names could be bogus too."

Hirsch looked at my two favorite narcotics officers and said, "I think it's time we learn all about the 98Mob."

Vincent added, "I have a call into the FBI organized crime task force. They've helped us before; they might be able to assist again."

Rourke said, "We can put a line in to the feds too. They keep an eye on the 98Mob, and we have regular meetings. But in the meantime, we can provide an overview of the 98Mob organization to you."

"This is getting more complicated each day," I said, realizing the depth of the situation. "I also want to know if my brother Clark is entangled in all of this."

Rourke and Kiva exchanged glances. "We were wondering when you would ask about him."

"I'm asking," I said firmly.

"He's in it too. Let's set up some time with the rest of our team, and we'll go over everything. I'll check around to see who is available and if I can get ahold of the feds. If they have any ongoing operations, they may have insight into why Toby and Ace were killed and why they put a hit on Darren."

And with that, I knew we'd get to the bottom of things with the help of CoCo County's narcotics division and half of the old Cold Case Squad.

The team was getting back together.

After Rourke and Kiva hurried off to assemble the team, I pivoted to Vincent and Hirsch and said, "We have some time before we'll get the details on the 98Mob. Let's make it count."

Vincent gave a knowing smile. "I know who I'd like to talk to."

"A certain disappearing eyewitness?"

Hirsch nodded. "Let's find a room and give her a call. I, for one, would like to get to the bottom of all of this."

"Ditto." The sooner we could put all the pieces together, the sooner my family would be safe.

31

CANDACE

My hands kept the flaps of the box down as Talia placed a strip of packing tape over the seam. With a smile, I said, "I think that's the last one."

"Great, now we can get you back to my place. The security system has been installed, and the spare room is now yours. All we have left to do is load up the cars and move you in."

"Thank you so much for your help."

"That's what sisters are for," she said with a warm smile.

Yesterday, my emotions had been all over the place after the call from Detective Leslie, telling me to be careful. Like the man who showed up to threaten me wasn't warning enough. Was the detective a dirty cop? Why did she tell me *not* to talk to Martina Monroe? Was it because Martina was Darren's sister or because the detective was worried about what Martina would find? It didn't matter. I was putting everything from that time behind me. I wasn't looking back. Even if they reopened the case, I would simply say exactly what I had said before. *No worries.* Onward and upward.

My phone rang, and Talia asked, "Are you expecting a call?" Her tone was overly protective.

Who could that be? Maybe it was work. "No."

"Do you want me to answer it for you?"

"Sure."

Talia answered, "Hello. No. This is her sister." She paused, then put the phone down and whispered, "It's Martina Monroe."

I shook my head back and forth vigorously, and she responded into the phone.

"No, I'm sorry, Candace isn't available right now. Can I take a message?" Talia stared at me, her expression filled with concern. "Okay, I'll give her the message."

Despite my newfound optimism, my heart raced, and I wondered why Martina Monroe was calling. What did she want? Should I tell Detective Leslie? On second thought, I didn't want to get involved further. "What did she want?"

"She said it was important to call her when you get a chance."

"Well, Miss Monroe, sorry, but I don't have any chances to call you back," I muttered under my breath.

"That's the shooter's sister, right?"

"Yeah, the detective said I shouldn't talk to her."

Before I could describe the intensity of the conversation I had with Martina Monroe at the hospital, my phone rang again. I motioned for Talia to answer it.

"Hello. No, my name is Talia. I am Candace's sister." Talia's mouth dropped open, and she gave me a look far more serious than when Martina Monroe had called. "Okay, um, yeah, here she is." She lowered the phone and said, "It's a sergeant at the CoCo County Sheriff's Department. I think you should talk to him. I don't think you should avoid talking to the police."

Feeling a mix of fear and guilt growing inside of me, I said, "Okay, give me the phone." Standing up straight, I put the phone to my ear. "Hello."

"Hi, Candace, my name is Sergeant Hirsch at the CoCo County Sheriff's Department. How are you today?"

"I'm doing well, thank you for asking."

"That's good to hear. I have you listed as a witness in a shooting back in February. Is that correct?"

"Yes, that's correct."

What was he getting at? Why was he calling? Detective Leslie did say they may be reopening the case, and all I had to do was keep my statement the same as it was before. Everything would be okay. This sergeant must be working with Detective Leslie.

He said, "Well, there's been some new information that's come to light, and we're reopening the case. We would like to have you come down to the sheriff's department so we can talk to you. Are you able to come down to the station this afternoon?"

"Today's not really good," was the only thing I could think of to say, a way to stall, really not wanting to go to the sheriff's station again. I shook my head, realizing I had nothing to worry about. All I had to do was tell them exactly what I had said before. There was no reason to be nervous.

"Would you be able to come down tomorrow, or even Saturday? Whatever works best for you."

"I can come down tomorrow, sure."

"What time?"

I shrugged. "Four-thirty."

"Great, thank you so much. We'll see you when you get here. At reception, ask for Sergeant Hirsch, and I'll come and get you."

"Okay, sure thing."

The call ended and I took a breath. All I had to do was tell them what I told them before. Darren *was* a killer. He was exactly where he deserved to be, right? No reason to be nervous or feel guilty.

"They want me to come down to the station to talk about the case. They're reopening it."

There was worry in Talia's eyes, and I understood why. "Just do what Detective Leslie told you to do. Everything will be okay."

I certainly hoped so. If it wasn't, I didn't know what would happen to me. I had to keep optimistic and believe everything would be fine. If I stuck to my statement, no more scary men would visit and threaten me. All would be right in my world. *I hoped.*

32

MARTINA

Perplexed as to why Candace wouldn't take my call but would talk to Hirsch, I was more suspicious than ever. It didn't make sense. Maybe she figured she had to talk to Hirsch since he was law enforcement and I was inconsequential. Whatever the reason, it bugged me.

"Penny for your thoughts?" Hirsch asked.

"It's weird Candace wouldn't take my call, right?"

Hirsch shrugged. "Maybe."

Three tall, well-muscled men entered the room, Kiva, Rourke, and another I hadn't met. Following them was Jayda. She sat next to me. "I guess I can't get away from you two," she said playfully.

"Never," I teased.

Kiva and the other two sat. "Hey, all. Most of you know my colleague, but for Martina and Vincent, this is Buck. He's a recent Narcotics transfer from OPD. He's been working on 98Mob for a few years."

"It's nice to meet you, Buck. I'm Martina and this is Vincent."

Vincent chuckled. "I hope our identities were obvious! Hey."

Buck gave a wide grin. "I figured. I'm no rookie."

A few grins cracked around the room.

Hirsch stood up. "Thank you all for gathering here. As all of you know by now, we're reopening the Toby June murder case. Toby June was a known member of the 98Mob, a low-level street dealer who worked with his alleged shooter, Darren Kolze. The eyewitness testimony placed Kolze at the scene of the crime and identified him as the shooter, and with his own confession, the case was closed."

Nods ensued.

"However, since our dear, tenacious friend Martina started looking into the case because Darren's her brother, she found some unsettling discoveries. One, Narcotics was not consulted on the motive or to gather any information about both parties. The motive is listed as a turf war, but Martina confirmed with Narcotics that both men worked for the 98Mob. Secondly, there was absolutely no physical evidence to corroborate Darren Kolze's confession. The gun was never recovered, and there was no gunshot residue on him when he was brought into the station." He glanced over at me, and I nodded in agreement.

"We have since learned that one of our own, Detective Leslie, had been blackmailed into fingering Darren Kolze as the shooter and was told by her blackmailer to not interview any other witnesses or talk to other departments. As you know, that's not how we operate here. Because of the breach in protocol, we are reopening the case. Now, I'm going to let Martina go over some key items, and then we'll have Narcotics discuss the structure of the 98Mob. After that, Jayda will take over and tell us what she knows about the murder of the informant, Ace, the person who blackmailed Leslie into closing the case."

It was a mouthful, but it was a great summary of where we

were at. "Thank you all for working on this case. Like Hirsch said, it's personal. My brother was charged and pled guilty to the murder of Toby June. The only thing pointing to Darren's guilt was the eyewitness testimony of a woman who was at the scene. More about her later."

After acknowledging nods, I said, "So, I started looking into the case because I had gotten an anonymous phone call shortly after Darren's arrest, saying he wasn't the shooter. And my mother begged me to clear Darren's name. We weren't able to trace the call. Subsequently, my brother pled guilty and begged me to stop looking into the case. Since then, I've received two anonymous, untraceable phone calls telling me to stop working on the case. Now, my brother is fighting for his life in a hospital bed after an attempt was made on his life. After learning of Leslie's role in the investigation, we attempted to reach out to the CI who blackmailed her, but he is dead. Our open questions are: Why would the CI, Ace a.k.a. Anthony Hernandez, a member of the 98Mob, rat out Darren if he was the shooter? And because Toby is a member of the 98Mob, why would Darren shoot him? Subsequently, why would they attack Darren in prison to kill him, and why would the CI also be killed? My gut is telling me something much bigger is going on than I originally suspected. I'm hoping between our Narcotics team and Jayda, we can shed some light on what could be happening."

Vincent said, "And to add to that, I do have a call in to the FBI's organized crime task force to see what they know. Have you gotten a chance to talk to them?"

Kiva said, "I just got off the phone with them and the DEA. I told them we're working with you. They say 'hey' and said if you need anything beyond what the DEA is providing, to call. They also told me there's big stuff brewing."

Like what?

Hirsch said, "Nice transition. Take it away, Kiva."

Kiva pushed out of his seat and picked up a dry erase marker. "Welcome to 98Mob 101. I'm your instructor Kiva."

A few chuckles sounded before he continued, "Okay, at the top, we have the mob boss, Jaime Ragnar, and I call him a boss because he's trying to create his own organized crime syndicate. He's created a typical organized crime structure: lieutenants at the top and a few levels below working for them. All the money gets gathered at the low levels—drug dealing, prostitution, and we suspect human trafficking. All the money filters up through the different levels, ultimately feeding into the boss's pockets, making him a very wealthy young man. He's only thirty-five."

Where did Darren and Clark fit in?

"Toby is at the bottom, Darren one level above that. Ace, Anthony Hernandez, is two levels above Darren—a lieutenant. The feds were suspicious when three of the 98Mob were either killed or had an attempt made. That's three out of about thirty 98Mob members."

How did Candace Mason fit in? Would they get to it? I hoped so. "What did the feds say?"

"Well, with flags raised, the feds reached out to their pals at the DEA. Turns out there's some rumblings that a secret coup is taking place within the 98Mob. Some people don't like how the boss is running things. Jaime thinks he's pretty hot stuff and is rubbing a few folks the wrong way. Some real bad, dangerous folks. The current theory is that there's a division within the organization and those not in favor of the new king are being eliminated."

Again, how was Candace involved? "Who's the new king?"

"At this time, that is *the* million-dollar question."

Jayda said, "It makes sense. There weren't any witnesses at the scene of Anthony Hernandez's murder, but he was shot once in the head, just like Toby June. The gun hasn't been recovered. Ballistics is running the bullet to see if the gun was used in any other crimes. But considering it was a hit very similar to Toby June's, we're guessing it's a 98Mob hit. Which side of the coin is unclear."

Vincent threw his hands in the air and said, "Are we in the middle of a mob war?"

Kiva said, "It's very possible. We don't know Darren and Toby's side in the war. But if the DEA is correct, it may be Ace is with the new king and took care of Darren and Toby who are on team Jaime."

"Then why take out Ace?"

"A few theories. One, Jaime took him out as retaliation for Toby and Darren. Two, the new wannabe king took him out to silence him. Or three, my personal favorite, Ace was killed as a punishment for June Bug's case being reopened. Too messy. The new king may not be a merciful one."

Was Darren part of the coup? Was he the shooter? "Okay, let's assume one of the theories is correct. Toby June was taken out because he's on Team Jaime—if Darren killed him, wouldn't that put him on Team New King? And Ace is on Team Jaime? And then was killed by Team New King?"

"This is getting confusing," Vincent commented.

It was confusing because it didn't feel right. There was only one scenario that fit in my head. But it could be my own bias wanting it to be true. "Or, bear with me. How does this theory sound? Toby and Darren are on Team Jaime. Ace is on Team New King. Toby is killed by one of the new king's men, who turns around and frames Darren. They threaten Darren to keep quiet and take the rap or they'll kill him too. The new king gets nervous and decides to take out Darren so he can't recant. Or Jaime takes him out as retaliation for Toby. Ace could be a target for the new king or old."

Kiva nodded. "It works ... except for the eyewitness."

But if the eyewitness lied, it would explain why they'd shown up at her house to threaten her, to ensure her statement didn't change. "Speaking of the eyewitness. She's an interesting one. Can't get her to tell us why she was at the park that day, but we've learned that her husband was a drug addict and Toby was his dealer. There's no sign that she's actually a user herself, but she was known by a few dealers at the park. They said she'd been there to buy for her husband six months ago. He died nearly two *years* ago."

"Okay, so that's in the confusing column. Is she cooperative?"

"Not with me, not anymore. I met with her, and when I asked her why she was at the park that day, she ran off. I called her recently; she wouldn't pick up. Hirsch called a few minutes later, and she talked to him and agreed to come in tomorrow for an interview. She's avoiding me, but why?"

"Another question in this crazy case," Vincent said, adding a bit of levity to our conversation.

Hirsch said, "We can ask her when she comes in. Let's make sure we get the most out of that interview. If she can tell us why she was at the park, maybe she can tell us if she really did see Darren shoot Toby. Sounds like we have our work cut out for us."

"One more thing," I said. "Where does Clark Kolze, my other brother, fit into all of this?"

"Clark is the same level as Ace, a.k.a. Anthony Hernandez. So, not a street-level dealer. He's a lieutenant, which means he's deeply involved."

An uneasiness settled over me. My brother was a lieutenant in an organized crime group? "He came by the hospital to see Darren. He told me to be careful. Any idea which side he's on, Jaime's or the new king's?"

"We don't know the details yet. The DEA and FBI have an

operation going, and with the number of bodies dropping, it's becoming a top priority for them."

Vincent chuckled and shook his head. The entire room turned to him.

"What's so funny?" I asked.

"If they framed your brother, boy, did they frame the wrong person, huh? You don't mess with the friends and family of Martina Monroe," he said, continuing to laugh.

Hirsch smirked. "No kidding."

It was true. If it hadn't been for my brother and my mom begging me to investigate the case, we may never have discovered that there was actually an internal mob war. But who was on which side? Were Darren and Clark on the same side? Would I lose Clark in all of this? Gang wars were dangerous, and I didn't know if my mom could handle losing one or *both* of her sons.

Jayda said, "Martina, you've got the gift."

"That keeps on giving." And sometimes I wished it didn't.

Hirsch pulled us back on task. "Okay, we have the eyewitness coming in tomorrow afternoon. Maybe she'll be able to answer a few open questions. How about we meet again after Narcotics gets an update from the feds and the DEA?"

Buck said, "We'll let you know as soon as we hear anything."

"Till then." I let out a sigh of relief. It wasn't just me investigating this case. It wasn't just Vincent and me. It was the FBI, the DEA, the narcotics department, Jayda, and Hirsch. There wasn't a better team. About to thank everyone and say goodbye, I was halted by an incoming call. "I have to take this." I stood up and stepped to the side. "Hi, Mom. What's up? How's Darren?"

"He's awake!"

Thank you, Lord. "That's great, Mom."

"I told him about the case and how Hirsch reopened it."

"What did he say?"

"He says he'll talk to you."

Not believing it, I said, "Are you sure?"

"Yes. Come and talk to him, Martina."

It was a long drive. "Is Zoey with Ted?"

"Yes. Is it okay if she comes too? She really wants to meet him."

I glanced over at Hirsch, and he gave me a puzzled look. "Let me talk to Darren first. If he's sincere, Zoey can visit."

"Oh, Martina! Thank you! I'll see you in a few hours!"

Ending the call, I walked over to Hirsch and explained.

He said, "You want some company?"

"I do."

"Let me call Kim and tell her I'll be late."

33

MARTINA

Charging down the chilly, sterile halls of Marin County Hospital, I prayed Darren would recover fully and have useful information for us. Information that could put an end, or at least bring some clarity, to the multitude of questions that plagued me. Questions about his involvement with the 98Mob and whether our family was in danger.

As we approached Darren's hospital room, Hirsch said, "Is that one of your guys?"

"Sure is. Have you met Otto?"

"I don't think I have. He looks formidable."

It was an understatement. Otto was 6'4", with fair hair, blue eyes, and built like a tank. Personally, I wouldn't want to go up against him, but I was glad he had volunteered to watch over my brother's hospital room, ensuring there were no further attempts on his life.

Our steps pounded down the hall as we approached Otto. I smiled and waved at him; he smiled back, eyeing Hirsch cautiously, as if assessing if he was a threat. "Hi, Otto, has everything been quiet around here?"

"It has. Your mom's inside with your brother."

"Great. Otto, this is Hirsch. Hirsch, Otto."

There wasn't much more needed for an introduction. The team at Drakos Monroe Security & Investigations knew of Hirsch, considering he was one of my best friends and my partner at the CoCo County Sheriff's Department.

"Nice to meet you, Hirsch."

"It's good to meet you as well. I hear Darren is in good hands with your presence."

"I aim to serve," Otto stated, his tone reflecting his Army Special Forces training, a common trait at Drakos Monroe. With his size and skill, nobody would get past him.

Entering Darren's room, I saw my mother sitting beside him, her eyes closed, possibly in prayer. Darren was asleep, but there was a noticeable improvement in his complexion, a healthy color had returned to his cheeks.

Mom's eyes fluttered open, widening upon seeing Hirsch. "Oh, I'm so glad you're here," she whispered. "He just went to sleep, but he kind of goes in and out. He's tired, as you can imagine," she added softly.

At the sound of my mother's voice, Darren's eyes flickered open. He glanced at his hand, cuffed to the bed, which rattled slightly.

"Hi, Darren. I brought a good friend of mine to talk to you today. This is Sergeant August Hirsch of the CoCo County Sheriff's Department."

"Mom calls him August," Darren mumbled, voice hoarse.

It wasn't surprising Mom had spoken of Hirsch. "Yes, both Zoey and Mom refer to him by his first name, but I can't seem to do it. He's just Hirsch to me."

"OK," Darren replied, his voice gravelly, likely sore from the previously inserted breathing tube. It was a relief to see him looking more human.

"I'm glad to see you're awake, and it sounds like you're going to make it, as long as nobody else comes for you," I said, a hint of caution underlying my words.

He nodded ever so slightly, a clear sign of his lingering weakness. I knew whatever conversation we had needed to be brief, and I had to make it count. He didn't seem to have much energy, and we needed to extract as much information as possible.

"Mom said you wanted to talk to me about what happened. About who tried to kill you. And what really happened to Toby."

His eyes shifted toward Hirsch.

I said, "Yes, he has the authority to charge you, but considering you've already pled guilty, what do you have to lose?"

"My life," he said quietly.

"Based on our conversation with our narcotics department, if you don't talk to us, we can't help you, and your life is over anyhow. The fact that you're lying in that hospital bed proves the point," I said matter-of-factly.

"Fair enough," he conceded.

He was the one who said he was ready to talk. Why was he dancing around the topic? "Who attacked you in prison?"

Maybe he wanted to talk but was realizing it would be harder than he expected. He was struggling with the words, and I didn't think it was solely due to his medical condition. "I can't let it get out, not until everyone is safe."

"I don't know if you've met Otto, who's standing outside your door, but nobody's getting past him. And I have a whole team just like him. You don't need to worry about us," I assured him.

"Zoey."

"Ted's with Zoey, and they've got full security. Ted may be a bit older, but he's a trained police officer. They're fine," I assured him and myself.

He let out a breath and said, "It was a guy they call Lil Jon. He's not big, maybe 5'6". I knew him on the outside."

"Is he with the 98Mob?"

Darren nodded. "Yeah."

Hirsch scribbled notes in his notebook, but I knew I wouldn't forget the details. "Did he say why he attacked you?"

"No. We used to be friends, or acquaintances, anyhow. We were just talking. I didn't even see it coming,"

"Do you know anything about people not wanting to work for Jaime Ragnar anymore? Maybe looking for a new boss, a new leader?"

He gave a slight shoulder shrug, then winced, indicating that even minimal movement caused him pain.

Hirsch said, "We have reason to believe there's a war going on inside the 98Mob."

Darren furrowed his brow. "I'm not sure about that. Maybe. That would make sense."

"How so?" Hirsch inquired.

"Well, the fact that I'm here, the fact they told me if I didn't plead guilty, they'd come after my mom."

My mother gasped at the revelation, and I turned to her, offering a reassuring look.

"Any idea why they would do that?" Hirsch asked.

"I don't, but I wasn't going to take any chances."

Refocused on Darren, I said, "Who told you to take the fall?"

Darren exhaled deeply, clearly troubled by the prospect of ratting out his fellow gang members. "It was Ace. He's not someone you mess with." His eyes fluttered, betraying his exhaustion from the conversation.

Hoping to keep him awake a bit longer, I revealed, "Ace is dead."

His eyes popped open, startled. "Seriously?"

Unflinching, I said, "Yes." Upon hearing the news, I hoped to instill a sense of security for Darren, enough for him to be truthful about Toby's murder. It was time for the million-dollar question. "Did you shoot Toby?"

He moved his head from side to side. "I didn't. And I didn't understand why they were pinning it on me. I would've never killed him. He was my boy."

That lined up with Toby's mother's interview. "Did you see Toby get shot?"

"Not the actual shooting. I was across the park when I heard the shot but ran toward Toby after. I saw a tall guy with dark hair run off. It was too far away to see his face or tell if he was white or Hispanic."

It was the same description Candace had given. "Do you know why anyone would want to kill Toby?"

He shook his head again. "I don't. I mean, I knew Toby had money problems—like he owed the boss, uh, Jaime. I thought maybe that's why he got capped, but it didn't really make sense. Not Jaime's style to kill one of his own over something so small. But you never know."

I looked over at Hirsch, who gave me a look indicating he was surprised by all the information Darren was giving us, but I could tell he wasn't fully convinced it was all true. And he had every right to be skeptical, considering my brother was, in fact, involved in organized crime.

But if what Darren was saying was true, how had Candace picked him out of the lineup? "Do you have any idea why the eyewitness would've said you were the shooter?"

He shook his head. "No, it's weird. I remember that woman. She used to buy for her husband. But maybe somebody got to her, told her she had to pick me. I don't know."

That was a possibility. Hopefully, it was something Candace could explain when she came into the sheriff's station the next day. "Do you have any idea who's been calling me with an anonymous, untraceable phone?"

"Honestly, I don't." Darren's eyes closed once again.

Was he avoiding eye contact or really drifting back to sleep? My mother placed her hand on my arm, and I pivoted toward her.

With pleading eyes, she said, "He's tired, honey. It's just like I said. I knew he didn't do it, not Darren. Maybe you should let him rest."

A quick glance back at Darren, and I saw his eyes were still closed. "Has Clark been by again?"

"No."

Clark was higher up in the 98Mob organization. It didn't take long for me to realize he might be the brother who could answer more of our questions. Because if he was as deeply entrenched in the 98Mob as the FBI and DEA believed, he knew exactly what was going on within the organization. Like if there was infighting because of a new king trying to steal the crown, and maybe more importantly, who was on which side. Was Clark part of the side that tried to kill Darren? Would he really try to kill his own brother?

34

MARTINA

It was a nice neighborhood, with well taken care of yards and maintained homes, definitely a nicer part of the city. I didn't know exactly what I was expecting, but I would have been less surprised by a run-down dilapidated neighborhood. In hindsight, that picture didn't really fit. If my brother Clark was high up in the 98Mob organization, then he had some money. And from my experience, the higher one is on the organized crime food chain, the less they appeared to be living a life of crime. It was part of the cover to keep everyone protected.

It had taken some coaxing to get my mother to give me Clark's address, but finally, she relented when I explained he might be the only one who could help us, outside of law enforcement, of course. It helped her decision right along when I had agreed to allow Zoey to visit Darren in the hospital since he would be there for quite some time. In some ways, it was a blessing. The longer we kept him in the hospital, the more time we had to clear his name and get his plea deal thrown out.

What would happen then? I wasn't sure if Mom would let him move in with her and Ted or if Ted would want that. It wasn't the time to worry about it, and I realized it would be a nice problem to have to solve. My brother, out of prison and on a new path of sobriety and faith. Wouldn't that be something?

As I pulled up to the curb at my brother's quaint, one-story home with a rock garden and rosemary bushes adorned with tall grasses, I thought, *I might get one brother back, but I don't think it will be Clark.*

He had found a pretty cushy life, albeit a dangerous one. Parked, I reached over to the glove compartment to pull out my gun and place it in the holster under my arm, and a second, smaller weapon in my ankle holster. Clark didn't know I was visiting, and I didn't know who would be in the house with him. Showing up unannounced at a mobster's home, family or not, I was walking into a potentially dangerous situation.

To ease any possible tensions, as much as I could anyhow, I chose to go in alone. If I had Vincent or Hirsch by my side, Clark and whomever was in the house could deduce they were law enforcement and refuse to talk to me, or worse. It was the one perk of being Clark's sister and a civilian.

Hirsch didn't like the idea of me going in alone, but we came to an agreement. Hirsch and a backup team were set up a few blocks away, ready to come in if something went wrong.

It was a family matter after all, not just about justice and right or wrong.

Strapped, I exited my car and surveyed the neighborhood. It was quiet for a Friday morning, likely because most of Clark's neighbors went to a job that didn't involve drugs or crime. Kids were out for summer vacation, but maybe they were inside reading or playing at a nice park, or more likely playing video games or watching TV.

It wasn't a neighborhood where you would expect gang violence. It was possible the situation wasn't as dangerous as I theorized, but I knew looks could be deceiving, and I wasn't taking any chances.

At the front door, I knocked and stepped back a few paces. That way, whoever looked through the peephole would get a good look at me and hopefully think I wasn't a threat.

The door cracked open, and my brother Clark peeked his head out. He opened it farther and stood there, staring at me. "What are you doing here?"

It's good to see you too, bro. "I wanted to talk to you face-to-face."

From inside the home, I heard a woman's voice ask, "Who is it, Clark?"

He sighed and replied, "It's my sister."

"You have a sister?" she responded, sounding surprised.

Next I heard footsteps, and a woman appeared next to Clark. She had blonde hair, brown eyes, and freckles on her nose, giving her a wholesome look. Did she know who my brother really was and what he did for a living?

"Yeah, this is my sister, Martina. Martina, this is Naomi."

I waved and stepped forward. "Hi, Naomi, it's nice to meet you." I didn't take offense to the fact this lady was clearly my brother's romantic partner and had never heard of me.

"Aren't you going to invite her in?" Naomi asked.

He gave me a perturbed look and said, "Come on in."

The interaction was going better than I expected.

Inside, the place was clean and organized. A new modern looking set of living room furniture was to the left and a fireplace to the right. There were paintings on the walls, one of which looked like an Ansel Adams, featuring black and white landscapes. Clark motioned to the living room, and I stepped inside. "Have a seat," he offered.

"Can I get you anything?" Naomi asked.

"No, I'm fine, thank you," I replied.

Clark took a seat, and I followed suit.

"So, what's this about?"

"I wanted to let you know that Darren is awake, and it looks like he will make a full recovery."

Without emotion, he said, "That's good to hear." He glanced over at Naomi and said, "Babe, do you mind getting me an iced tea?"

"Sure. Martina, you want one?"

"No, I'm fine, thank you."

With that, Naomi hurried off to the kitchen, deeper in the house. Clark turned back to me and said, "You shouldn't have come here, Martina. I told you that you need to drop this."

"Even if I stopped looking into the case, it's not going away."

"What do you mean?"

"Look, I'm just trying to keep our family safe. I know you and I haven't been in each other's lives, and we live very different ones. But word on the street is that someone threatened to hurt Mom if Darren didn't cooperate. You chose your life, and Darren seems to want to turn his around. But Mom is innocent in all of this, and so is my daughter, and Ted, and everyone we care about. I don't appreciate them being threatened."

Naomi popped back in and announced, "We don't have any."

Clark rolled his eyes and said, "Can you make some?"

"Of course, give me a sec."

I smirked. "She seems nice."

"Yeah, she's all right," Clark replied nonchalantly.

"Look, I know more than you think I do. I'm here begging for help to keep our family safe. They threatened Mom."

Clark shook his head. "I don't know what you want me to tell you, Martina."

"I know both you and Darren are part of the 98Mob, and I know that the 98Mob's mortality rate is rising. Someone put a hit on Darren and now Ace is dead. We've got witnesses being threatened. And I want to know why."

I wasn't going to share with him that we thought there was a power struggle within the gang. The 98Mob had no idea law enforcement was onto them.

"There's just things you don't understand, Martina," Clark replied evasively.

"Oh, I understand far more than you think, Clark. I have friends in very high places," I countered confidently.

"Look, you could get me killed by showing up here. Do you understand that? Not only me but you too. They don't want exposure. Okay?" Clark's tone was laced with worry.

"I'm not police."

Clark laughed bitterly. "They're not afraid of the police. That's not the exposure they're worried about."

His statement made me speculate on the true motive for the recent murders. If they weren't afraid of law enforcement, who were they afraid of? Was it all an attempt to cover up something big, a massive takeover? Were they trying to blindside the boss and I was getting in the way?

Pleading, I said, "Is there anything you can tell me? Who are they afraid of?"

"I can't say anything else. You're messing with people you don't want to mess with. I mean it. For your sake, for Mom, for Darren, for me. This is bigger than all of us, and they don't care who gets hurt as long as their interests are protected." Clark's cheeks turned crimson.

Naomi returned and said, "Here you go, honey."

He picked up the iced tea. "Thanks."

"Are you sure I can't get you anything, sweetie?" Naomi seemed nice. What was she doing with Clark?

Clark interjected, "No, she was just leaving."

I supposed that was my cue to go. "It was nice to meet you, Naomi. And Clark, it's good to see you."

He simply tipped his chin and didn't bother to get up as I exited his house.

Shutting the door behind me, I glanced around the neighborhood once again. As I began walking toward my car, a dark sedan was driving rather slowly down the street. That wasn't a good sign. They could be scoping out the place or getting ready to fire shots.

The driver's face was difficult to see because they were wearing a baseball cap. Was it surveillance? Was it somebody from the 98Mob watching over Clark's house or someone following me? I hadn't picked up on a tail on the way there, but anything was possible. I hurried to my car and crept down as the car drove past. With my heart nearly beating out of my chest, I caught the license plate number and quickly put it into my phone.

With the suspicious vehicle out of view, I crab-walked over to my door and stood up, taking a look around once more. The coast was clear and I hopped into my car. Phone in hand, I called Hirsch. "I have a license plate we need to run. The car was driving too slow past Clark's house. I don't know if they're after me or watching out for him or the other side."

"What's the plate?"

As I rattled off the license plate number, I felt uneasy but also like we were one step closer to finding the truth.

35

CANDACE

Sweat trickled down my back as I sprinted toward the front door. Fumbling with my keys, my nerves rattled as it took far too long to fit the key into the lock. With a short prayer, I was able to unlock the front door and scamper inside to safety. With a quick slam behind me, I locked the deadbolt and hurried over to the alarm system to re-arm it. Out of breath, I wondered if I was being paranoid or if somebody was really following me.

I had been so confident everything would go back to normal, to my new normal, but I wasn't so sure anymore. Maybe I was being paranoid and jumping at my own shadow but, I would swear it was him.

Terrified of being followed, I'd left the groceries in the car. Would they be ruined? Certainly not. It had only been a few minutes. All I had been concerned about was getting inside the house and locking myself in, to get away from that man. Why was he there? I hadn't changed my testimony. I hadn't done anything to make him come back for me. Concerned he was outside waiting for me, I crept over to the window, next to the door, and peeked out.

There was no traffic coming, and there was not a soul in sight.

Had I imagined it all? No. I swore I hadn't. Chewing my bottom lip, I decided that if nobody showed up in the next ten minutes, I would go back and retrieve the groceries. Surely they'd be fine. And if there was a threat outside, forget the groceries. Hunger pangs were preferred over death.

I paced the house, trying to rid myself of nervous energy.

If he was following me, what could I do? I can't go to the police. That might only trigger him and they may ask questions I can't, or won't, answer. But then again, Detective Leslie told me I could call her if something went wrong or seemed off. Maybe I should call.

It seemed like a solid idea. I was supposed to go to the station that afternoon to talk to the sergeant. Maybe I could go early, or would that be suspicious?

No, I'd call Detective Leslie. She hadn't steered me wrong yet. I pulled out my phone and called her cell phone.

"Detective Leslie. How can I help you?"

"Detective Leslie, this is Candace Mason."

"Hi, Candace. Is something wrong?" she asked.

"I think I'm being followed."

"Can you tell me why you think you're being followed?"

"I was at the grocery store, shopping like I normally would. But I was in a new grocery store because I moved in with my sister. This store is near her place. Anyway, when I was in the cereal aisle, I swear I could sense somebody behind me, but when I turned around, nobody was there. Then, after I finished buying my groceries and was loading them into the trunk of my car, I swear I saw him—the man who came to my house and threatened me."

Detective Leslie didn't say anything for a moment, but I

could hear her breathing. She was still there. "Okay, I'll make a note of this. Where are you now?"

"I'm at my sister's. I don't see him here, and I'm inside the house. I looked outside, and there weren't any people or any cars that I could see."

"Sometimes, this happens with witnesses of violent acts. Paranoia and seeing things that aren't there. It's a form of PTSD. Chances are, everything's fine."

Was it? Maybe I should make that appointment with a therapist. It wasn't a bad idea. Truthfully, I had been through a lot and might find therapy useful. "Do you think so?" I wasn't entirely sure I had hallucinated the man. It was *the man.*

Detective Leslie said, "If he was there, he probably would have approached you in the parking lot or at your sister's. Just give me a call if you see him again, OK?"

"Oh, OK," I replied, unsure if I agreed with her.

I ended the call, pondering whether Detective Leslie was right. Could it be PTSD? The man I saw didn't have a weapon that I could tell.

After I gathered up my courage, I looked back out the window. There was no sign of anyone near the house. With a deep breath, I unlocked the door and deactivated the alarm.

Stepping out onto the porch, I glanced around. There wasn't anybody in eyesight, it was just me. It must've been a man who happened to look like him in the parking lot. Perhaps it was a touch of post-traumatic stress disorder. I would be fine. Everything would be fine.

At my car, I grabbed the two bags of groceries and shut the trunk before heading back inside the house. With the door secured behind me and the alarm on, I headed to the kitchen to unpack the groceries.

My nerves were on edge, so I thought maybe some music would calm them. I went over to my phone and started up my favorite playlist. Singing along to my favorite song, my heart rate steadied as I placed the eggs in the refrigerator and put away the last of the canned goods. I folded the paper bags and placed them in the recycling.

Everything was going to be *just* fine.

Everything *would* be fine. I had moved into my sister's house, already unpacked, and filled up the house with groceries. Maybe in a few days, or another week or so, I could go back to work, get back to living, and stop hiding. Travis would have wanted that. He would have wanted me to live my life fully. Travis, before the drugs got to him, the old Travis, was incredible—sweet, loving, kind, a gentleman.

Satisfied I was safe and tucked in for the day, I still had a few hours before I had to be down at the sheriff's station to give a statement. In front of the mirror, I practiced it again and again, so I wouldn't forget a single detail. There was no need to throw suspicion on me.

Settled onto the couch, I picked up the paperback novel on the coffee table and began to read a tale about a young witch with magical powers. A small smile formed on my lips. Wouldn't that be nice, to have magic powers, to transport yourself anywhere you wanted to go, no limitations? I thought that was a silly thing to think about and continued reading.

Thirty minutes passed when a knock sounded on my door. Not expecting anyone, my guard was up as I hurried over to the door and looked through the peephole.

My eyes widened, and I ran back toward the living room, my heartbeat thumping in my ears. But I didn't know where to go. I had to call the police—no, they wouldn't arrive in time. What should I do? Run out the back? Could I get away? Did he know I was home alone?

As I stood paralyzed, deciding which direction to run, a

loud explosion sounded, and I remained stunned as the front door flew open with splinters flying in all directions.

And there he stood, those eyes, and that gun.

Despite my fear, I found the courage to speak. "I haven't changed my statement. I have no intention of changing my statement."

He smirked. "I know you won't," and he raised his arm, and in a flash, there were stars before my world faded to black.

36

MARTINA

Sitting on the sofa across from the kitchenette housing the beloved coffee maker, I sipped on my coffee as I waited for Hirsch and Vincent to arrive. It was the coziest spot in the entire sheriff's department. There weren't many times when I wasn't in a conference room or an office, or just stopping by the kitchen for some much-needed caffeine. But the couch was comfy, and it was what I needed to rejuvenate before we met to create a game plan to interview Candace Mason. There were so many questions I had for her, starting with why she was at the park the day Toby June was killed, and why she had told the other dealers she was buying drugs for her husband who had passed away more than a year earlier. And was she affiliated with the 98Mob, or had they threatened her family if she didn't go along with their plan? Or was it something even worse?

I waved as Hirsch and Vincent approached. "You're looking awfully relaxed," Hirsch said with a hint of amusement in his voice.

More like exhausted. "I don't know if I'd use the word relaxed. Spent is probably more accurate. It's been a long day."

After the morning at my brother Clark's house, I returned to meet up with Hirsch to figure out who was slow rolling past Clark's residence. The license plate search was used to identify the registered owner of the vehicle. To my surprise and disappointment, the registered owner, Doug Kendle, aged sixty, didn't have much of a criminal record aside from a few parking tickets. That didn't jive with the behavior I witnessed. Usually a slow roll was surveilling or getting ready for a drive-by shooting.

I was the first to admit my nerves were on overdrive and could be seeing things that weren't there. Mr. Kendle may have been lost or was just a really bad, slow driver. Or I was rationalizing and Mr. Kendle had nefarious reasons for driving past Clark's. Unsatisfied with the initial information on the black sedan, I requested for the research team to perform a full background on Douglas Kendle. If Mr. Kendle or anyone associated with him was involved in criminal activity, we'd know in a day or two.

"And it's not over yet," Vincent added.

Not budging from the soft cushions, I said, "Nope. If you need some caffeine, get your fix, and then we'll go huddle in the conference room."

"You're so bossy." Vincent smirked. "I like it."

With a grin, I said, "Good."

Hirsch shook his head like he wasn't sure what to make of Vincent. But I knew he enjoyed Vincent's sunny demeanor as much as the rest of us. And his sunshine was just what we needed in times like these.

Vincent went over to the counter and pulled two mugs from the cupboards. He set one under the spout and stepped back, bowing to Hirsch. Hirsch pressed the button and said, "Finally. Some respect around here."

I wadded up my napkin and tossed it at Hirsch, hitting him in the arm.

"Hey!"

"Grab your coffee and quit complaining," I said with a wink.

Vincent doubled over laughing. It was as if he was surprised Hirsch and I could be funny too. Hirsch picked up his full mug and said, "Yes, ma'am."

Vincent grabbed his mug, still chuckling, and said, "Okay, enough of this fooling around. Have we heard from Rourke and Kiva yet?"

We giggled. A sure sign we were exhausted. Hirsch said, "Kiva said they haven't heard from the FBI or the DEA yet."

After another sip of coffee, I returned to a more serious tone. "I for one can't wait to get some intel from them. Maybe all the little pieces I've gotten from my brothers will make sense and we'll finally understand what's really going on." I had my suspicions, but I thought it best to keep them confined to my brain until we heard more from the DEA and the FBI. There was no reason to go off on tangents with no more than a gut feeling to back them up. Plus, it was my family, and I knew that if it was someone else, not me, investigating a case involving their family, I would take whatever they had to say with a grain of salt.

"Do you have any plans for the weekend?" Vincent asked as he retrieved his afternoon pick-me-up.

I stood up and said, "Nope, just hanging around Mom and Ted's, but likely working if I need to."

"How about you, Hirsch?" Vincent asked as we took steps toward the conference room.

"We're planning to take Audrey to the Oakland Zoo this weekend. Should be fun. She loves animals."

"Zoey was like that when she was Audrey's age. Actually she still loves animals."

"Still wants to be a veterinarian?" Hirsch asked.

"Oh yeah, she's pretty sure we'll be referring to her as Doctor Zoey Monroe in eight years. It was why she chose to attend the University of California at Davis. Even though she's just an undergraduate, she's hoping that if she attends for undergrad, it'll give her a leg up to get accepted to the vet school."

"Boy, she's a clever one. Not even in college yet and she has her future figured out," Vincent said.

"Oh, I know. I certainly didn't have it all figured out when I was her age." Learning was a lifelong pursuit. With each new lesson learned, our thoughts and decisions and perspectives were influenced. Zoey was sure she'd become a veterinarian, but maybe she'd change her mind and decide she was destined to be the president of the United States instead. I wouldn't be surprised. My girl could do anything.

Vincent said, "Neither did I. I feel like I'm still making my way through life, figuring it out as I go."

I was surprised to hear that, considering he had been with the firm for six years and before that was at the CoCo County Sheriff's Department for a few years. And he had recently gotten married. "Yeah, sometimes I feel that way too. It seems like things are always changing."

After a huge gulp of coffee, a very animated Vincent said, "Yep." He propped the conference door open, and led us in. Inside he said, "Are you ready to get this brainstorm party started so that witness will tell us everything we want to know?"

With another swig of brew, I glanced at Hirsch and back at Vincent. "I'm ready."

AN HOUR AND A HALF LATER, the three of us looked at one another, perturbed, and Vincent said, "OK, I'll call it. She's an hour late. No call, nothing. Maybe try calling her *again*?"

Hirsch made the call from his cell phone, for the third time. We waited and waited some more. He shook his head. "She's not answering."

Was she caught in traffic or forgot we had an appointment? Or was it something worse? "We should go by her house."

"That's a bit of a leap. She's only an hour late. She could be stuck in traffic," Hirsch countered.

"Yeah, but it could be a lot worse considering Detective Leslie told us that a man went to her house and threatened her."

"Well, what if she's perfectly safe, and we leave here, but she shows up and we're not here?" Hirsch asked.

It was a logical question, and I wanted to believe it was a possible scenario, but something was telling me this was all wrong. Everything about this case had been wrong. Nothing was as it seemed. "Well, maybe tell one of the team she's coming in. Her sister's house isn't far from here. We would be back soon. We'll get Rourke or Kiva to hold her, or even Jayda if she's still around, until we get back."

Hirsch looked skeptical, but Vincent said, "I'm with Martina. Let's go check her house."

"Since I'm outnumbered," Hirsch said, "I guess it's decided. Let's go find Jayda and then head out."

I hoped I was wrong, but I had a bad feeling I wasn't.

HIRSCH DROVE QUICKLY, and as we saw the flashing lights in front of Talia's house, Vincent and I exchanged glances. Hirsch parked the car, and before he could even turn off the engine, I climbed out and rushed toward the front door. It was guarded by a police officer, but I could see inside the home and the bad feeling I had earlier was realized. The front door was splintered and cracked, barely hanging on the hinges, and most ominous was the pool of congealed blood in the entryway.

It was a lot of blood.

Was Candace dead? Was it because she had agreed to talk to us?

Hirsch ran up, flashing his credentials to the uniformed officer. "I'm Sergeant Hirsch from CoCo County. What happened here?"

"The security alarm was tripped. The security company called the homeowner, who wasn't here at the time, to ask if everything was okay. But when she called her sister, who should've been inside, and didn't get an answer, she told security to call the police right away. Officers arrived and found the door kicked in and a woman lying in a pool of blood. It looked like a single gunshot wound to the head."

My stomach flipped. "Any witnesses? Security footage?"

"No cameras that we can see. Robbery Homicide hasn't arrived yet. But the homeowner, Talia Davis, isn't here to answer any questions."

My stomach flip-flopped. Candace was dead. Or not. A flash of hope. If Candace was dead, her body would be in place for the medical examiner to evaluate. "Where is the victim now?"

"Mount Diablo Medical Center. She's in critical condition. The homeowner is her sister and said she was on her way there."

"Do they think she'll pull through?" I asked in disbelief.

"It's a long shot, but it's possible."

I shook my head. Somebody was eliminating persons associated with the Toby June murder. Why? If it wasn't to avoid police attention, then what? What was the 98Mob up to?

37

MARTINA

THE DAILY VISITS to Bay Area hospitals were grating on me. The stale air and the prevalent sadness were depressing. But it was unavoidable because we needed to find out if Candace had survived and the events leading up to the shooting. Amongst the worried, we spotted a uniformed officer speaking to a distraught woman. We briskly approached them. Hirsch pulled out his badge. "Hi, I'm sorry to interrupt. My name is Sergeant Hirsch from the CoCo County Sheriff's Department."

"I'm Officer Angelo with the Alameda County Sheriff's Department."

"We're here inquiring about a shooting involving Candace Mason. She's a witness in an open investigation in CoCo County."

"Yes, of course. This is her sister, Talia Davis."

Talia, with dark hair and tears shimmering on her cheeks, shared the same bright blue eyes as Candace.

"How is she doing?" I asked.

"She's in surgery. It'll be a few hours. They said they're not sure if she'll make it."

"I'm so sorry to hear that. Do you mind if we ask you a few questions about what happened?" Hirsch asked gently.

Talia hesitated, glancing between me and Hirsch before agreeing, "Sure."

We thanked Officer Angelo and stepped aside with Talia. "This is one of my partners, Martina Monroe, and like I said, I'm Sergeant Hirsch."

"She's your partner?" Talia asked, obviously surprised.

"I'm contracted with the CoCo County Sheriff's Department to solve cold cases. Hirsch and I have been solving cases together for, what, nine years now?"

"Just about," Hirsch confirmed with the slightest hint of a smile.

"Oh, I thought you were a private investigator. That's what Candace said," Talia remarked.

"I'm also a private investigator with my firm, Drakos Monroe Security & Investigations," I clarified.

Talia seemed confused. "Yeah, that's what she said. But I thought we weren't supposed to talk to you."

That was surprising and unsettling to hear. Hirsch said, "Who told you that?"

"Candace said she got a call from Detective Leslie. She mentioned you might be reopening the case and advised her to not talk to Martina Monroe because she's the shooter's sister."

Hirsch and I exchanged glances, my blood heating up. Detective Leslie, our friend and colleague, had advised Candace *not* to talk to me. Talk about a gut punch. What else didn't we know about Detective Leslie? And what else was she hiding from us?

Hirsch clarified, "Detective Leslie must've misspoken. Martina is working the case with us. Yes, she is the accused's sister, but she is actively involved in the investigation. If she asks you a question, I would appreciate you answering her."

Talia nodded in understanding.

Hirsch continued, "Is that why your sister wouldn't take Martina's call the other day but took mine?"

"Yeah, that's why. I'm sorry. I guess Candace must've misinterpreted what the other detective said."

Detective Leslie's withholding of information troubled me. Was this related to Clark's assertion that the 98Mob wasn't worried about police exposure because they had Leslie under their thumb? We had recently taken her son, Ethan, into protective custody and questioned him. He didn't have much to tell us other than how to buy drugs and physical descriptions of those he bought drugs from. He was safe, so I had to wonder what leverage the 98Mob could have on her, or had she turned dirty all on her own?

"Why don't we take a seat."

Talia nodded, and we headed over to the beige leather visitors' chairs. Talia sat down, and Hirsch and I took seats next to her.

"What can you tell us about what happened today?" I asked.

"I got a call from the alarm company. They asked if it was a false alarm or if they should call the police. At first, I almost brushed it off, but then I realized Candace was supposed to be home. I called her but she didn't answer. I knew something was wrong, so I called the security company back and told them to call the police."

"Where were you when the security company called you?"

"I was at work. I'm a dental hygienist in Pleasanton," she replied. "After I got off the phone with the security company, I drove home, but the police were already there. I saw the blood... I thought she was gone. But the paramedics were en route, and they said they found a pulse. They brought her here. They don't know if she's going to make it," she said, her voice breaking as she broke into tears.

"I'm so sorry, Talia," I offered sympathetically.

"After all she's been through, I can't believe it. I mean, I guess we should've known," she said, wiping her eyes.

"What do you mean? You should've known?" I asked, glancing at Hirsch. I quickly pulled some tissues out of my backpack and handed them to her.

"Thanks," she said, taking a tissue to wipe her eyes. "About a week ago, we were at Candace's house, and this man showed up. He was big, tall, with dark hair. He threatened her, saying she better not change her testimony about the shooting. She said she wouldn't, and he left, after warning her he'd come back if she did. But she wasn't going to change her testimony, so I don't know why he came back."

"Have you told this to any of the officers today?" I asked.

She shook her head.

"Do you think you could describe the man who showed up at Candace's house?"

Talia nodded. "Oh, yeah. I stared at him the whole time he was talking to her. He was big, around six foot two, medium build, like he worked out. Dark hair, brown eyes, thin lips. He was tan skinned, like he could be Italian or spent a lot of time in the sun. He had really bushy eyebrows."

"If we brought down a sketch artist, do you think you could help us put together a picture of this man?" I asked.

Wiping her eyes with the tissues, she said, "I could try."

"Did the man say anything else other than 'don't change your testimony or I will come back'?" I probed further.

"No, he just said it looked like she didn't want him to come back. She agreed, and that was it. We decided she was going to put everything behind her and just move forward."

"Put what behind her?"

"Oh, well... She told me about her husband's overdose," Talia began, her voice laced with sadness. "We thought his death was due to complications from a car accident, but she's been lying to the family. Before he died, he was draining their bank accounts to buy drugs because the pain was unbearable, and the doctors wouldn't prescribe more. One day, he overdosed and died. She was devastated. For a whole year, she just swam through life in slow motion. She started to perk up about six months ago, right after the one-year anniversary of his death. And that's when she came up with a plan."

Hirsch and I exchanged a glance. "A plan?" we echoed in unison.

"I don't remember all the details," she said.

Suddenly, we were interrupted by an older couple approaching. "Oh, Talia!" they exclaimed.

"Those are my parents," Talia said, standing up and rushing over to an older man and woman who embraced her.

Under my breath, I said, "What do you think Candace's plan was?"

"I don't know, but I sure would like to find out."

We stood and caught up with Talia to meet Candace's parents. "We got here as soon as we could," they said, clearly distressed.

Hirsch introduced himself and then me.

"Who did this to our baby? Are you going to find them?" the woman asked, her voice filled with anguish.

Looking Mrs. Davis straight in the eyes, I said, "We will absolutely find out who did this, and they will be brought to justice."

"Good. I just can't believe all this is happening. Was it a home invasion? Did they take anything?" she questioned.

Talia's face crumpled. "Yes and no. There are some things

you should know. Things Candace didn't want you to know," she said solemnly.

Mrs. Davis turned to us. "We would like some privacy, please."

"Of course, ma'am," Hirsch said, and we walked over to the corner, on pins and needles. I was eager to hear what Candace had to tell her family and what she had been keeping from them. It had to be tied to Toby June's murder somehow. Or had she gotten mixed up in drugs herself? The truth was, we wouldn't know until Talia or Candace told us. But considering they may lose Candace, it wasn't the right time to push. Hirsch and I made our way back to the visitor seats. "Do you know who will be assigned the case?"

Hirsch said, "I can call over to Alameda County and find out."

While Hirsch contacted the Alameda County Sheriff's Department, I glanced around the hospital waiting room. Nurses and doctors were bustling around in their scrubs and lab coats, yet there was a somber tone in the place, not surprising given the circumstances. Hirsch set down his phone, "Detective Olivio is at the scene. He said he'll call us with an update when he's done with his preliminary assessment."

Excellent. We'd worked with Detective Olivio on another case several years back. It was good to have friends *everywhere.*

"What do you make of the family?" Hirsch asked, his tone reflective.

"They're devastated. We'll have to wait to talk to them to find out what Candace has been hiding. Or hopefully, Candace will make it and tell us herself. In the meantime, we should get a sketch artist down here to talk to Talia."

"Agreed. The man who threatened Candace is likely the person who shot her. I'll call the station and get the artist down here."

Hirsch handled the logistics within the sheriff's department while I spent my time making a call to Zoey, sent a message to my mom, and said prayers for Candace to make it through. A gunshot to the head was a difficult thing to survive, but miracles happened every day, and we couldn't give up hope.

Finally, a surgeon in blue scrubs with gray hair pulled into a tight bun lowered her mask. Candace's family rushed over, and we followed. "I'm Talia, Candace's sister. These are my parents, Haley and Donavan Davis."

"I'm Dr. Potter, her surgeon. And you are?"

"I'm Sergeant Hirsch and this is my partner, Martina."

With a knowing nod, Dr. Potter said, "It was a tricky surgery, but we were able to remove the bullet lodged in her brain. She made it through the surgery, which is a very positive sign. However, the next twenty-four hours are critical."

The family's cries of relief filled the room.

Turning to us, Dr. Potter said, "I presume you want the bullet fragment?"

"Yes, we do," Hirsch confirmed.

"We'll have it out for you shortly," she assured us before hurrying away.

Talia turned to us. "Do you still need me to sit with the sketch artist?"

It was good to hear she was focused on helping us find who shot her sister. "Yes, she'll be here soon. It will be critical for finding out what happened to Candace."

Talia gave a slight nod.

With a soft tone, I said, "We know this is a difficult time, but you were telling us about Candace's plan."

Candace's mother interjected, "We're not going to discuss Candice's plans or what happened in the past. My daughter will provide a description of the man who came to Talia and Candice's home, but beyond that, we have nothing else to say."

What was Candace wrapped up in?

Hirsch, ever the diplomat, said, "We understand this is a difficult time, but any information you can give us about what Candace has been doing over the last few months could help us figure out why this happened to her."

"The sketch should be sufficient," Mrs. Davis stated firmly, pulling out a business card from her handbag and handing it to Hirsch. "I'm a lawyer. I know my daughter's rights, and at this time, we are not going to make any statements on behalf of Candace. My daughter Talia will provide a description for the sketch. Now, if you will respect our wishes, it would be appreciated."

"Of course," Hirsch agreed.

Whatever Candace had been involved in prior to the shooting must have been criminal in nature, otherwise, why would her family refuse to tell us about it?

38

MARTINA

In the parking lot of the CoCo County Sheriff's station, I spotted Hirsch approaching the entrance. I waved and ran to catch up to him. "Good morning."

"Is it morning? I don't recall sleeping," he quipped with a tired expression.

"Come on, you love it."

Hirsch sighed. "Martina, I'm getting too old for this."

"Oh, stop. You've got a few good years left in you," I teased, trying to lighten his mood.

"Thanks."

Shifting the conversation, I said, "Still planning to go to the zoo today?"

"If we can get out of here by noon, the zoo is still a go. If not, I think I'll lose major daddy points."

Listening to Hirsch talk about Audrey was heartwarming. He was such a natural, loving father. It was amusing to recall how, when we first met, he was staunchly anti-kid and anti-marriage. Years later, he had transformed into a happily married man, and a father whose little girl was clearly the apple of his eye. "Who's meeting us?" I asked, curious about the day's agenda.

"Rourke and Kiva will be here," he began, "and I asked Leslie to come in. It's her day off, but I think we need to have a conversation with her."

No kidding. "How's her son doing?"

"Well, it sounds like he isn't thrilled about being locked up, but he also likes being alive. Until we can figure out why those associated with the 98Mob are being gunned down, he's safer where he's at."

"Maybe while he's locked up, Ethan can get help for his drug problem?"

"Leslie's talking to the resource center to see what they can do for him while he's here. I can't imagine what she's going through. If Audrey were ever in that position, I don't know what I'd do."

I knew exactly what Hirsch would do. As much as he loved Audrey, he would do everything in his power to ensure her safety. But then, he wouldn't just cover it up and continue as if nothing happened. He would bring those responsible to justice and seek help from his friends, like me and the rest of the sheriff's department. There's no way he would let them off the hook, continuing to threaten him and his family. "I think you do, Hirsch."

"You're probably right."

It was troubling to learn that Detective Leslie had told Candace not to speak to me. I couldn't help but worry about what else she might be hiding. During her interview, I had sensed she was holding back, but I wasn't sure what to ask to pry it out of her. But it was a new day, and I was armed with a list of questions up my sleeve, determined to uncover whatever else she was hiding and why she advised Candace to avoid me.

Inside the station, it was unusually quiet for a Saturday

morning. People were likely at their desks, writing up reports, or out in the field. All official business was on hold, other than emergency services.

We headed toward the narcotics office area and spotted Rourke and Kiva right away. They were standing together, drinking from mugs of what I surmised was coffee.

Kiva greeted us with a six-hundred-watt smile. "If it isn't our favorite troublemaker *and* sergeant."

That elicited a chuckle out of Hirsch. Heat rose to my cheeks as I grinned. "Good morning. What do you have for us?"

"Right down to business. I like it. We took a look at the sketch you sent over. It's not somebody we know."

Well, that was a letdown. "He doesn't match anybody in the database or the gang books?"

Kiva motioned for us to go into the conference room to the right. Inside, we all sat down, and he explained, "Here's the thing. I went through the roster of the 98Mob and he's not in it. He's not a known associate, nothing."

"Could it be that Candace's shooting was unrelated?"

"There's no way," Kiva countered. "Candace's sister said the man who had threatened Candace told her not to change her testimony."

Rourke added, "And if our theory is correct, that it's the new kingpin who wanted to take her out, he could be using outside help. It fits."

"What do we do now?" I asked, feeling a sense of urgency.

"We could go to the press. Put his face on the news. 'Anybody seen this man?'" Kiva proposed, though he seemed unsure.

Rourke said, "No, I don't think we want to draw attention to the fact we know he exists. We want whoever is behind Candace's shooting, and maybe others, to feel safe, comfortable. We sent over the sketch to the DEA and the FBI. Obviously, we haven't heard back yet, but if they know who he is, it could unlock a lot of unanswered questions."

Fingers crossed.

"How is Candace doing? Any change in her condition?" Rourke asked.

I had called over to the hospital earlier that morning, so I explained, "She's still unconscious, recovering from the surgery. She made it through the night which is a good sign. But the doctors say these kinds of injuries are really unpredictable. Best-case scenario, she wakes up in a day or so, able to talk, responds well to physical therapy, heals up, goes on with life. Worst case, she never wakes up, or she does wake up and has lost her ability to walk, to talk, and has a long, long recovery ahead of her."

Kiva said, "Hopefully she recovers and can move on. Speaking of, I heard you talked to Clark Kolze."

"I did. Not entirely fruitful, except for the fact he told me that whoever is behind all the violence is not afraid of the police."

"That's concerning," Hirsch commented, his brow furrowed.

"For more than one reason," I agreed. "But my thought is, if they're trying to keep everything quiet, maybe they're trying to cover up there's a coup about to happen. Or maybe it's not a coup. Maybe it's an outside force deciding to take over."

"That would explain why the guy in the sketch is unknown to us," Kiva suggested.

"Exactly. If it's an external force, outside the 98Mob, it's possible they're taking everybody out. Maybe they promised to bring some of the existing folks, like Ace, into the new organization, but once his usefulness expired, they took him out. That kind of makes sense too," I concluded. "And no peep from the feds or DEA on who they think could be trying to take over the 98Mob?"

"No, but it has me thinking about the car that drove slowly past your brother's house."

"Is the background check done yet?"

"Not yet," Kiva replied. "We've got researchers on it. Hopefully, they come up with something useful. It could have been just a lost guy driving around."

"But if it wasn't, and if this new kingpin decides to take out the existing hierarchy, including all the lieutenants, the entire 98Mob could be in danger," Rourke added.

If someone wanted to eliminate the existing 98Mob, that would include my brothers. I couldn't help but worry about my mom because I didn't think she could handle losing two children in a drug war, or for any reason.

"Let us know when you hear something."

"Will do. Is the ballistics report back on Candace's shooting?" I asked, searching for any new leads.

Hirsch said, "I haven't heard back from Olivio yet. But I'll follow up with him this morning to get an update."

"Who knew the first time we met, you, Martina, we would be seeing so much of you," Rourke joked, a slight smile on his face.

Was he flirting with me? He was handsome in a linebacker kind of way.

Hirsch quipped, "She has a way of sticking around like gum on your shoe."

"Hey, I take offense to that," I retorted playfully.

As long as Hirsch and I were working on cold cases, and my investigations overlapped with theirs, they'd never fully get rid of me. But I knew they loved it.

Turning to Hirsch, I said, "Ready to go talk to Leslie?"

"As ready as I'll ever be."

We said our goodbyes, each of us hoping the sketch of the

man who threatened Candace would provide something useful in understanding what was going on within the 98Mob.

39

MARTINA

After Hirsch spoke with Detective Olivio from Alameda County, we were disappointed to learn Ballistics hadn't processed the bullet from Candace's shooting yet. In the meantime, we found Detective Leslie waiting in Hirsch's office. "Good morning, Sarge, Martina," she greeted us warmly, but worry was written all over her face.

We walked inside, and I shut the door behind us. Taking a seat next to Leslie, I tried to maintain a composed demeanor. "Hopefully, it is a good morning, Leslie."

"What's up?" Leslie asked, her voice tinged with nerves.

As it should be.

Scooting my chair over to face her, I said, "That's exactly what we would like to know. We were at the hospital last night, speaking with Candace's sister. Do you want to know what Candace's sister told us?" I asked, watching her reaction closely.

Leslie shook her head slowly, her eyes widening with concern.

"She told us the reason Candace didn't take my phone call was because you told her not to talk to me. I'd like to know why you told Candace not to talk to me about the investigation."

"Maybe she misinterpreted..." Leslie started, stumbling over her words as if deciding whether to continue lying.

Hirsch, with a firm tone, interrupted, "Leslie, it's time for you to come clean. This is your very, very last chance. If we find any more inconsistencies, or that you're tampering with witnesses or still in contact with the 98Mob or whoever is trying to take out witnesses and members of the organization, you're done. We're talking possible jail time. But if you come clean now, we can see if we can have you avoid prison."

It was rare to see Hirsch so fired up. Usually, he was the level-headed one who calmed me down when I got overly passionate about a case. "Well?" I pressed, eager for her to speak.

Leslie dropped her head, and I heard her sniffles, followed by the sound of her wiping her eyes. "I'm so sorry. I am. I'm sorry. I've just been in so deep," she confessed, her voice cracking with emotion.

Hirsch, not letting up, demanded, "I need you to tell us absolutely everything you know, and what you're currently involved in."

She nodded, a mixture of relief and fear in her eyes. "Ace was my contact, that was true. He's the one who told me to pull the photo of Darren Kolze, and that he was the shooter, and to not look any further, to close the case, no more questions asked. He's the one who held my son hostage until I did what he wanted. But of course, people like that don't stop there."

Hirsch signaled for her to continue.

"So, after I got my son back, they kept calling me, dropping by our house. They wanted information. They knew that Martina was looking into the case and figured that eventually the case was going to be re-opened. Ace had been calling me to find out what was going on with the investigation."

"How often are they contacting you?"

"We have a daily check-in," she replied, shaking her head as tears streamed down her face. "I'm so sorry, I'm so sorry."

Hirsch's face was beet red with anger. It was evident he was furious—we had a mole, a dirty cop. Leslie hadn't always been corrupt, but because she had been compromised, every case she worked on could also be compromised. That was disastrous, not just for this case, but if it became public knowledge, those she put away in her homicide investigations or cold cases that we closed together could be put into question and those criminals set free because of her indiscretions. Hirsch's anger and disappointment were appropriate.

"Ace is dead. So, who is calling you now?"

She looked at me and said, "It's your brother, Clark."

My brother was a traitor? My brother, on the side trying to silence Darren? Did he really try to kill his own brother? If that was true, then why did he warn me to stay away? Maybe he didn't have a choice? This was overwhelming, but I had to power through. "When does he usually call you?"

"In the evening, ten o'clock. I have a burner phone they gave me."

"What does he ask? What do you tell him?"

"He asks about the case details. I told them everything about reopening the case, the evidence we have, and our conversations," she admitted, her voice barely above a whisper.

Hirsch shook his head in disappointment. "Stay here, Leslie. Martina and I need to speak outside for a moment."

We didn't speak until we were halfway down the hall. Huddled together, he said, "I can't let her go, Martina, but if your brother is really shaking her down, he could be doing so on behalf of whoever killed Ace, and maybe Toby, and attempted to kill Candace. Your brother—he could be on the wrong side, the new king's side."

As if I hadn't considered that awful scenario. "I know, and if the theory is the new king is taking out anybody part of the old regime, under Jaime, they could go after Clark. They could be using him and when he's done, he's gone."

"You're right."

We needed to get to the bottom of this because I didn't have much fight left in me for this battle. Attempting to think clearly, I said, "What if we put Leslie in a holding cell? She's got the burner phone. We'll keep her here. Listen in on the next call and trace it."

"And if it's Clark?"

"Then it's Clark, and we keep a close eye on him." One, because he may have critical information and two, because I wanted to keep him safe.

"After we get confirmation Clark is her connection to the 98Mob, I'll need to report all of this to Internal Affairs and let them know what's going on. They'll likely want to start the process to let her go."

There was no way Leslie was keeping her job, and she may have just kissed her pension goodbye. Leslie likely knew this, which meant she needed to be watched closely. "Do you think she's a risk for suicide?"

"I don't know. I thought I knew her, but now I'm not so sure," Hirsch admitted, his voice heavy with disappointment. "I'm going to go back in. I'm taking her badge, her gun, and putting her in holding. I'll tell her what the plan is, and we'll have her wired up."

"I'm sorry, Hirsch."

He was taking this harder than he would admit.

Hirsch smirked, a hint of sadness in his eyes. "So much for the zoo."

"Sorry."

"All right. I'll let you know if I hear anything."

My heart hurt from all angles of the investigation. Hirsch was losing a once trusted friend and detective, and my brothers were criminals putting all our lives in danger.

40

CANDACE

My eyelids flickered open, but the lights above were too bright. I moaned softly and heard distant voices. "Her eyelids moved. I think she's waking up," someone said.

Who was that? Where was I? My mind was a blur, and I couldn't remember what had happened. I tried opening my eyes again, and slowly, shapes materialized before me—my mom, my dad. I shifted my gaze, noticing a window and hearing the steady beeps of a machine. I glanced down and realized I was in a hospital bed. "Candace, can you hear me?" That voice, unmistakably my mother's, broke through the haze.

I looked over at her. She clasped her hands together in relief. "You can hear me, can't you? Donovan, Donovan, she can hear me!" my mother exclaimed jubilantly.

Why wouldn't I be able to hear them? What happened to me? I moved my hand slowly up to my head, feeling the soft bandages. What happened to my head? Why was I so tired? Perhaps I was drugged. It would explain the fuzziness and the muffled voices.

My attention drifted back to my mom and dad. I noticed someone rushing out of the room—it looked like my dad.

I watched as a woman in a white coat approached, shining a light in my eyes. It was bright enough already. I blinked furiously until she finally moved it away. "Candace, my name is Dr. Potter. Can you hear me?"

It felt like a colossal effort to talk, but I managed to nod my head slightly.

"That's really good, Candace, really good. Can you say anything? If you can, say 'yes'," she encouraged.

I swallowed hard, mustering every ounce of energy to croak out a barely audible, "Yes."

Tears appeared in Mom's eyes. Why was she crying because I said 'yes'?

"That's a wonderful sign. You're doing fabulous," the doctor reassured me.

I tried to speak again, more clearly this time. "What happened?" My words came out slow and laborious.

"You suffered a gunshot wound to your head. We took you into surgery and removed the bullet. Now you're in the hospital. You've been here for two days."

I was shot in the head? He must've come back. I couldn't remember, but I did recall a feeling of being followed at the grocery store. I wasn't imagining it. Detective Leslie had told me not to worry, and yet there I was, lying in a hospital bed. I couldn't trust her after all. What a time to realize it.

The doctor leaned in, asking gently, "Do you remember who shot you?"

I hesitated. I didn't remember the actual shooting, but the memory of the man who had threatened me was clear. Was that enough? Unsure, I nodded slightly.

"That's great news. We're going to call the detective, and he's going to come down here to talk to you, along with the sergeant, okay?" the doctor said, sounding hopeful.

I nodded again, feeling a sense of urgency. Surely, this man needed to be stopped, or he might come after me again.

The regret was overwhelming. I thought I could leave it all behind, but I was so wrong, naively thinking I could escape.

The doctor said, "You take care. I'll be back to check on you in a little bit," before leaving the room.

My mother returned to my side, Talia next to her. The relief that Talia was safe washed over me. I hadn't been sure if she was home during the incident.

Talia greeted me softly, "Hi, Candace."

"Hi," I replied weakly.

"Oh, honey, we're so glad you're awake. You had us worried," my mother said, her voice laced with relief.

They were worried, and so was I. My mother turned away for a moment, then faced me again. "Honey, I want you to know, Talia told us everything—everything. She gave the police a sketch of the man who threatened you. They're going to look for him. But you're not going to tell them anything else, okay?"

Confused, I managed to ask, "Why?"

"Trust me. I'm not only your mother, but as you know, I'm also a lawyer. If they know everything, you could get into trouble, honey, and we don't want that to happen. It's not going to bring anybody back. I'll be here with you when the detective comes back, okay?"

I nodded, processing her words.

Turning back to Talia, I wondered if keeping silent would be another mistake. Perhaps sticking to my initial statement and trying to move on was wrong. Maybe the only way to truly move past it was to confront it head on, to finally tell the truth, whatever the consequences might be. That would be better than constantly fearing for my life. If I told the police the truth, maybe it would stop them from coming after me.

Unsure if it was the right thing to keep quiet, I was too tired to fight, and said, "Okay."

Exhausted from the conversation and the heavy realizations of where I was and what had happened, I closed my eyes and allowed sleep to take me away.

41

MARTINA

IN the dimly lit hospital parking garage, Hirsch shared the latest developments with me. "Leslie's officially on leave until the investigation into her role with the 98Mob is concluded. We're holding her at the station for her own safety. The ten o'clock phone call confirmed what she said—they were able to trace the call back to Clark's house."

Not news Mom would put in the holiday newsletter. "What did they discuss on the call?"

"Leslie gave Clark details on the investigation into Ace and Candace's shootings and the status of Toby June's murder. She told him they hadn't made much progress but were suspecting it was a rival gang. That seemed to make him happy."

The thought of my brother involved in such nefarious activities was disheartening, solidifying his position in the "bad guy" category. "At least she told us the truth."

"True and she didn't give him anything too useful but kept him talking long enough for the trace."

"What does this mean for Clark?"

"Well, he didn't technically break a law asking her about the case. But if it goes to trial and we don't pick him up on something else, we can likely get him for a charge relating to the other crimes by the 98Mob—at the very least as an accessory after the fact," Hirsch explained.

The reality hit me hard. No matter how this whole thing played out, I would have at least one brother in prison, if not two. "Well, now you know why I haven't kept in touch with my brothers," I said with a hint of resignation.

"Have you told your mom about Clark's involvement?"

The thought of telling my mother was more than I could handle. "No, it's better she doesn't know. At least for now." I didn't want to put her in the same difficult position that had compromised Detective Leslie.

As we passed the reception desk and stepped into the elevator, I changed the subject. "How was the zoo?" I knew Hirsch had made a deal with Audrey to go to the zoo on Sunday instead of the planned Saturday, in exchange for an outing to the ice cream shop.

"Audrey loved the monkeys," Hirsch replied with a soft smile.

"Yeah, who doesn't love monkeys," I said, trying to lighten the mood.

"Do you think she'll talk to us?"

"I don't know. If her mother's there, we might get shut down."

When we heard the news that Candace was awake and could speak, it was a huge relief. Surviving a gunshot wound to the head was rare. The doctor had told us she had been one of the lucky ones. With some physical therapy and a lot of rest, she would fully recover. It was the best-case scenario for Candace.

As we approached Candace's floor with a ding of the elevator, we stepped out and walked toward the hospital room. Hirsch and I entered without warning.

Candace was propped up halfway in her bed, her head bandaged, attentively listening to her mother and sister discussing plans for a vacation once she recovered. I waved at her and greeted her warmly, "Hello, Candace. It's good to see you awake."

"Hi," she managed weakly.

"This is Sergeant Hirsch. You spoke with him on the phone a few days ago. Do you remember that?" I asked, trying to ease into the conversation.

She nodded in recognition.

"We're working with Detective Olivio from the Alameda County Sheriff's department on the shooting. We spoke with your sister, Talia, and she gave us a sketch of the man who threatened you and was most likely the one who shot you."

Candace nodded in understanding. I pulled out a photocopy of the sketch and placed it in front of her. Her eyes widened. "That's him. That's the man who threatened me."

"Is he the man who shot you?"

"I don't remember. I don't remember the shooting."

It was common for shooting victims to have memory gaps about the incident or the moments, or even hours, leading up to it. "Had you seen this man before he came to your house and threatened you?"

Candace glanced over to her mother and sister, seemingly seeking approval or guidance, indicating she might have seen the man before but was hesitant to disclose more. "He... I don't... I can't say," she hesitated.

"Is this the same man who shot June Bug?" I asked, watching her reaction closely.

Her eyes grew even wider, a mix of fear and recognition flashing across her face. Her mother, sensing the intensity of our questioning, intervened. "That's enough. If you don't have any other questions, I'm going to have to ask you to leave. My daughter's in a very delicate state, and you're here interrogating her," she said, her tone firm and protective.

I stepped back, addressing her mother directly. "There's a person running around free who almost killed your daughter. Don't you think it's important we try to find that person and stop them?"

"We gave you a sketch. She said she doesn't remember. I don't see how else she can help you," her mother retorted.

"We believe Candace knows a lot more than she's telling us about the shooting of Toby June," I said, glancing back at Candace.

Candace looked increasingly nervous, her eyes shifting away, avoiding our gazes.

Ignoring her mother's protests, I pressed on. "Candace, we know that you were down at the park, allegedly buying drugs and telling the dealers they were for your husband. But your husband had already passed. Why were you really down there?"

She remained silent, a clear indication she wasn't going to answer any more questions.

Not surprising.

"Miss Monroe, that is enough," Candace's mother interjected firmly. "She's very tired. If you don't mind, I would like both of you to leave."

Hirsch, maintaining his composure, glanced over at the mother and responded, "We will leave so she can rest, but this situation isn't going away. We will find the truth, with or without Candace's help. Do you understand what I'm saying?"

"Have a good day, sergeant," Mrs. Davis replied curtly, her tone indicating that the conversation was over.

Hirsch, undeterred, turned back to Candace and said, "There are very dangerous people out there who will not stop just because you're in a hospital bed. If you choose to remain silent, you're not only putting your own life on the line but possibly your family's too."

Candace shut her eyes, no doubt trying to block out the harsh reality of her situation. Her mother, red in the face, warned us, "Now if you don't leave, I will get security."

I couldn't hide my disdain and neither could Hirsch. He glared at her and said, "We'll go, but as a lawyer, I'm sure you understand that obstruction of justice is a criminal offense." And with that, Hirsch led us out of the hospital room, leaving a palpable tension in the air.

Candace's reluctance to speak to us only piqued my interest more. Clearly, she was hiding something, but what?

42

MARTINA

Cornered in my mother's kitchen, I contemplated how much to divulge. Mom couldn't know her son was not only part of organized crime but also involved in the shakedown of a homicide detective. A detective who was once a friend but then flipped when her only child was threatened. Clark didn't only go after bad people; he went after the good too. I think that was why it was more difficult to deal with.

"How's the case going?" my mother asked, her eyes filled with hope.

After what we'd learned about the 98Mob, I had come around to her side of thinking on Darren's innocence. But it wasn't a sure thing yet, and I didn't want to get her hopes up. "We're gathering a lot of information, which is good news."

Even if Darren was cleared of the shooting, it didn't mean he wasn't involved. I knew he was there the day Toby June was killed, and we still had an eyewitness claiming he did it.

"That's all you're gonna give us?" Zoey asked, looking perplexed. Considering we were staying with my mom and Ted, Zoey was around for all the conversations about the murder investigation and the attempt to clear Darren's name. It was a little too close for comfort for me. Zoey had always been interested in the investigations I was working on, even as a little girl, but she didn't need the gory details.

"Sorry, it's an active investigation."

Mom protested, "But it's my son."

Ted stepped into the kitchen, greeting everyone cheerfully, with Barney wagging his tail beside him.

"Good morning, Ted."

Mom turned to Ted. "Martina says she can't give us any details of the case because it's an active investigation."

I gave Ted a look, hoping he understood that it was better I didn't give any details at that point.

"Well, Betty, sometimes that's just how it has to be. It could compromise the investigation," Ted reasoned.

Mom's face was turning an awful shade of fuchsia. "We're family!"

A member of our family could be the reason Darren was in a hospital bed, but I didn't have the heart to tell her, and I didn't want her to slip any details of the investigation to Clark.

"Betty, if Martina says she can't tell you details, then it's probably best you don't hear the details. We have to trust Martina," Ted said.

I mouthed a "thank you" to Ted and quickly excused myself. "Anyway, I need to get to work."

"OK, go to work with your secret investigation," my mother retorted, her tone tinged with frustration.

"You know that's uncalled for. I'm doing my job to the best of my ability, and I have a lot of people helping me," I replied, feeling a sting of hurt.

"I'm sorry, Martina, I just..." Mom's voice trailed off.

"I have to go," I said firmly.

Zoey's eyes widened. It wasn't often I argued with my

mother. I gave Zoey a kiss on the cheek and said, "I'll talk to you later," before hurrying out of the house.

To be honest, I didn't like keeping details from my mother, Ted, or even Zoey, but until we understood what side Clark was on, I couldn't jeopardize the DEA and FBI's operations. It wasn't just about Darren anymore.

VINCENT ENTERED the conference room and took a seat next to me. "Hey, you're here early."

"Yeah, it was getting a little hot in my mom's house."

He raised an eyebrow. "Oh?"

"Mom doesn't like that I'm not discussing details of the case."

"She clearly doesn't understand what's at stake."

"No, she doesn't. At least Ted came to my rescue." I explained how Ted had come to my defense, taking some pressure off me.

"The original Sarge..." Vincent said wistfully.

It was strange to think Ted and I used to work together and Hirsch held his old position. "Any word from Narcotics?"

"Nope, just said they wanted a meeting."

Hirsch stepped in, and I waved and said, "Anything from Detective Olivio?"

"Not yet."

Great. No progress. *My favorite.*

"I really would like this to end quickly. I know I say that in every case, but this one is too close to home." I paused, then added, "Like, *in* my home."

Hirsch said, "I get it. I think everyone's doing as much as they can, not only to help you but to stop the bloodshed on the streets."

"I know. I'm grateful. It's just getting to me."

"Understandable."

Our narcotics pals entered. "How's it going, y'all?" Rourke said with a Texas twang.

Not great. "It's going. You?"

"Not too shabby. We have some details that I think you're going to want to hear."

"Yeah, what is it?"

"We finished the background on the driver, the one you spotted going past Clark's house. The car is registered to a Douglas Kendle, aged sixty, but background found that although he is the car's registered owner, he has a son named Jeremy Kendle and is listed as a driver on his car insurance policy. And you want to know why that's interesting?"

Vincent said, "Because he's a gangster?"

"Bingo, and Vincent wins the game," Rourke declared with a wry smile.

Vincent pumped his fists in the air like he had just won a poker tournament.

"Who is he with?" I asked.

"He's one of our known 98Mob members. Low-level, doesn't deal, more of a recruiter for dealers."

"What do you think he was doing at Clark's house? Do you think he's friend or foe?"

"To Clark, you mean?" he clarified.

I nodded.

"Well, that's completely unknown at this point. But I was talking to Hirsch, and he told us Clark has taken over for Ace in his dealings with Detective Leslie. Between these two things—him shaking down a police officer *and* being a known member of 98Mob—we're thinking he may be in cahoots with the new king. We propose twenty-four-hour surveillance at Clark's. We could pick up something valuable."

I let that sink in.

We were putting my brother, Clark, under surveillance.

Up until that week, I hadn't seen him in twenty years, and now we would be watching him twenty-four hours a day in order to catch him, to put him in jail. Mom was not going to be happy about this.

"It makes sense. I think we should do it. Do we have enough people?" I asked.

Vincent volunteered, "I could do surveillance."

Rourke said, "We have some folks from Narcotics, but yeah, if you have anybody from any other departments, Hirsch, it could help out."

Hirsch added, "We've got some folks we could use. Vincent, for one. But Martina, I think you should sit this one out, obviously."

Gladly. "Agreed. Clark would recognize me."

Rourke straightened up in his seat. "Okay, we're agreed on surveillance at Clark's house, and we're gonna talk to a judge to see if we can get wiretaps too."

"A solid plan." Not only could it give us valuable information about the case to end the madness, but maybe it would keep Clark safe too. If Jeremy Kendle was a foe, he could be watching Clark's house to take him out. Clark was still my brother, even if he was on the wrong side of the law—the really wrong side, the opposite side—in the shadows. He was still my brother, and I loved him. I just didn't love his choices and how he chose to live his life.

We made a plan, and Hirsch and I stayed behind to work as Rourke, Kiva, and Vincent left to set up surveillance at Clark's house.

"How's your mom doing?" Hirsch asked.

After I explained my morning, he said, "Did you tell Ted what's going on?"

"No, I don't want to put him in a position to have to lie to my mom. He got the hint that it's serious. He knows better than to ask for details."

"Well, hopefully, we can get to the bottom of this soon. The DEA has the sketch that Candace's sister provided, and we're still waiting on ballistics. Hopefully, once those results come through, we'll get some answers."

"Amen."

43

MARTINA

Hirsch and I had just returned from lunch when we spotted Kiva in the cubicle area. He waved and jogged over. "I just heard from the DEA. Sounds like they got something. You have time for a call?"

"Yes, please," I replied eagerly.

Rourke and Buck entered behind Kiva, and we all returned to the table while Kiva dialed the number. "This is Rourke, Kiva, and Buck from the narcotics team, and I'm also here with Martina Monroe and Sergeant Hirsch."

"Figured this is a Martina and Hirsch case," the voice on the other end responded.

I smiled despite the nerves and anticipation of what was about to unfold. "Bishop, is that you?"

"Sure is. Boy, are you great at just stepping right into it."

"It wasn't my fault this time."

A chuckle emanated from the speaker. "I heard Clark and Darren Kolze are your brothers."

"Yes, sir."

"You might not like what we have to say, but we definitely have some news."

I didn't like the sound of that. "Well, let's hear it, Bishop."

We had worked with Agent Bishop and his partner a few cases back when a drug dealer was hanging around the Sonoma coast, pretending to be a commune leader.

"We received the sketch of the man who threatened your eyewitness, Candace Mason. It took us a few days, but we confirmed his identity. His name is Jax Carvallo. That's the good news. The bad news is he's a hired gun used by a Mexican cartel. The cartel is led by a guy named Eddie Domingo. The interesting thing about that is Domingo's a supplier for Jaime and the 98Mob. This is where our operation came into play."

"Are we allowed to ask the nature of your operation?"

"Yes, you've all proven you can keep things quiet. We have a few undercover agents working within the 98Mob, and a few who have been deep undercover in the Mexican cartels for a few years now. We have increased contact because of the number of bodies dropping. We finally learned what, we believe, is really going on."

"And?"

"Turns out Domingo, who's no big fan of Jaime's, has decided he wants the 98Mob's Bay Area operation. And he's using Jax to take out any 98Mob members not willing to join his crew."

"So basically, he wants the territory currently controlled by the 98Mob."

"Exactly. This is really bad news. We do not need Mexican cartels operating out of the Bay Area."

"What does this mean for our case? Do we think Jax and Domingo are tied to Toby June and Ace's murders, the attacks on my brother and Candace Mason, our eyewitness in the Toby June murder?"

"Rumors are yes, Domingo and his crew are responsible for all of it."

The gravity of the situation settled over us. A tangled web of crime, reaching from local gangs to international cartels, was now at the forefront of our investigation. As I digested the news, I said, "You said I wasn't going to love the news. I mean, this isn't great. But did you mean something specific about my brothers?"

"Yes. Our people think Domingo approached different members of the 98Mob, higher-level members like lieutenants, to see who's willing to stay on under Domingo's reign. Rumor has it Clark and Ace were approached."

"So, if I have this right, Clark is now working for a Mexican cartel? And these people are about to take out the 98Mob including Jaime Ragnar?"

"That's what we think is happening."

More details for my family's holiday newsletter. "What do you think about Jeremy Kendle? Is he with Domingo or loyal to Jaime?"

"We're not sure which side he's on."

Kiva chimed in, "This morning, we put surveillance on Clark's house."

Vincent had been updating me every hour since he set up camp. It was good to have one of my Drakos Monroe team in there.

"Smart."

"Do you think Darren is still in danger?" I knew it wasn't exactly at the top of everybody's priority list, but he was my brother and was darn near the top of mine.

Bishop said, "It's likely he's still a target."

"I have a guard on his hospital room."

"Someone you trust?" Bishop asked.

"He's from my firm. He's solid."

"Good."

"Is it possible they'd go after my family, considering they've gone after Darren and have maybe been scoping out Clark?" I asked, concerned for Zoey and my mom.

"Domingo's not really known for going after family members. They're usually pretty focused on mission-based hits. We're not entirely sure why they tried to take out your brother Darren. It could've simply been a way of eliminating the current 98Mob structure," Bishop explained.

"All right. What do we think is going to happen next?"

"We think there's going to be a coordinated attack against Jaime and anybody else who's still with him as part of the old 98Mob."

At least it sounded like my family was safe, with the exception of my brothers who were both 98Mob members. It was, at least, *some* good news. "Anything else you can tell us?"

"Not at this time. We have a major operation going on, so all of this stays in this room. We want to take them down if we can. If we play our cards right, we could prevent the Mexican cartels from taking up residence here in the Bay Area."

"Sounds good."

The phone call ended, and I said a silent prayer that my family would stay safe. It sounded like they were, but I couldn't be sure so I supposed I'd be a houseguest for a bit longer.

Hirsch's phone rang, and so did the narcotics team's phones. Something major had to be going down. My cellphone vibrated, and I saw it was Vincent. Quickly, I answered. "Hey, what's up?"

"Shots fired at Clark's. Shots fired."

My heart pounded. "Can you see anything? Has anyone been hit?"

Like my brother.

"The surveillance team went in and took down the shooter, but there are a couple of bodies. Paramedics are on their way."

Please let Clark be okay. "I'll be right there."

The urgency in Vincent's voice was obvious. I grabbed my gear, knowing that every second counted. The situation was escalating, and I had to be there to help contain it and protect my family.

44

MARTINA

Hirsch offered to drive me to Clark's house, but I refused. If something had happened to Clark, I would need to see my mother in person, and Hirsch, as a sergeant, would have other duties to attend to. As we pulled up to the neighborhood, the scene of the carnage was unmistakable. Sirens wailed, and a dozen black and white police cars lined the streets. I parked in the first available spot and hurried toward a man who looked like Vincent. As I jogged toward him, he waved, standing next to a man who held himself like a police officer.

Vincent didn't hesitate. "Martina, this is Officer Danbury. He works in Vice. He was here for the surveillance."

"Nice to meet you. I'm Martina Monroe."

We shook hands, and he said, "Your reputation precedes you."

"Thank you, but do we know the situation going on in there? You said there were bodies."

Vincent said, "There were two hit by gunfire. One was your brother, and the other was the shooter."

"Is he OK?"

"He's alive. The paramedics took Clark and the shooter a few minutes ago. They're en route to the hospital."

I silently thanked God. "What happened here? Do we know?"

"A car pulled up to the curb, a tall man, about six feet with dark hair, went up to the front door, knocked, but nobody answered right away. When no one opened the door, the man looked in through the window, pulled a weapon from the back of his trousers, and opened fire inside the house. Fire came from inside the house to the shooter, who was running back to the car. The driver attempted to get away, but the surveillance team was fast, and they took him down. Like I said, the shooter is en route to the hospital, the driver's in custody."

"Did you get an ID on the shooter and driver?"

"The shooter didn't have ID, claimed to not speak English."

Could it be Jax, the hitman? "And the other? The driver of the car?"

"Jeremy Kendle."

A foe. "That's who I saw driving past the house when I was here a few days ago."

"Sounds like he was scoping it out for an attack."

Was this part of the coordinated attack the DEA suspected was in the works by Domingo and crew? "Have you contacted the narcotics team?"

"Oh yeah, everybody's been contacted. We think this is just one of many going on right now. Everyone's on high alert and assembling the troops."

I raked my fingers through my hair and looked over at Vincent. "Did they say which hospital they're taking Clark to?"

"Mount Diablo Medical Center."

Nerves rattling, I said, "Did it look like he'll make it?"

"It all happened really fast, Martina. From where I was, it looked like a hit to the chest. That's all I know."

"He's your brother, huh?" Officer Danbury asked.

"Yeah, and I've got another one in Marin County Hospital."

"I'm sorry to hear that. I hope he pulls through."

I felt my nose tingle and forced back the tears. If that wasn't bad enough, I had to do something I really didn't want to. I had to call my mom and tell her another one of her sons was headed to the hospital with a life-threatening injury.

Vincent spoke up, "Do you want me to go with you to the hospital?"

Just then, Hirsch jogged over. "Hey, Martina, Vincent. Are you about to head over to the hospital to see Clark?"

"Yes, but I need to call my mom before I head over."

"I'll go with you," Hirsch offered.

I turned to Vincent. "Maybe you should stick around in case there are any questions about the surveillance."

"You got it, boss. Good luck, and I hope everything works out," Vincent said, patting me on the arm.

"Thanks."

And with a heavy weight on my shoulders, I pulled out my cell phone before heading to my car.

45

MARTINA

In the emergency room with Hirsch, I asked to speak with Clark's doctors.

"Are you family?"

"Yes, but I'm also with law enforcement. He came in with a gunshot wound. His name is Clark Kolze."

"Oh yes, the doctor will be right out," the receptionist replied.

Footsteps hurried toward us. Over my shoulder, I saw my mom with Ted and Zoey. Why had she brought Zoey? She had never even met her uncle Clark, and this wasn't exactly a great day for that. "Hey."

"How is he? Is he gonna make it?" my mother cried.

"The doctor should be out to talk with us soon."

As if on cue, a man in dark blue scrubs and a white coat approached. "The family of Clark Kolze?"

My mother rushed over, and Hirsch and I exchanged glances as we followed. "I am Sergeant Hirsch of the CoCo County Sheriff's Department, and this is my partner, Martina, who happens to also be the victim's sister. This is her mother,

Betty, stepfather Ted, and daughter Zoey." Hirsch hesitated, as if just realizing Zoey was there too.

"What can you tell us?" I asked.

"Mr. Kolze was lucky. He suffered a gunshot wound to the shoulder, just missed his heart. It was a through-and-through; the bullet's not lodged in him. We bandaged him up. He should be fine to go home in a few days—or wherever he's going," the doctor said, glancing at Hirsch.

"Thank you. Can we see him now?" my mother asked.

"You can. He's awake. He's a little grumpy, but he'll live."

"Thank God," my mother exclaimed.

Hirsch said, "There was another man brought in. Gunshot wound."

The doctor said, "Yes, he's still in surgery. You can let reception know you're waiting to hear his condition."

Hirsch said, "Thanks," and faced me. "I'll go with you to check on Clark and then head back to wait to hear the shooter's status."

"Thanks."

The doctor escorted my mother and the crew, but I stopped Zoey. "I don't want you going in there right now."

"But he almost died, Mom."

"I don't know if I'm comfortable with you talking to him right now. This case is very dangerous, and your uncle is part of it," I said quietly.

Hirsch stood a few paces away, waiting for us.

Zoey protested, "So, I'm just going to sit here by myself while my whole family's in there?"

She had a point. "Do you really want to meet him?"

"Yes. Please, Mom. If he's really in a world that is so dangerous, this might be my only chance to meet him."

Zoey's plea formed a giant ball of guilt inside me. "Okay. Fine. But I'll introduce you."

Hirsch gave me a look that conveyed his understanding of the turmoil I was going through.

Inside the room, Mom was holding Clark's hand, with Ted standing by as if guarding her. Hirsch walked in and introduced himself, but Clark didn't seem very pleased by his presence.

Keeping Zoey behind Ted, I said, "Hi, Clark, I see you've met Sergeant Hirsch. He's one of my partners."

"Great," Clark responded dryly. "Are you here to question me?"

I glanced over at Zoey and said, "We will do that in a few minutes. First, I wanted to make sure you were okay."

"Doc says I'm gonna live. Lucky me," Clark said grimly.

I glanced at Zoey, her expression reflecting my own concerns. "Before Sergeant Hirsch and I talk to you about what happened today, I want you to meet someone."

Clark's eyes widened in surprise as I pulled Zoey next to my mother. "Clark, this is Zoey, my daughter. Zoey, this is your uncle Clark."

Without a trace of shyness, Zoey greeted him enthusiastically. "Hi. It's nice to finally meet you."

"Hi, Zoey, it's nice to meet you. I wish it was under different circumstances," Clark said, his voice carrying a tone of regret.

Talk about an understatement.

Zoey and Clark studied each other as if trying to paint a mental picture they could keep with them for the rest of time.

Noticing that we were running out of time, I decided to move things along. "Okay, now that we've seen that Clark's okay, Hirsch and I need a few minutes to talk to him alone."

"Martina, is this really necessary right now?" my mother interjected.

Her attitude was starting to wear on me. "There are very dangerous people out there, and we need information from Clark to make sure nobody else gets hurt. I hope you can understand, Mom." Facing Zoey, I said, "Go with Grandma and Ted. I'll see you soon." Thankfully Ted seemed to understand the seriousness of the situation and ushered them out of the room.

"I'm surprised you brought her here," Clark said, his voice trailing off.

"Mom did. I would not have."

"She looks like you except for the bright blue eyes."

Jared's eyes.

"She does."

"It's cool. I get it. But thank you for letting me meet her."

Trying to keep my composure, I said, "Sure."

Thankfully, Hirsch jumped in. "Members from our narcotics team, as well as the DEA, will be here shortly to speak with you, but I want to hear from you what happened today."

Clark sighed. "If I talk, they'll kill me."

I looked him dead in the eyes. "They're gonna kill you if you don't. They already tried once."

He shook his head. "I'm not talking without a deal. Sorry. If they don't kill me, they'll make me wish I was dead."

Before we could press further, Kiva and Rourke appeared in the doorway. Hirsch motioned them in. "Come on in. He won't talk to us. Maybe he'll talk to you."

But I remained skeptical, knowing the gravity of Clark's situation and the imminent danger he was in. Before I could argue further with Clark, my phone vibrated in my pocket. I hurried out of the room and answered. "Jayda, what's up?"

"I got a call from Detective Olivio. The ballistics are back on the bullet from the Candace Mason case."

Why did Detective Olivio call Jayda? Whatever the reason, I couldn't wait to hear what she had to say.

46

MARTINA

I HURRIED BACK to where Hirsch, Rourke, and Kiva stood. "Hold on," I said into the phone, turning to Hirsch and the narcotics team. "I have Jayda on the line. Detective Olivio called her with the ballistics report on the Candace Mason hit."

Without hesitation, they stepped out of the room, and in the hallway, I relayed who I was with to Jayda. "Okay, what did they find? And why did Olivio call you?" I asked into the phone.

"Detective Olivio called me because the bullet from the Candace Mason case was a match for two other homicides, one I'm working."

Two other cases? I repeated this to the team, my voice low. "What are the other cases?"

"Toby June and Anthony Hernandez, a.k.a. Ace."

My mouth dropped open, and my heart raced. I shared the news, stepping a few spaces farther down the hallway but still keeping an eye on Clark's room. "It's likely all the same shooter," I said to Jayda and the guys.

Jayda replied, "It's a strong possibility, considering we never found the gun in the Toby June or Anthony Hernandez murders. It looks like your brother may be innocent after all."

At least Darren was innocent. Clark, however? "Thank you, Jayda. Thank you so much."

"I didn't do anything. It was all ballistics. How's Clark doing?"

"He'll pull through, but he won't talk to us."

"Well, that's not a shocker, is it?"

"Not really. I'll talk to you soon." I pocketed my cell phone, then said, "We should let the DEA know that it's a match for the Toby June and Ace Hernandez murders."

"I'll give them a call. Afterward, I'll go in and question Clark," Rourke said.

"The shooter is in surgery."

"We'll follow up with him later."

"Good luck."

Hirsch stepped closer. "Looks like maybe Darren didn't shoot Toby after all."

"Then why did Candace say that he did?" A realization struck me. "What do you say we go visit our other *friend* in the hospital?"

"Candace."

I nodded.

"Let's go."

47

MARTINA

Adrenaline pumping, I hurried with Hirsch toward the elevators. Assuming Candace was in the same room as before, we knew exactly where to find her. I charged in. Candace was alone in the room, her parents likely taking a break. *Finally, some luck.* "Hi, Candace. How are you feeling?"

"Better, but they said I might be here awhile."

Nodding, I played the sympathy card. "You're lucky to be alive."

"That's what I'm hearing. Did you find the guy from the sketch?"

"The man matching the description was involved in a shooting earlier today. He's in surgery. Once he's healed up, he'll be in jail." I purposefully left out the tidbit that he was in the very same hospital as her.

With wide eyes, she said, "He tried to kill somebody else?"

Was she surprised? "Yes. We think he's a hitman who was hired to kill you," I revealed, noticing the fear on her face. She needed to understand the full seriousness of the situation.

Hirsch said, "Candace, we're also here to tell you there has been another development in your case. The bullet they retrieved from your head matches a bullet from two other crime scenes."

"Do you want to guess one of them?" I asked.

Candace closed her eyes, took a deep breath, and then looked at me. "Is that man going to jail?"

"Yes, he opened fire on a home in front of police officers. He's not getting out of jail probably ever," I assured her. "We know you were threatened before you were shot, and we think you haven't been telling us the truth, at least not all of it. These people are very, very bad. We need you to tell us what you know. If you don't, we can't protect you."

Candace lowered her head. "You're right. I haven't been telling you everything. It's time. I'll tell you everything."

Hirsch and I exchanged glances, and I thought, *it's about time.*

48

CANDACE

As I WAS ABOUT to share my story, my parents returned to the room. Mom quickly interjected, "We already told you Candace has nothing more to say. What are you doing here? Why aren't you out looking for the man who shot her?"

Hirsch replied, "With all due respect, ma'am, we believe the man who shot your daughter is in surgery. After that, he'll be in custody."

"Mom, Dad, it's okay. I want to talk to them."

Mom glared at me. "Candace, we talked about this. You're not to say a single word to them."

Enough was enough. "It's my decision. It's my life. It's my story to tell. I want to tell them my story. I want to tell the truth."

Mom shook her head, clearly disappointed. "This could ruin your future, Candace."

"I'm in a hospital bed with a gunshot wound to my head. I don't think I could get more ruined. It's lies and negative energy that got me here. I don't want to be this person anymore. I thought I could put it behind me, but I can't. I need to tell the truth—it's the only way I can ever move on. I hope you understand. I really don't want to have this on my conscience anymore."

Eventually, Mom conceded and took a seat with Dad on the chairs to the right of my bed. "Go ahead," she said reluctantly.

Sergeant Hirsch and Martina Monroe stood next to my bed. "I'm listening, Candace," Martina said, encouragingly.

I swallowed hard and chose to be brave. It was time to put this behind me, but the only way to do that was to tell the truth. Someone once said the truth will set you free. That's what I needed—a clear conscience, a clean soul.

"It started after my husband died. He became addicted to fentanyl after a really bad car accident, and during the last six months before he died, we argued and fought because I found out about the drugs. He was draining our bank accounts. We were fighting, and I barely recognized him anymore. I tried to get him help. He'd say he would get help and then he wouldn't. It was the hardest time of my entire life. And then when he overdosed, I think part of me died or just maybe fell through the cracks."

Martina said, "I'm so sorry. To have lost your husband... It's very difficult to move on."

"It was. I felt like a shell of a person, and I lost my desire to do anything, to work. I was just lost."

Martina took my hand and said, "I understand. I've been there. Believe me, I've been there."

I nodded, sensing a genuine understanding in her eyes. There was something about her that made me trust her, and I knew she wouldn't judge me. It's strange how sometimes you barely know a person but can sense who they are on the inside.

"Before Travis died, I had followed him a few times to see where he would go and buy his drugs. That's one of the first times I confronted him because he denied the drug use. But on the anniversary of his death, I got this crazy idea in my head that

I would get revenge on those people who sold him drugs. I decided I was going to go back, and I was going to pretend I was buying them for Travis, even though he'd been gone for a year. So, I started going to the park. I met June Bug and Darren. And I began to understand how the operation worked. I'd give my money to Toby, and then Darren would come out with the drugs. It's funny, though. The first time I went, I had no idea how much the drugs cost. After I explained they were for my husband, Darren actually gave me a pill to tide him over until I could come back with enough cash. If they weren't drug dealers, I would've thought they were kind. But I was so full of anger and rage, I wanted them to pay for what they did to my husband. They sold him the drugs that killed him. I blamed them for his death."

Martina nodded again, and said, "It sounds like you had a lot of anger, but maybe you now see the situation differently."

"I do, but one day I was at the park, and I was just watching them. I was going to get my revenge, and I couldn't quite figure out how. I thought maybe I'd record them selling drugs, then I could call the police, and they'd get arrested. I was crouched behind the bushes, and that tall man with the dark hair walked up to Toby and just shot him. I didn't know what to do. That's not what I wanted. Not at all."

Sergeant Hirsch said, "Was this the same man who visited your home and threatened you?"

"Yes, it was the same man. That's why I was so scared. It was *him*."

"Then why did you say it was Darren who shot Toby?"

"I didn't, at first. I told the detective that it was a tall man with dark hair, but then when she showed me the photographs, and Darren was one of them, I figured it was a way to get back at him for giving drugs to Travis. So, I said it was Darren. I'm so sorry." Tears began to escape, and I tried to wipe them away, feeling so ashamed.

"And then what happened?" Martina asked.

"I went back to the station the next day for the lineup, and there was Darren again, so I pointed him out again. Honestly, I didn't think twice about it until you came asking me questions at the hospital, and then Detective Leslie called about the case. And then I had the threat from that man, and here I am."

"So, you don't know the man who shot you?"

I shook my head in response. "I don't know his name. I never saw him before the day he shot June Bug and didn't see him again until he came to threaten me."

"Do you have any other affiliations with June Bug, Darren, or that drug organization?"

I shook my head again. "No, I was just... I was pretending to buy drugs for Travis, to learn about how their operation worked so I could figure out a way to get back at them for killing him. I should've known better. It was a terrible idea."

I could tell Martina was fuming. Of course she was.

"I'm so sorry. I know that Darren is your brother, and I heard they tried to kill him too. I'm so sorry. I was wrong. I'm just... I didn't want anyone to die. I'm so sorry."

The two talked amongst themselves, but I couldn't hear what they were saying. Were they talking about arresting me? Was that what I deserved? "Will I go to jail for lying? For saying Darren shot June Bug?" I asked anxiously.

Sergeant Hirsch said, "I'll have to discuss this with the rest of the team, but the fact you're coming forward now could be really useful in an ongoing investigation. If you agree to testify, and sign a sworn statement, we can probably work something out."

"Are you saying she won't go to jail?" my mother interjected. The ever-present defense attorney.

The sergeant said, "I'm not making any promises, but it's not likely that she'll see the inside of a jail cell."

Relieved yet still feeling foolish, I realized that if I had just told the truth initially, I could've avoided all of this. My own fear of going to jail or getting into trouble was so stupid. "I'll testify. I'll sign a statement. I'll do whatever I can to make this right. I'm so sorry." I'm sure I sounded stupid, but it was true. I was more sorry than I could ever convey.

After thanking me, they left my hospital room. I glanced over at my parents and apologized to them too. "I'm sorry. I realize how wrong I've been."

My mother took my hand, her voice full of support. "We love you, sweetheart. We'll stand by your side through anything."

Although the guilt continued to consume me, my heart was full of gratitude.

49

MARTINA

Back in the hall, I was stunned and could barely process what I had just heard. The eyewitness to Toby June's murder had lied. If only she had told us the truth sooner. On the other hand, perhaps it was because of Candace's lies that we kept digging and digging, until something made sense. And because of that persistence, the DEA and FBI were about to take down an entire drug cartel from Mexico attempting to infiltrate the Bay Area. But the investigation had almost cost my brothers their lives.

"What do you make of that?" Hirsch asked.

"My brother was innocent all along. How many other people knew? For one, the person who called me anonymously. It has to be Darren's girlfriend, right?"

Hirsch shrugged. "We won't know until somebody tells us. You could ask Darren."

"When I asked, he said he didn't know who was calling me. Maybe it doesn't matter at this point. Jax killed Toby. Between the eyewitness testimony, assuming she's telling the truth this time, and the bullet from Toby's murder matching the type of gun they found on Jax after the shooting at Clark's house, we know the truth."

Ballistics hadn't had a chance to process Jax's firearm, but it was the same caliber as the bullets found at Toby, Ace, and Candace's crime scenes. All signs pointed to Jax. Of course, we'd have to confirm for sure.

"Are you going to tell your mom?"

"Not yet." Not until we knew for sure everyone was out of harm's way. We hadn't heard from the FBI or the DEA and I wouldn't feel my family was safe until I knew they had rounded up all suspects.

As I was about to suggest to Hirsch we should check in with Rourke and head back down to my brother's hospital room, he received a call and nodded.

"Hello." A pause. "I'm at the hospital. I'm here with Martina. Kiva and Rourke are with Clark. OK, I'll gather the troops and meet you down at the station." Hirsch said goodbye and turned to me. "We've got to go. Big stuff is happening."

We rushed back, taking the stairs down two flights to Clark's hospital room. Mom was outside the room, speaking with Kiva. "Well, there they are. Where have you been?" Mom asked.

I tried to signal Hirsch silently, asking for his help to restrain her and stop her from asking so many questions about the case. "We had to talk to someone," I said evasively.

Hirsch added, "Kiva, we need you and Rourke. There's a meeting down at the station we need to attend."

"Do we both need to be there?" Kiva asked, concern evident in his voice.

I wondered if he was worried about Clark's safety. "We'll send a uniform to stand outside his door," Hirsch assured.

Kiva explained, "The doctor stopped by to let us know the shooter is out of surgery. We'll need to question him when he's awake but also someone to guard his room so he doesn't try to escape."

Hirsch said, "I'll call in backup."

Kiva said, "All right, but let's wait until they get here."

I appreciated that Kiva was taking no chances with my brother's life. If there had been a coordinated attack that day, and Domingo's team decided to make a pit stop at the hospital, Clark could be in danger.

My mother shook her head and said, "I don't like any of this, Martina, and I don't like not knowing what's going on."

It was a good thing Ted was retired when they got married. I didn't think she could've handled being married to an active police sergeant. Glancing around, I realized something was off. "Where is Zoey?"

My mother said, "She went down to the cafeteria to grab something to eat."

"By herself?"

Before I could say more, Ted interjected, "Since you're up here, I'll grab Zoey and bring her back."

"Thank you," I replied, grateful yet still concerned. How could they be so careless and let Zoey go to the cafeteria by herself?

As Ted hurried down the hall, Zoey came bouncing up, a fry in one hand and a greasy bag in the other. She waved and smiled. Maybe I was overreacting. Tensions were high, but I didn't like the idea of not knowing exactly where my daughter was in a time like this. Sure, the threat against her was probably very low at that point, but still.

Mom said, "I'm so sorry, Martina. Clark said that we are... he said they weren't going to come after us and that we were safe."

She chose to believe her son, a member of organized crime, that we were all safe. I shook my head again, disbelieving the entire situation. I gave my daughter a quick squeeze, and she stepped back. "Are you okay?" Zoey asked.

Was I OK? *No, I am not.* I was in the middle of an organized crime murder case that was going after both of my brothers, and my daughter was just traipsing around a hospital, free to be attacked at any moment. Maybe I was overreacting, but she was my only child. I couldn't even think about the fact that she was going off to college next month and would be away from me all the time. "I'm fine. We just have somewhere we need to be," I said, trying to sound calm. Not sure if I succeeded.

As if on cue, a uniformed officer scurried over.

"Okay, we have to go. I'll talk to you later. I love you, honey."

"Love you too."

After giving the orders to the uniformed officer, the four of us headed back to the CoCo County Sheriff's Department.

50

MARTINA

Situated in the war room, a new person stood chitchatting with Vincent. The unknown man was, my goodness, 6-foot-4, bald, and brawny. "You must be Martina Monroe and Sergeant Hirsch," he said.

I hesitated, "Yes."

"I'm Bishop. Nice to meet you in person," he greeted warmly.

A smile dawned on my face, and we shook hands. "Good to see you, Bishop."

"Well, as you can imagine, a lot of stuff is going down today. I want to show you what we have so we can make sure we've got everybody. We need to cross all our Ts and dot all our Is. Cool?" Agent Bishop asked.

We all nodded in agreement.

Vincent added, "We're definitely cool," before taking his seat.

Agent Bishop walked over to the projector, pressed a button, and the machine whirred to life. Lights flickered, and the screen displayed an org chart. "Thanks to your help, and working with Kiva and the narcotics team, we think we have unraveled a major clue about the 98Mob war." He went on to describe all the players in Domingo's crew, pointing out Jax, the hitman, several lieutenants, and their underlings. Then another color highlighted the 98Mob, with Jaime at the top, my brother on the next level with the other lieutenants, and two levels below, my other brother Darren. There were circles around Darren and Clark and a macabre 'x' through Toby and Ace's names.

My body practically vibrated in anticipation of the reveal.

"So, as you can see, we've got the Mexican cartel here, and the Bay Area 98Mob here. You can see where the overlap is and where we believe the targets have been. We have every single member of Domingo's US-based team in custody, aside from Jax who is still in the hospital. But the DEA has a close eye on him."

There was a mix of hoots and hollers—it was excellent news.

"As for the 98Mob, we've arrested a few of them, mostly on weapons charges, just to hold them and see if we can get them to talk to us. After we captured Domingo creeping up on Jaime's compound in Byron armed with six men, Jaime agreed to come in and talk to us. But he's not under arrest."

"So what you're saying is, you had a busy day?" Vincent said with a playful smirk.

"You have no idea. Let me tell you, for Domingo's crew, they all had weapons that weren't registered. Half of them are not US citizens, so they'll be easy to deport. This is a big win for the DEA, so again, thank you very much." He paused to tip his head in gratitude and started up again. "As for the 98Mob, they're a little trickier. If we had some insiders, it could give us additional context about what went down over the last few months. So far, we don't have any takers. But we are certain the lieutenants were approached by Domingo's team, and even some of the lower levels. Not everybody was cool with the plan. And since word was getting around, some started catching bullets due to loyalty issues. Loyalty to Jaime was not acceptable to Domingo. He wanted those who were willing to do his dirty work, like Ace, and we believe, Clark too." Bishop hesitated and then added, "I hear he's still in the hospital. Do you think he'll talk to us?"

With regret, I said, "He's refusing to talk without a deal. He says they'll kill him."

Hirsch added, "It sounds like you've got it all figured out. Do you need him?"

"If we have an insider who is willing to talk, it would absolutely help. We don't think Domingo and his crew in the Bay Area are acting on their own. We're fairly certain he's tied to a bigger cartel in Mexico. If we can get insight into that, it could be valuable to both the feds and us."

"Well, you can try talking to him. We also just had an interesting visit with the eyewitness to the Toby June murder. She is recanting her testimony that it was Darren. She says it was Jax, based on his photo, who shot Toby June and threatened her."

"Why did she lie?" Vincent asked.

It was hot off the press news, and we hadn't had time to brief him. "She lied because she hated my brother, and she hated Toby. Both sold drugs to her deceased husband. She blamed them for the overdose. And when Detective Leslie brought out the photo of Darren, she picked it out, thinking it was her lucky day—a way of getting her revenge. She's obviously regretful now, as she's recovering from a brain injury due to a gunshot wound to the head, courtesy of, we believe, Jax."

"The drug business is a dangerous one," Bishop said. "But if Clark's willing to talk for a deal, we'll call our pals at the feds. See if we can get him into WITSEC. Chances are he is keeping information that may require extreme measures to protect his safety."

How would my mom feel about that? She would never be

able to see Clark again, as if he were dead. But she'd likely prefer him alive at an unknown location than actually dead. "Go for it," I said.

"OK, sounds like we've got everything wrapped up, but I'm definitely interested to hear what Clark has to say."

As was I. Not only that, I certainly would like to know who was making those phone calls to me about Darren's case. It had to be somebody in communication with Darren. "I know this isn't a high priority, but is there anybody who could check prison records to see who is visiting my brother, Darren? We still haven't identified the person who was calling me and telling me he was innocent and then telling me to drop the case."

Agent Bishop said, "We've got a few friends. Not that it really impacts the case much, but it'd be good to know. It could be someone who knows what's happening. More witnesses is always better."

"Exactly."

Darren said he didn't know, but that didn't mean he didn't suspect someone in particular. It was a case of a job well done, and I'd be cheering a little louder if I didn't have two brothers currently in hospital beds and my mom a total wreck.

51

MARTINA

VINCENT GRIMACED. "YIKES, ROUGH NIGHT?"

Indeed, it had been a tumultuous evening. Not necessarily in a bad way. There were tears—of happiness, frustration, and anger, a mix from both me and my mother. As I had suspected, she was far from pleased about our efforts to secure a deal for Clark that would place him in witness protection. It meant she might never see or hear from her son again.

Ted had tried to explain to her it was the only way to keep Clark safe. The discussion went on, punctuated by tears, tissues, and cups of tea. Eventually, Mom accepted it, assuming Clark would agree to the terms. The feds were presenting the deal to Clark later that day. Of course, it all hinged on whether he had material information that could help infiltrate and dismantle the 98Mob and Domingo's contacts in the Mexican cartel. If he didn't know anything, if he wasn't important to them, Clark might be able to return home. Did that mean he was safe? *Probably not.*

I had to explain to my mom you don't just walk away from organized crime. Often, the only way out was in a coffin. That revelation hit her hard. I thought she had been in denial about the extent of her son's criminal involvement until then. He wasn't a low-level dealer trying to scrape by; he was deeply entrenched in serious criminal activities.

On the flip side, there was some good news. The ballistics report came back proving the bullet found in Toby June was fired from Jax's weapon. Proof Darren was innocent and hadn't killed his friend.

Mom had always believed in his innocence, and the confirmation brought happy tears. But she was quite unhappy that Candace Mason, the eyewitness who lied and said Darren was the shooter, would not be facing any charges in return for her testimony against Jax, the actual shooter. Nor was Lil Jon, Darren's prison attacker, whom the DEA suspected had once been in the 98Mob but had switched sides and had been working on behalf of Domingo. But the only witness willing to talk was Darren, and well, that wasn't enough. But on the flip side, Lil Jon was already serving a life sentence and couldn't go after Darren again, assuming we could get Darren out of prison.

It was a roller coaster of emotions at Mom's place. In some ways, I was glad Zoey was present, so she could understand the complexities of my family. Over the years, she had questioned why she never met her uncles, and why, in her earlier years, I wasn't close with my own mother, who struggled with alcoholism. Not all families provided warmth and comfort. Some put your life in danger by prioritizing their addictions and their lifestyle choices above you.

Zoey admitted she was glad to have met Clark when she did, to have seen his face and spoken to him. She didn't express a desire to see him again, possibly knowing it might be brief and potentially the last time. She told me she was okay with that but was definitely keen to meet Darren, especially since he'd been vindicated, although still technically a convicted murderer in the hospital.

My next challenge was to reach out to the district attorney to figure out how we could get him out of prison once he recovered from his wounds. It was disheartening to hear about the difficulties in releasing someone from prison even when a mountain of evidence proved their innocence. Thankfully, he was protected in the hospital and not back in a jail cell, where his attacker might go after him again.

I summed up the night to Vincent: "It was a night."

"How did your mom take the news?"

"She was happy to hear about Darren, but not so thrilled about how difficult it may be to get him out of prison."

Vincent winced. "That's our justice system for you. You'd think it would be simple, but it could be years before they actually let him out."

I wasn't about to let that happen. "Over my dead body," I muttered under my breath. Thankfully, I had contacts within the justice system that would hopefully expedite the process. My contacts included a direct line to the district attorney who had penned the original deal for Darren's twenty-five-year sentence. It was my turn to plead and beg with the higher-ups to get the ball rolling and clear Darren's name.

"Guessing you need this more than I do," Vincent said, lifting a fresh mug full of piping hot coffee toward me.

"Yeah, and if you can keep them coming, I'll be grateful," I said, accepting the mug. "More news?" I raised an eyebrow.

"Yep, I heard from Agent Bishop. He's got the roster of who has been visiting your brother in jail. I thought one name in particular might be of interest to you."

"Oh?" I perked up. "And who might that be?"

"Ever heard of an Isabel Henderson?"

After nearly spitting out my coffee, I said, "Izzy?"

"Perhaps," Vincent hinted.

My brother and I needed to have a conversation. Part of me

felt I should see him in person, let him know we had cleared his name despite his reluctance for us to continue working the case and to question him about Izzy. "Maybe I'll go see Darren with my mother today and ask him about her. Or not."

"No? He must be more cooperative now. I mean, come on, his sister saved his life."

That was sweet. But I had no idea how helpful he would be. Maybe he didn't want us meeting Izzy. "I don't know. Zoey wants to meet him. Maybe I should go and get two birds with one stone."

"Sounds like a decent plan."

Was it? Truthfully, I had been hiding at work. I couldn't wait to be back in my own home and get some distance from my mother. My love and appreciation of her was deep, but her all up in my investigation was too much. "They're presenting Clark with the deal today. I was thinking of going and saying goodbye. I can't do both."

"Tough one. But if Darren gets out, you'll have many opportunities to see him."

True. Vincent, *the wise*. "If he gets out soon." Before another inmate could attack him.

"Well, if Greggs won't move fast enough, you could reach out to the Innocence Project. They have a branch in Santa Clara. They could start the wheels turning if nobody else will. But honestly, you've got a lot more friends in the system than most."

"True. And I suppose it's my time to call in a favor."

What a complicated case this had become. When I started, I thought maybe there was a glimmer of hope I'd find the truth and we would all be a family again. But after all we learned, I knew that was an impossible mission. One brother, Darren, could get out of that life and re-join our family. He was already halfway there, finding his faith and getting clean. But my other brother—there were only two paths for him: witness protection by turning on the 98Mob or rejoining it and ending up dead. One path meant we'd never see or talk to him again; the other was worse.

Decision made. "I'm going to see Clark."

"If I was in your position, I'd do the same. Have faith. Sometimes things work out the way they should, you know? And I've got a feeling about this one. I think you'll get your happy ending," Vincent encouraged.

Usually, we accepted a bittersweet ending, but if Clark was safe and Darren rejoined our family, clean and sober, away from a life of crime, that would definitely be a happy ending. The challenge—make it all happen.

ACCOMPANIED by District Attorney Greggs and a member from the FBI Organized Crime Task Force, we entered Clark's hospital room. I waved at him. "Hey, Clark, how are you feeling?"

"Decent. They said I could go home today."

"We're glad to hear that," Agent Hammer said.

"Who are you?"

"Agent Hammer, FBI, Organized Crime Task Force. This is a colleague, District Attorney Greggs from the CoCo County Sheriff's Department. We would like to offer you a deal," Hammer explained.

Clark looked back at me.

I said, "You tell them everything you know about the 98Mob, Domingo's crew, and their connections to Mexico, and you get a new life, a fresh start."

"Does Mom know about this?"

"She does, and she understands this could be the only way

forward for you. One way, you go back to the 98Mob, and you're on everybody's radar, right?" I glanced over at the FBI agent, who nodded. "The other option is you end up six feet under. Mom understands."

"Would I be able to say goodbye to her?"

Greggs interjected, "Yes, usually we can arrange for a final meeting with the family, covertly of course."

Clark scratched his chin and said, "Is that why you're here? Is this your final goodbye?"

"Are you accepting the deal?"

"I understand there is only one way I will survive all of this, and that's to talk. Seeing you, seeing your daughter, Mom... it reminded me of everything I used to have, or could've had if I had chosen a different life. I'm ready for a second shot."

"I'm glad you're taking it."

"Well, it's been good to see you, little sister. And to meet Zoey. She seems incredible," Clark said, his voice soft.

Fighting the tears, realizing this was the very last time I would ever see my brother, I used all my gumption to keep my composure. "She said it was really great to meet you too. You take care of yourself."

"You too," Clark replied with a hint of sadness.

Greggs said, "Sounds like we've got a deal."

With that, I turned out of Clark's hospital room, leaving him to start his second chance at life. I knew it was better than the alternative, but it was a lot to process that I would never see my brother again. But he'd be safe, and in my heart, he would always be with me and I with him.

52

MARTINA

THREE MONTHS LATER

Mom peered into the oven to check on the turkey while I mashed the potatoes. She shut the oven door and said, "Full house today."

With a warm smile, I replied, "Yep."

The doorbell rang, and Zoey's voice echoed through the house, "I'll get it!" as did Barney's alert barking as he followed her.

Zoey was back home, and I was grateful. It had only been a few months since she'd left for college, but her presence in our home again filled my heart. Her college was just an hour and a half drive, and I had visited her several times, but seeing her in her pajamas and fuzzy slippers, helping us prepare for Thanksgiving dinner, made everything seem right with the world.

She called out, "It's Darren and Izzy!"

They appeared in my living room, and I greeted each of them with a warm hug.

Three months ago, I wouldn't have believed I'd be hugging Darren and his girlfriend in my home. If Clark had been there, I would have thought I was dreaming. But he wasn't. He had testified against both the 98Mob and Domingo's operation and was in witness protection, starting a new life somewhere unbeknownst to us.

Darren's journey home had been a tumultuous one. I'd pushed hard, using Gregg's influence and a presentation to the Governor of California, and it took two weeks to clear his name. To our family, two weeks seemed like forever. But in reality, Darren had been fortunate. His lightning-fast exoneration was undoubtedly due to my connections within the criminal justice system. Without those, he might still be incarcerated, desperately seeking help from the Innocence Project to get him out of jail.

Izzy's loyalty to Darren was unwavering, and she even started rehab to get clean, inspired by his transformation. It turned out she was the one who had been calling me and had been present at the park on the day Toby had been shot. Her call was an attempt to prove Darren's innocence, but when she learned Darren's life was in danger if I continued my investigation, she begged for me to stop.

Over the last couple of months, Izzy had become like family to me. I'd never had a sister, but Izzy was quickly filling that role.

Zoey was over the moon to have an uncle and auntie in her life. It was understandable, given her limited family connections due to her father and my small families.

Of course, we had found our own special family over the years. With Hirsch and Kim, Audrey, Vincent, and Amanda by our side, we had much to be thankful for this year. I had even made a new friend. And we had also lost one—namely Detective Leslie, who was terminated from the sheriff's department. But she avoided jail time. She was fortunate and likely to be safe at home with her son, no longer threatened by Domingo and his crew.

The doorbell rang again. "I'll get it," I said, making my way to the door.

"Is that your friend from the rehab center?" Zoey asked curiously.

My mother glanced at me with a mix of intrigue and concern. "A friend from the rehab center? Is this the one you've been telling me about?"

"Yes, it is," I said, trying to keep my cool. "He doesn't have any family in the area, so I invited him over."

"I think that's great, Mom," Zoey said with a smile, her voice filled with approval.

Approaching the door, I felt butterflies swarming around my belly. A deep breath later, I opened the door and there he stood—a man with dark hair, olive skin, and a broad smile.

For months, I'd tried to shove the butterflies away, but they wouldn't relent. He had been sober for less than a year, so dating was out of the question. Nevertheless, we had a brief conversation about relationships and agreed that being friends would have to be enough for the time being. Friends was good. And friends could come over for Thanksgiving with your family, right?

"Happy Thanksgiving."

"Happy Thanksgiving. Most of the gang's already here," I said with a stupid grin on my face.

"Oh, I see one," he said, noticing Barney. He knelt down and gave Barney some loving scratches, which the pup clearly enjoyed.

He shut the door behind him, and I led him into the living room where my family had gathered.

Although some guests were still expected, he was the last of the early arrivals. The group stood around, observing him with a mix of curiosity and intrigue, their expressions reflecting more surprise than anything else. Hirsch, always perceptive, gave me a knowing smirk. He was all too familiar with my tells.

Turning to the group, I began introductions. "This is my mom, Betty, her husband, Ted, my brother Darren, his girlfriend, Izzy, and of course, my daughter, Zoey. And over here, we have Hirsch, his wife, Kim, and their daughter, Audrey. Rocco, Vincent, and Amanda might be coming a bit later, but this is most of the crew."

"I've heard so much about all of you," he said warmly. "It's so great to be here. Thank you for sharing your holiday with me."

Zoey nudged me and whispered, "You didn't introduce him."

Shaking my head, I chuckled at my oversight. "I'm so sorry. I didn't actually introduce him, did I?" The room shared a lighthearted laugh at my expense, but it was a comfortable, loving laughter. After all, they had already heard about my new friend.

Our connection was unexpected yet profound. I often pondered if our bond was due to our similar experiences with heartbreak and addiction or because we both were blessed with bright daughters, gifts from above that made us question our worthiness. The way he spoke about his daughter, Selena, with such devotion and hope, it was clear he was a man striving to be the best version of himself, yearning for her acceptance back into his life. He was a blend of strength and sensitivity and admittedly, easy on the eyes.

Catching my gaze, Hirsch gave me a playful wink.

With my nerves rattling, I finally introduced him. "Everyone, this is Charlie."

The group then eased into casual conversation, everyone wanting to learn more about Charlie and expressing their happiness he joined us that year. As they chatted, a profound sense of wholeness overcame me. It was a feeling I hadn't experienced since Jared's passing.

Surrounded by my family, a group that was continuously growing, I realized I was ready for whatever the future held. In that moment, with my loved ones around me, I felt prepared for anything and everything that life might bring next.

THANK YOU!

Thank you for reading *Lies She Told.* I hope you enjoyed reading it as much as I loved writing it. If you did, I would greatly appreciate if you could post a short review.

Reviews are crucial for any author and can make a huge difference in visibility of current and future works. Reviews allow us to continue doing what we love, *writing stories.* Not to mention, I would be forever grateful!

Thank you!

ALSO BY H.K. CHRISTIE

The Martina Monroe Series —a nail-biting crime thriller series starring PI Martina Monroe and her unofficial partner Detective August Hirsch of the Cold Case Squad. If you like high-stakes games, jaw-dropping twists, and suspense that will keep you on the edge of your seat, then you'll love the Martina Monroe crime thriller series.

The Selena Bailey Series (1 - 5) — a suspenseful series featuring a young Selena Bailey and her turbulent path to becoming a top-notch private investigator as led by her mentor, Martina Monroe.

The Val Costa Series —a gripping crime thriller with heart-pounding suspense. If you love Martina, you'll love Val.

The Neighbor Two Doors Down —a dark and witty psychological thriller. If you like unpredictable twists, page-turning suspense, and unreliable narrators, then you'll love *The Neighbor Two Doors Down.*

A Permanent Mark A heartless killer. Weeks without answers. Can she move on when a murderer walks free? If you like riveting suspense and gripping mysteries then you'll love *A Permanent Mark* - starring a grown up Selena Bailey.

For H.K. Christie's full catalog go to: **www.authorhkchristie.com**

At **www.authorhkchristie.com** you can also sign up for the H.K. Christie reader club where you'll be the first to hear about upcoming novels, new releases, giveaways, promotions, and a free e-copy of the prequel to the Martina Monroe Thriller Series, *Crashing Down*!

ABOUT THE AUTHOR

H. K. Christie watched horror films far too early in life. Inspired by the likes of Stephen King, Jodi Picoult, true crime podcasts, and a vivid imagination she now writes suspenseful thrillers.

She found her passion for writing when she embarked on a one-woman habit breaking experiment. Although she didn't break her habit, she did discover a love of writing and has been at it ever since.

When not working on her latest novel, H.K. Christie can be found eating & drinking with friends, walking around the lakes, or playing with her favorite furry pal.

She is a native and current resident of the San Francisco Bay Area.

To learn more about H.K. Christie and her books or simply to say, "hello", go to **www.authorhkchristie.com**.

ACKNOWLEDGMENTS

Many thanks to my Advanced Reader and Street Teams. These wonderful readers are invaluable in taking the first look at my stories and helping find typos and spreading awareness of my stories through their reviews and kind words.

To my editor, Paula Lester, a huge thanks for your careful edit and helpful comments and proofreaders Becky Stewart and Ryan Mahan for catching those last typos. To my cover designer, Odile, thank you for your guidance and talent.

To my best writing buddy, Charlie, thank you for the looks of encouragement and reminders to take breaks. If it weren't for you, I'd be in my office all day working as opposed to catering to all of your needs and wants such as snuggles, scratches, treats, and long, meandering walks. To the mister, thank you, as always, for putting up with me especially when I'm approaching one of my overly ambitious, self-imposed deadlines.

Last but not least, I'd like to thank all of my readers. It's because of you I'm able to continue writing stories.

Made in the USA
Coppell, TX
21 April 2025

48511238R00163